CROOKED FENCES

A Novel

By C.J. Heigelmann

COMMON FOLK PRESS

CROOKED FENCES
Copyright © 2020 by C.J. Heigelmann

For information contact:
Email: cj@cjheigelmann.com
P.O. Box 801 Lexington, SC 29071-0801
https://www.cjheigelmann.com
ISBN: 978-0-9994898-1-9
First Edition: Jan 2020

PREFACE

This literary work was inspired by firsthand knowledge of the devastation and suffering caused by Post Traumatic Stress Disorder. Although this book deals primarily with PTSD, as it affects returning war veterans, it also acknowledges the full causal spectrum which afflicts millions of individuals around the world.

Crooked Fences not only explores the journey of a war veteran's internal and external challenges after returning home, but also examines their personal and intimate life before the horrific events of battle. This aspect of the story illustrates their moral, ethical, and psychological state of mind before the war. It also describes how unresolved life issues will ultimately compound the effects of PTSD. Sadly, destructive behaviors, the separation of families, and suicide are all hallmarks of the untreated victims of the disorder, whether military or civilian.

The main character's primary ethical flaws are racism and homophobia. While *Crooked Fences* handles these subjects with care, it remains honest and truthful. The book deals with multiple personal issues and situations with true-to-life characters expressed in their pure flawed form, because all of us are flawed.

As with all my novels, I don't shrink from using stereotypes, whether positive or negative. Instead, I promote them and in the next breath, completely shatter them. This exposes the error of subjugating individuals into intellectually lazy social labels and compel the reader to confront the true empirical nature of the individual, while lending insight into understanding them.

It is my hope that this novel can answer many questions for the reader and promote discussions pertaining to several related social issues as the first page is turned. Without further delay, I present you with *Crooked Fences*.

DEDICATION

Dedicated to Shaney

IN LOVING MEMORY

Johnny Michael Pate
United States Army
August 12, 1957 ~ July 3, 2019

George A. Tolliver
United States Army
June 27, 1944 ~ October 31, 2007

Viventem in Sempiternum

CHAPTER ONE

PREMONITION

Big black eyes stared at me. Two minutes had passed and neither one of us had moved or flinched. I felt a sudden pain deep inside my lower stomach. Finally, it was ready to come out. I groaned with a sigh of discomfort and exhaled a breath of relief. Suddenly, the locust disappeared out the hatch as it took flight with a faint hum from its wings trailing behind. I heard Tucker, my squad leader and best friend, yelling.

"Todd! What are you doing in there, praying? Let's wrap it up! We are Oscar Mike in five!" he said.

"I'm coming out now, Tuck! Ten pounds lighter!" I replied, as someone in the bay started an MP3 of our battle hymn, "Highway to Hell" by the rock band AC/DC. As the heavy metal guitar riff started to crank out the opening chords of inspiration, I cleaned myself and secured my trousers, along with the rest of my gear. I picked up my M4 Colt and walked out to see Tucker standing in the middle of our bay, along with my two other best friends, Thomas Shirikjian from Boston, who we called Tom, and James Barber from San Diego, who we called Jay. All were head-bobbing to our anthem, pumping themselves up for the mission.

Tuck looked at me as he began to play air guitar with his rifle. He was speaking to me without words, but I knew what he was saying. I walked over to the group and joined my brothers in our solemn pre-mission ritual. Whether praying or doing things in a specific order, superstitions ran deep. Every warrior has some sort of routine. It might seem like bullshit to a civilian, but then again, we are talking about civilians. If they experienced even one day of carnage in this desert hellhole, they would believe in superstitions too. However, they aren't here, we are, the Devil Dogs. The Almighty has blessed us to become United States Marines.

The way I saw it, the only thing a civilian needed to worry about was what movie to watch on Friday night, or where to go out to eat. Back home in the United States, what we call the "World," exists a different reality than where we four Marines were living, fighting, and dying at for the past two years. As we rocked out and let the music take control of our minds and bodies, our spirits joined in unison, becoming one. We were one group, one purpose, one machine. We loved each other and we wouldn't hesitate to die for one another. We were a family.

The song ended, and Tuck turned off the music player. It was time to earn our paychecks. An honest day's work, for an honest day's pay, was the motto. Tuck walked back to us with his military bearing in overdrive. He stood tall and blond with blue eyes and a stone-cleft chin. He was from Tennessee and had a strong southern drawl when he spoke.

"You know the drill fellas, this ain't our first rodeo. Now, ain't that right?"

"Oorah!" We all sounded off in unison.

My adrenaline was high as my breathing increased. I was ready, and we were prepared for anything.

Tucker continued. "The mission briefing this morning was cut and dry. We got two buildings to clear in Sector 2a and one more in 7e," he said.

Tom spoke up. "Tuck, why the hell didn't they give us adjoining sectors? Echo Squad is hitting sector seven and sector three. Why can't we just swap a sector with them? It makes more sense than driving way the hell across the damn city."

Tucker frowned. "Ain't gonna happen. Nothing's gonna change, so suck it up and quit pissing and moaning."

Jay looked at Tom and smiled. "Too bad, so sad. You want my hanky, Tommy?"

Tom shook his head. He was getting pissed off. "Do you want me to stuff it up your ass?" he yelled.

Tucker broke up the skirmish.

"Enough with all that! Shit, Tom, what's with the attitude? Speak up like you got a pair, what gives?"

Tom just shook his head again. "Nothing, I'm cool. I just don't like driving through the city when we don't have to. Makes sense, right? Of course not, I'm a jarhead!"

We all laughed, except Tucker.

"You're right, it does make sense. But it's too late in the game now to change the plan. It sucks, but what else is new? We got a job to do. The sooner we get her done, the sooner we can come back to the house and kick our feet up. Now, are you good?"

Tuck was right. It sucked, but what else was new? I had something on my mind, so I spoke up.

"This whole day has been FUBAR. Did you see the replacements for Fire Team Charlie? They're all new blood and have never been out with us before. That's messing with my head. Something doesn't feel right about this one." I said.

Tucker looked over at me in surprise. "Not you too, Todd? They'll be on point, so no worries. Look, they're gonna be covering our entry and egress to the Humvees. You were a cherry once upon a time, just like the rest of us."

"Still feels like something is wrong. I mean, besides being cherries, they are all black. We don't know them dudes! You got to admit, it is strange to have an all-black fire team." I said.

"You stow that shit right now! Ain't nothing strange about that at all! Stop with the superstitious bullshit already!" He paused for a moment, frowned, shook his head, and sighed.

I stopped complaining, but what Tucker had said didn't change my mind or the way I felt. "Aye, aye, Tuck. I hear you, but I'm not riding with any of them! Us four are all riding together, just like always. That's all I have to say."

"I didn't know you got promoted to squad leader Todd, congrats." Tucker smiled, put on his helmet, and fastened the strap.

Jay and Tom laughed. Jay grabbed me by the shoulder and whispered in my ear. "Hey, bro! When we get back, can I borrow that Spring Break bikini picture of your girlfriend? I just need it for like two minutes, I'm about to bust!" I laughed and pushed him away. We all walked out of the barracks behind Tucker to the three Humvees parked single file. Bravo and Charlie Fire-teams were milling around their vehicles.

Tuck signaled to them. "Marines! Mount up! We are moving out!"

Bravo and Charlie Teams got into their vehicles, as we climbed in the middle Humvee in our usual positions. Tom rode with Tucker up front, while Jay and I were seated in the rear. Charlie Team took the point position as we made our way toward the front gate, followed by a thick trail of dust behind us. I noticed it was scorching hot today, dryer than usual. We had made this trip hundreds of times before, but this time it felt different. I turned to see Tucker staring at me. He could tell something was eating at me; he had no trouble reading any of us.

"You good?" he asked.

"Whatever, man, I don't give a shit. Let's just get the damn job done," I answered.

I looked back out the window. I wasn't the type to complain about something repeatedly, like some sissy. I spoke my piece at the barracks, and that was the end of it for me. A few seconds later, I heard Tucker on the radio calling out to the lead vehicle.

"Charlie Team, when we pass through the gate, fall back to my position. Alpha Team is taking the point, do you copy?"

A few seconds later, Charlie Team acknowledged, followed by Bravo Team.

"Ten-four, copy that."

I glanced over at Tucker, who was looking forward. Why did he do that? I couldn't let it go.

"What the hell Tuck? Why are you changing formation?" I asked.

Tucker looked at me.

"You ain't frosty, Todd! You're acting spooked! You said something didn't feel right. You're worried about Charlie Team. Well I just took care of that for you. Now we're on point! How do you like that? Satisfied? Now get your head out of your ass!"

We exited the base and Tom immediately passed Charlie Team. Tucker looked at him and knocked on his helmet like a door.

"Tuck to Tom! How about you put some lead in your foot? I want to see the pedal to the metal, baby boy!"

This was Tucker-the-squad-leader escalating aggression in the atmosphere. It was one way of ramping us up and pushing us to where we needed to be. We had prepared ourselves to kill or be killed.

"I can't drive! Fifty-five!" Tom yelled out.

I looked at Jay, who was staring out of his window. He was nodding to a song in his mind. He was always quiet like this while en route to our first stop. We made a left turn two blocks before the East market, trying to avoid the primary traffic. We had six miles left before reaching the first objective. The first breach and clear of the day was always stressful, but as the day wore on it would become more routine, but not safer. Complacency on the team could cause mistakes which could kill all of us. I started to feel like my old self again as my adrenaline and aggression took control of me and turned the knots of fear inside my stomach into harmless butterflies.

"Oorah!" I yelled out.

Everyone else sounded off after me. "Oorah!"

Tucker looked back at me and nodded his head in approval.

"It's all good brother! It's all g—"

There was a flash of light, a jolt, and then darkness. That is all I remember.

• • •

I woke up to bright lights. My head felt ready to explode. I laid there for what seemed like hours, looking up at a white ceiling. I tried to comprehend simple thoughts and understand what was happening. I remembered I had feet connected to my legs. Yes, I had arms and hands with fingers. I tried to move each one, before I noticed a beeping sound. It must have been there the whole time, but now it was faster. I turned my head in the direction of the sound and felt a painful, burning sensation. It was coming from what connected my head to my body; my neck. Of course, I had a neck!

How the hell did I get here?

Reality flooded my consciousness and overwhelmed me. I realized I was in a hospital. What happened? A roadside bomb? A rocket-propelled grenade? I closed my eyes tight and tried to remember. Where's Tuck? Where's Jay…Tom?

"Corporal, can you hear me?"

The voice startled me and took my breath away. I opened my eyes and saw a woman standing next to me. I stared at her.

"Corporal, can you hear me?" I nodded; she leaned closer. "Can you talk?"

I tried to swallow, but even that was difficult. I took a deep breath and whispered, "Yes."

She smiled. "Good. Can you tell me your name?"

I knew that I had a name, but I couldn't recall it. I remembered the names of my buddies, so why not my own name? The next minute which passed was exhausting and a struggle, but I could not remember it.

"Take your time, there is no rush." She spoke gently. Her voice was soothing, but I gave up.

"I don't know," I replied. My vision blurred as tears rolled from the corners of my eyes. I closed them and began to quietly cry. Shame and embarrassment were the least of my worries; I thought that I must have brain damage. The nurse saw my distress and held my hand.

"Everything is fine. It may take a while. I'm going to take your vitals and the doctor will see you shortly, to explain your condition. I will let your unit Commander and 1st Sergeant know you've woken up. Just relax and try to stay calm." I opened my eyes and looked at her.

"Todd Goodson. My name is Todd Goodson," I whispered. Still groggy, I drifted back to sleep.

• • •

Bam!

"*Domino!*" *Jay hollered, as he slammed his last one on the table and stood up. "That's game bitches! Pay up right now!" he yelled.*

Everyone tossed their money on the table except Tuck.

"*Man, all I got are fifties," Tuck said as he looked away. Jay's eyes widened.*

"*You lying sack of shit! You reneging Tuck? Where's your damn honor, Marine?*"

Tuck laughed at him.

6

"I didn't say I wasn't gonna pay, I just don't have change is all. Let me go to the canteen first. Dang! It's only five dollars bro! You act like I'm trying to stiff you out of a car payment!"

Jay gathered up the rest of his money. I couldn't help myself. I had to instigate.

"I never thought I would see the day that Tuck would re-nigger on a bet! Uh, I mean renege…That's a damn shame!" I laughed, shaking my head. Tuck snapped.

"That shit ain't funny!" Tuck looked at me. "I've done told you before about talking like that. One day you're gonna say that around the wrong person and get your face punched in," he said. I stood up from the table.

"What? Do I look scared? I don't give a damn man! It's just a freaking joke!" I replied and walked over to my footlocker. He shook his head.

"You need to wake up and smell the coffee punk," he said.

I reached inside and grabbed my MP3 player, walked over to my bunk, and laid down. I always needed to get the last word in.

"You need to stop being so sensitive. You sound like an old woman," I said, while putting my earbuds in and turning up the music. He was staring at me, so I stared back over at him. He started talking, but I couldn't hear him over the music, so I shouted out. "I can't hear you! Speak up like you got a pair!" I laughed.

Tuck stood up and started throwing dominoes at me. Tom and Jay joined in the stoning as I did my best to block the incoming projectiles. They circled me as I tried to get up…

"Lay down. Lay down Corporal! Corporal Goodson!" I opened my eyes and saw three figures standing over me. Two of them were holding me down. It was my 1st sergeant and a doctor. The third person was my commander Major Truesdale. I quickly gathered my thoughts along with my military bearing.

"Sir, yes, sir. I must have been dreaming." I said.

The doctor smiled.

"I'm Captain Horowitz. You are one lucky Marine, Corporal." He looked down at his clipboard. "I want to give you a rundown of your injuries and condition, none of which are life threatening."

"Yes sir." I nodded while glancing at my 1st sergeant and commander out the corner of my eye. Both were silent and stone-faced as the doctor continued with my report.

"You have sustained a level three concussion and have been unconscious for the last fourteen hours. You have several minor first- and second-degree burns, as well as two separate stress fractures on your lower right fibula." He flipped to another page. "Also, you have experienced a severe flexion-extension motion of the neck. This is similar to what you may know as whiplash." He turned to another page. "You have no internal bleeding detected at this time—which was one of our main concerns in your case. Regardless, we are going to continue monitoring you over the next few weeks as you recuperate and heal. If all goes as planned, we'll draw up a specific rehabilitation program for you. You can expect to be here for two to three months. Now that you are awake and conscious, tell me, how are you feeling?"

"Where's my team sir?" I croaked with a dry throat. The doctor looked at me with his eyebrows raised, then turned to my commander, who in turn gestured to my sergeant. The 1st sergeant nodded and walked over to my bedside and held on to the bed rail. He leaned over and spoke quietly.

"Son, I want you to brace yourself. It is not good news." My heart went dead. I could feel my eyes begin to water again. "Your Humvee was hit by an I.E.D. You and your fire team were ambushed. Corporal Thomas Shirikjian and Lance Corporal Jay Barber were killed instantly in the explosion."

"No. No!" I yelled out of shock. I closed my eyes tight and clenched my teeth as I lost my composure. I didn't believe it, but I knew it was the truth. The 1st sergeant rested his hand on my shoulder.

"I'm sorry, Corporal. They gave all." I barely heard his words as the thoughts in my head drowned out everything around me. *Why? Why am I still alive? This wasn't right. It shouldn't be happening. It was wrong. It was all wrong!*

"Sergeant Tucker Pearson was severely wounded in the blast. He's alive but in critical condition," he said.

I opened my eyes at the sound of his name. "Tuck is alive?"

"Yes he is, but he is in the fight for his life as we speak. They flew him out to Landstuhl Regional a few hours after the blast," he replied.

I desperately wanted to see Tuck, but realized I might never get the chance. I was exhausted and just wanted to close my eyes and die. All of this needed to stop, be over and done with. Sarge had told me the truth, but I didn't want to hear it. I closed my eyes and turned my head away. A few moments later, someone else's hand was on my other shoulder. This time, I heard my commander's voice.

"You rest up, Corporal Goodson. We all mourn this loss with you. It's another sad day for the Corps and for America. I want you to know we're all here for you. I promise you their sacrifices will never be forgotten." He patted my arm and I nodded without opening my eyes. I couldn't handle it anymore. Soon I heard their footsteps as they moved away, talking.

"The mission de-brief will wait until he is ready. He's going to need some time," Captain Horowitz said.

I lay there alone and thirsty, hoping I could blackout, sleep, or just fall unconscious. However, I felt the need to urinate. I looked around the bed for a call button and pressed it. A short while later, the nurse came by my bedside.

"How can I help you?"

"I'm thirsty and need to go to the head."

"Corporal Goodson, we don't want you trying to walk just yet. I will bring you some water now, but if you feel the need to urinate or have a bowel movement, you can do that now. You have a catheter inserted, and your urine bag is only a quarter full. I'll also recheck your incontinence diaper and change it if necessary," she said.

I hadn't realized any of this. The weight of reality smothered me. I was wearing a diaper, two of my brothers were dead, and my best friend was clinging to life. Somehow, I needed to escape this hell.

"Nurse, could you give me something for the pain? My head and neck are killing me. The shit is almost unbearable and I need something for the pain right now. Please!"

"Of course," she replied. "I'll inform Captain Horowitz. Try to relax and I'll be back shortly with something for the pain." She left and returned with a tumbler of water and some medication. I sipped on the water slowly as she patiently waited.

"Don't drink too much. Your mouth is very sensitive right now. Even water may start to hurt," she advised. I didn't believe her, but after I handed the tumbler back to her, the roof of my mouth began to ache.

"I see what you mean," I mumbled.

She produced a vial and began to unwrap a needle.

"This will help you with pain and also allow you to sleep. Are you ready?"

"I'm ready. Where do you want to stick me?" I replied. I didn't care for needles.

"No sticking. I'm going to take it easy on you this time," she said. As the nurse injected the drug directly into my I.V., it began to work immediately. I felt a rush of relief pulsate through my mind and body. I stared at the light directly above me in the ceiling. The light; so soft and bright, guided me safely away from the pain of this world.

• • •

Three weeks had passed and I was healing well. It was great to walk and eat. My body began to feel better, but inside, I still felt like crap. I inhaled depression with every breath. If it were not for the pain meds helping me to temporarily forget, I believe I would have lost my mind.

Captain Horowitz would not release me back to my unit. He said I was not ready physically or psychologically. I was going to physical therapy daily, with counseling sessions twice a week. To me, it was a waste of time and I couldn't understand why, or what good came from talking about my thoughts or feelings. The present reality was set in stone. Nothing about the past could change the here and now.

None of the bullshit therapy was helping me or Tuck, wherever he was. I found out after staying two weeks at Landstuhl that they flew him stateside.

There were two months left on my service contract and I had previously planned to re-enlist. All four of us were going to do at least twenty years. This was our life. We were career professional soldiers, but now I knew I wasn't going to re-up. Why should I? I couldn't go back without my brothers. No way.

Earlier in the day, two guys from my unit came to visit me. That was cool. They gave me some encouragement and I began to feel better for a little while, until they mentioned that Charlie Team came out of the ambush without a scratch. They should've had the point position that day and been blown to bits, not us! The shit wasn't fair. Everything about that day felt wrong. I had a feeling and I was right.

The more I thought about it, the more it pissed me off. I could see those black dudes now; sitting around the barracks, listening to their rap music, probably eating watermelon-flavored jellybeans or chicken-flavored potato chips, laughing it up and having a good old time. It made me sick to think about it.

I looked at my watch. I needed to wait another hour before taking my pain pill, but I walked to the water fountain and took it early. I sat down on a chair in the hallway to relax and let the magical meds do their work. They acted quickly and relaxed me, taking me to that place I needed to be. I hadn't talked to anyone back in the States since the attack. I tried getting a hold of my girlfriend, Angela, but her voicemail said she was out of the country and would return this week.

She was a pharmaceutical sales rep for a company based in Germany, traveling every few months from New York to work at the corporate headquarters. Memories of her hit me hard and I wanted desperately to hear her voice. I didn't believe she understood how much I loved her.

I got up and walked to the dayroom to watch television for a while. There were always three or four guys in there kicking back, shooting the shit. Thirty minutes later, it felt like I was wasting away and I had to get out of there. I walked out into the courtyard and called Angela again. Every ring that went unanswered depressed me and pissed me off. My neck began to tighten and I felt hot. The sensation of rage was growing stronger inside me.

"Shit!" I shouted. A few startled heads turned to the outburst, so I walked to a more secluded area of the courtyard with my cell phone to my ear. My heart jumped as I heard the line connect.

"Hello? Todd?" The sweet sound of her voice was pure nirvana.

"Hey babe! I've been trying to reach you all day!"

"Sweetheart, I am so sorry! I was in Stuttgart all week at corporate. Oh my God! How are you? Your voice sounds different. Are you all right?"

"No babe. I am in a world of shit right now. A couple of weeks ago my squad was hit. It was an ambush." I began to feel flush, almost lightheaded. I heard her shriek.

"Todd, no! What happened sweetie?" She started to whimper.

"Our Humvee was hit by an I.E.D. It's what you hear about on the news. Basically, it was a roadside bomb. Tom and Jay are dead, gone. Tucker is in critical condition. Last I heard, they flew him back stateside," I replied. She was clearly crying now.

"Oh my God, I can't believe it! Please, tell me about you. How bad are you? I need to know! Did you lose anything sweetie? Your arms? Legs?"

"No babe, I'm whole. I had a concussion, a few minor burns, and fractures, but I am all right." I felt weak and started choking up as my eyes began to water. I sat down on the grass. My chest felt tight and I couldn't seem to get enough oxygen. "I'm not good baby. I shouldn't be here. I should have died with them."

"What? Are you crazy! Don't talk like that! Do you hear me?" she screamed.

I closed my eyes while her words tore through me. I didn't like being yelled at. It was the first time in six weeks I'd heard her voice and she was fussing at me already.

"I hear you Angela, but I don't want to fight with you."

"I am not trying to fight with you. You say something like that and what, I'm just supposed to let that go by unchecked? You should be happy to be alive! I'm sorry about your friends, truly, I know you were close, but you're alive and that's what matters!"

I heard her but I wasn't listening to what she was saying. She didn't know, and could never understand, what was going on inside me. How could she?

"Okay Angela, you're right. I guess I'm just stressed out and trying to get my thoughts together."

She was quiet for a moment.

"Sweetheart, I don't blame you. I cannot imagine what you must be going through right now. Let's just change the subject. When are you coming back to New York? If I remember correctly, you should only have a few months before your contract is completed. Am I right?"

"Yeah, I have around two months left," I replied. I had never told her about my plan to re-enlist. She would have resisted the idea of becoming a military wife and it would have been a deal-breaker for her. I thought that over time, I could win her over to the idea.

"Awesome! Finally! Now you can begin submitting your application for the dream job you've always talked about! We can seriously begin to plan our future together."

She remembered that? The idea hadn't crossed my mind in years. A career as a New York State Trooper was no longer a dream, now it was a reality. Years ago, when we first began dating, I remember constantly talking about the idea. Right now, there was too much going on in my life, and Tucker's well-being stayed on my mind. The state police was something to think about someday.

"Yeah, you're right babe. Maybe it is time to start planning our future. Getting married, buying a home somewhere, having kids..."

She interrupted me.

"Hold on there! Before you start planning our future, you need to actually become a state trooper, silly!" She laughed. "I heard they have a waiting list, so you need to start filling out the paperwork soon. On second thought, you may not be able to pass the physical. How bad are your injuries?" she asked.

"I'm good to go, I told you! I wouldn't have any problems passing the physical; Besides, I have my technical college credits in HVAC, plus my years of military service. It's as good as done!" I replied.

"All right, fine. When you come back home you can start on it. By the way, you do know that when you get back you're staying with me, right?"

"Babe, I hadn't thought about any of that, but since you brought it up, hell yes! I can't wait!" The thought of sharing the same bed with her again gave me the first real dose of happiness I'd had since the ambush. I heard her moan with excitement.

"I can't wait either! You have no idea the things I am going to do to you every night, over and over," she added. I grunted in agreement. Her sexy voice always made me horny and she knew it.

"Oh! Have you spoken with your Dad yet?" she asked.

"Actually, I hadn't called him yet. I will after we hang up," I replied.

"I know he will be so happy to hear from you. He'll be proud of you after he finds out that you are going to join the NYSP. You should be proud as well, by following in his footsteps and becoming the third generation in your family to serve on the force. That will put a huge smile on his face!"

"Yeah babe, that's true. My old man will definitely be proud of that," I replied. Instead of ending that subject there, she kept talking about it.

"Yes he will and he deserves it too! After all the pain that he's been through." She paused, waiting for me to comment again, but I didn't, so she kept pushing. "You know what I mean by that. Like when your mom left the both of you." She just couldn't leave that subject alone and she knew damn well it would stir up a hornet's nest.

"Angie, I don't really feel like talking about any of that." I tried to remain calm as she huffed.

"I'm not going to say another word, just forget it. I won't argue with you either. We had a good conversation, so let's just end this call on a happy note," she replied.

"Okay babe. I'll talk to you later. Be careful out there. I love you," I said.

"You too sweetheart! Goodbye!"

I hung up the phone and sat there a few minutes, daydreaming while staring at the grass. My old man would be happy about me coming home. I couldn't help feeling a little excited, but the crappy feeling was still in the pit of my stomach. Tom and Jay were gone and Tucker was in a bad way, probably suffering. I honestly had no right to be alive, let alone a reason to be happy. I searched through my phone contacts and dialed my dad. It rang until his voicemail answered.

"Hello, you have reached the voicemail of Mike Goodson. I am not available right …" I hung up. My dad was old-school and barely used his cell phone. I dialed his apartment landline and within a few seconds, he answered.

"Hello," he said.

"Hello Dad."

"Todd! How in the hell are you, boy? I hadn't heard from you in months!" The happiness in his voice was contagious.

"I'm okay Dad. Damn, it's good to hear your voice again! Let me update you first. A couple of weeks ago, my squad got ambushed. An I.E.D killed my friends Jay and Tom. Tucker, my squad leader, is fighting for his life in the hospital back in the states."

"Holy shit Todd! How are *you*? Talk to me son!"

"I'm fine. I mean, I'm the only one who's walking around. I have some minor injuries, but they're nothing."

"Thank God! I had a feeling, you know. Like something wasn't right. Over the past month, I couldn't stop thinking about you over there. Those bastards! The military needs to just nuke that whole country and send them back to the stone ages." He became quiet, but I heard him sniffling. "I'm grateful you're alive."

Dad was a proud person and a real man who never used to cry, but he changed after Mom left us. I tried to cheer him up.

"Hey Dad, everything is all right, really I'm good. I have some other news you'll like. I'm coming home and joining the New York State Police. That's right! I plan to become the third generation of New York State Troopers in our family!"

I heard him hold the phone away from his mouth and shouting.

"Please tell me that you are not shitting me!"

"Hell no Dad! I'm not gonna re-up. I'm coming home in a few months and starting the application process."

"You just made my fricking year kid!" He laughed. "I'll get your room ready. I was storing some shit in there temporarily, but it'll be ready when you get home."

I hated to burst his bubble, but Angie had already spoken. I'd rather face my disappointed dad than my pissed off Italian girlfriend. Still, I had to let him down easy.

"Hey, about that; I just talked to Angie and she wants me to stay with her when I get back. I told her that I would, but that I also wanted to spend some time with you at your apartment. Just so you know."

"Ah, I understand. Whatever you want to do is fine with me. I don't blame you for wanting to stay with your woman. She is one hot number! You know that your room will always be here for you. Consider it a Base Camp. Whenever you two fight and she puts your sorry ass out, you can always come back home!" he said laughing.

"Thanks Dad. I appreciate that. I'll call you next week to check in on you."

"You make sure to do that. Hey, have you told your mother yet?"

"Na, I haven't called her," I replied.

"I can understand why not, but don't feel bad. The way you see her, well, she's done that to herself."

Now my dad was starting in on her, just like Angie. Even though I hated what my mom had done to us, and I definitely loathed her new husband, she was still my mom. I didn't like anyone to put her down or beat up on her. I wished everyone would leave her and our history buried.

"Yes Dad, I hear you. I'll probably call her later and let her know what's going on."

He grunted, not liking my answer.

"It's up to you. I don't even think about her anymore. I've moved on with my life, just like she did," he replied.

But he was lying; he had never moved on or gotten over her. Our shared past affected him as much as it did me. It was time to end the call before I regretted making it.

"Good for you Dad. I have to go to physical therapy now and then grab some chow. I'm starving," I said.

"All right, Toddy. That's a big Ten-four! I'll talk to you next week. Please, try not to get your ass blown up before you come home."

"Will do!"

"Todd?"

"Yeah Dad?"

"I'm sorry about your buddies. I'm not going to sugarcoat it; it's going to be hard for a while. Take your time and grieve. God bless each one of them. They are all heroes in my opinion, just like you."

I should have thanked him and said goodbye, but I had to correct him.

"Dad, they're the true heroes, not me. They gave all; I didn't. I gotta run now. I'll talk to you later."

"Okay. Goodbye Todd."

I was relieved to be finished talking to everyone and getting off the emotional rollercoaster. First, I'm sad, then happy, then pissed off, then depressed. I was a mess. I walked back inside and swallowed a few more pain pills before falling asleep.

• • •

We moved up the dimly lit stairwell, the floor littered with trash, with our rifles locked and loaded at the ready. As we passed each door, we could hear noise and commotion coming from inside. Jay was on point, while me, Tucker, and Tom brought up the rear. Jay stopped and signaled—we had arrived at our objective. All eyes were on Tucker as he nodded to Tom, who set the explosive charges and unwound the detonation cord. The air was thick and humid and my goggles started to fog.

Panic set in as I sensed that something was wrong. I tapped Tuck and signaled, No go. He smiled and shook his head. I touched him again, No go! Suddenly, he turned and pulled my goggles down below my chin. I struggled against him and grabbed both of his wrists, but he was too strong.

"Tuck! No go! Abort!" I whispered frantically. He laughed at me and began shouting.

"Off we go!" he yelled, just before a colossal blast engulfed the entire stairwell, along with the four of us.

I screamed and was somehow still alive and conscious, but blinded and burning. I couldn't breathe. The sound of my screams became muffled as I smelled my own flesh cooking; sizzling like a steak on a grill. The pain was unbearable. I felt someone trying to put out the flames consuming my charred torso.

• • •

"Wake up, Corporal Goodson! Corporal Goodson. Wake up, Todd Goodson!"

I opened my eyes, gasping for air and struggling to breathe. The nurse's voice had rescued me and brought me back. "You had a bad dream, but you're safe now."

I sat up in my bed, drenched with sweat, and looked around the room. The nurse rubbed my back while she dried my head with a towel.

"Relax and breathe normally, in and out. That's it," she said.

"I need to stand up for a minute," I said. The nurse helped me out of bed while fanning my face with the manila folder she was holding. "Wow, that was a bad one! It has to be the worst nightmare I've had all week. Thanks for being close by. This time I couldn't breathe. I was suffocating and being cooked alive," I said.

She listened attentively and shook her head.

"I hate to admit it, but for many of the soldiers I treat, this is all too common. It breaks my heart to see a person go through this. Most survivors are too afraid to go to sleep, not knowing what terrible nightmares are coming their way."

I nodded in agreement.

"Shit, I must admit it is a living hell," I replied. I looked down and felt my T-shirt. "Damn, everything is soaked. I can't remember any nightmares causing me to sweat like this."

She nodded and began removing my linens.

"You need to take a shower and change your clothes. I'll have your linen changed by the time you come back," she said with a smile.

"Thank you," I replied and stood up. The strong odor of urine and feces filled the room. "Man! Where is *that* smell coming from?"

Her smile morphed into a sad expression though she remained silent. I realized that the smell was coming from me. I had pissed and crapped on myself. She handed me a change of clothes, and I turned away in shame and walked to the shower. I felt emasculated and weak. For the first time since becoming a Marine, I didn't feel equal or worthy. I felt broken.

The shower washed away the filth and waste off my body, but did nothing for my pride. What was happening to me? I seemed empty inside with no center and no foundation. I was changed.

I finished my shower and walked back to my bed. It was freshly made, the top blanket folded back and exposing the clean sheets.

It reminded me of my mom; she used to do the same thing when I was a kid. She would always give me a snack before bed and then read me a short story. She and I were alone most nights while my Dad was on duty, patrolling the New York State highways.

I looked at my watch and saw it was 2330 hours, which would make it around 3:30 PM in California. Two months had passed since the attack, and I still hadn't called my mom to let her know. I grabbed my cell phone and walked outside to the empty courtyard. I sat down on a bench and looked through my contacts until I found her number. I breathed deep and dialed. It connected and my temper flared as *he* answered.

"Hello… Hello?"

"Hey, this is Todd. Is my mother there?"

"Hello, Todd! How are you doing out there?" I could hear the excitement in his voice as if he sincerely cared about how I was doing. I didn't know why. I certainly didn't care about him or how he was doing. To me, he was only blowing smoke up my ass.

"Uh, yeah, I don't have much time to talk; we're heading out soon. Is my mom there? I want to talk to her."

"Yes she is. Sorry. I'll get her. Hold on."

I heard him call for her.

"Sarah! Todd is on the phone." He got back on the call. "She's coming Todd. I usually don't even answer her phone, but I saw your name come up on the caller ID and didn't want her to miss it," he said. I kept silent. "Well, take care of yourself. It's good to hear your voice. Your mother will be ecstatic! When will you be able to come back to the states and visit? We can meet you anywhere you choose after you come back home. Just let us know."

"Yeah, okay," I replied.

I kept our conversation short. Every passing second talking to him was torture. Then, *she* picked up the phone.

"Todd! How are you doing?"

"I'm doing good Mom. Um, I had a little accident, but I'm about to be released from the hospital soon," I said. I heard her shriek.

"Oh no! What has happened?"

"I lost some of my friends in an attack on our squad. I'm all right, though, but I can't really say any more on the phone. I just wanted to let you know that I am not re-enlisting. I'm separating from the military. I'll be flying back to New York soon."

I could hear her sobbing quietly. Although our relationship had been strained for over a decade, I couldn't deny that we shared a deep connection. I couldn't bear to hear my mother weep.

"I pray for you every day Todd, and so does Herman. We ask that God protect you, keep you, and bring you home safely! I am so sorry for the loss of your friends. I cannot imagine what their families are going through. Can you give me their parents or spouses contact information so I can call them and give them my condolences? I want to offer them assistance or any type of help that they might need."

"I don't have any of that right now. I'll try and get that to you later when I get a chance."

I knew I was telling her a lie. This was my life and these were my friends. I didn't need her and Herman talking to any of Jay's or Tom's people, let alone Tucker's family.

"Please do honey, and please, please call me more often. I know you don't like to write letters, so I don't wait for a response from all the letters I send you every month, but at least let me hear your voice more often. I miss you! It's been over a year since we have talked to you, and even that was a very short conversation. Will you do that for me Todd?"

"Okay Mom, I will. I have to go now. Be safe," I said.

"I understand dear. Please be careful. Let me know when you return home. I love you Todd."

I usually avoided saying those words back to her, but I had to. For me, it was like pulling my fingernails out.

"I love you too Mom. Goodbye." I ended the call and looked up at the night sky. The half-moon was a bright beacon above. I remembered looking at the same moon from the top of our apartment building in New York. The same moon, but half a world away. It began to dawn on me that I was going back to the world, a place where everything made sense. I could fix myself there and find my center again, my foundation. I grinned for a moment and walked back inside, knowing that I was one day closer to going back home.

CHAPTER TWO

HOME SWEET HOME

*T*he Humvee rocked back and forth over the potholes, as we slowly rolled through the dirt alley. All four of us sat in our usual seats with our M4s locked, loaded, and resting on the door window frames. This gave us a good field of fire. It was dusty and the heat was excruciating, while the thick air made it hard to breathe, like someone was sitting on my chest.

"Just a little further," Tucker whispered to Tom. The tenement buildings towered over us and blocked out the sun. The alley became darker the farther we ventured. Fear crept up my back and caressed my neck. I shuddered and looked to see if Jay noticed. He was quiet, focusing on any movement from the buildings. Tuck was looking directly ahead and smiling, and then turned to Tom.

"Stop here. Turn off the engine."

Tom followed orders and we sat. I couldn't believe what Tucker was doing. We were like sitting ducks in the dark, so I challenged him.

"What are you doing Tuck? We should keep moving before we get hit!" I yelled. He started to laugh hysterically while Jay and Tom seemed oblivious to the danger. I tried to open the door, but it was stuck. I set my rifle on my lap and pulled on the door using both hands, but it wouldn't move. I began to panic. I leaned back against Jay and kicked the door with both feet.

Bam! Bam! Bam! The door remained closed. I stuck my head and shoulders out of the window, hoping to climb out that way. I twisted my body and caught ahold of the roof. As I lifted myself up and out, I saw rifles appear from every window surrounding the alley. I slid back inside the Humvee.

"Hostiles everywhere! Please! Let's go home!" I screamed as bullets ripped through the shell of our Humvee from all directions. I picked up my rifle to return fire, but nothing happened. I cleared and tried again. Nothing. I changed mags, but my rifle still wouldn't fire. No one returned fire as blood splattered, covering the interior of our vehicle. I looked out the front window and saw a hostile standing in front of our Humvee.

"Twelve o'clock!" I shouted.

The enemy combatant shouldered a rocket-propelled grenade launcher and fired it directly into our windshield.

"God, no!" I screamed as the RPG exploded.

I heard a woman's voice and felt a touch on my shoulder.

"Sir, please fasten your seatbelt and prepare for our final descent to LaGuardia," the flight attendant said.

"Yes ma'am," I replied and opened my eyes. To my surprise, it was a male attendant, not a woman. I fastened my seat belt.

"Sorry about that. I was out of it. I thought a woman was talking to me."

He chuckled and answered with the same feminine voice.

"Sir, to be totally honest, when I can save up enough money that will be a dream come true for me." He smiled and went on his way down the aisle. I shook my head in disgust, not wanting to believe a queer had actually touched me.

I moved into the empty window seat next to mine and buckled up. The plane was descending through the lowest layer of clouds, and I could see the landscape of my country below. This was what I had been fighting for all these years. The land of the free.

I was pumped up and nearly bouncing off the walls of the cabin. This was the happiest I had been since *that day*, and I could feel that things were starting to fall back into place. It was surreal and hard to believe that I was almost home!

I tried calling Tucker's phone in the weeks leading up to my return, but every time it went straight to voicemail. Finally, this past Tuesday, Tucker's little sister Tracy answered. Tucker had told me about her, and I knew that he worried about her all the time, especially the night of her high school prom. I was grateful to hear her voice, knowing she was a link to my best friend.

The news she gave me was bittersweet. He was alive, with all mental faculties intact, but he had lost his left leg at the knee and left arm at the elbow. He wasn't paralyzed, but due to the nature of his injuries and the shrapnel still lodged in and around his internal organs, he would have to use a wheelchair for the foreseeable future. She told me that despite being scheduled for several more surgeries, he was in good spirits. In her words, "You know how tough Tucker is!" She was right; he was as tough as they came.

She told me that he would be released from intensive care and coming home in a week, but she would call him at the hospital and let him know she had spoken with me. She apologized for not checking his voice mails, but she didn't have his password until he regained consciousness. My eyes watered after she let me know he was barely coherent, but he had asked about me, asking where I was. I told her I would call him once he was home.

I thought about our conversation and that brought a wave of guilt over me, drowning me in thoughts of how my friend was now disabled, while I walked around healthy and whole. Life wasn't fair, but what the hell could I do about it? A headache was coming so as we landed, I closed my eyes and turned my thoughts to Angie. She would be waiting for me at the airport.

I followed behind the slow-moving caravan of passengers through the tunnel and toward the gate, wondering which person in front of me was radiating a musty odor. I hoped the funky scent wouldn't linger on my clothes and ruin my reunion moment.

I was about to see my girl!

I reached the passenger pick-up area and looked around as the crowd began to disperse. Where was she? I turned to my left and saw her running up to me. It was like a movie. As I dropped my luggage, she jumped into my arms. I held her tightly and we hugged for what seemed an eternity. As our embrace loosened, our mouths came together and we kissed. I was lost in her spell.

She pulled away and stared into my eyes. "Let's find your bags and get out of here baby, I've got to get you alone."

"Let's go!" I replied and picked up my bags, while she led me by the hand to baggage claim.

Soon, we were in her car on our way to the city, first to see my Dad. I played with her hair as she drove, while she dug her nails in my thigh. At the first red stoplight, we started making out.

"Damn it Todd, I can't wait. We have to stop at a motel before we see your dad. I'm sorry."

"Let's go! I'm about to rip your clothes off in this car!" I demanded. We were like animals in heat and continued our mating ritual. She stopped at the first motel we saw and purchased a room for us.

Two hours later, we both found ourselves dehydrated, exhausted, and hungry. We checked out of the room and bought some food from Arby's on our way to my dad's apartment. As she drove, I couldn't keep my eyes off her. She was beautiful.

"I needed that so bad, you have no idea," she said while her eyes rolled upward.

"You and me both babe!" I replied. It felt great to finally get laid. I reclined my seat and closed my eyes. "I can't believe I'm home. I can't believe it."

"Believe it, baby. You're here with me now and you're not going anywhere."

I looked over at her and grinned. "I don't want to be anywhere else," I replied and kissed her cheek.

• • •

Forty-five minutes later, we were at my dad's apartment. I rang the doorbell and within seconds the door swung open.

"Hey Todd!" my dad shouted out before hugging me. He grabbed me by both shoulders and looked me up and down. "My boy," he cried, then hugged me again before turning to Angie. "I'm sorry, Angie." He let me go and hugged her. "Come on in you two."

We walked inside and I noticed how dark the room was. All the blinds were closed and there was only one small lamp on the table beside his recliner. His place was stuffy and the air had a faint sour smell. I was slightly embarrassed for Angie's sake, but she probably didn't notice.

"Sit down and make yourselves comfortable. Do you want something to eat? You must be hungry," he asked.

"No, thanks Dad. We stopped and picked something up already."

"Well then, how about something to drink? Angie, what would you like?"

"I'm fine, Mr. Goodson, thank you so much," she answered.

He looked at me again. "How about a beer son? Drink a cold one with your old man?"

"That's a big Ten-four on that, Dad!"

He smiled and hustled away before returning with two cold beers and handing me one. He held out his bottle for a toast.

"Here is to a warrior coming home from battle. Todd Goodson, a job well done!"

I smirked and tapped his bottle. "Roger that," I mumbled.

We stayed for nearly an hour. I updated him with what I knew about Tucker and Angie told him her plans for my living arrangements, as well as the academy. While they spoke, my eyes wandered around the room. Everything was just as I remembered, except for one familiar family portrait. He had long since taken it down, even before I enlisted with the Marines, yet now I saw it was displayed again. I didn't comment on it, knowing why he took it down in the first place. After Mom left us, he removed everything associated with her from the apartment. It told me, contrary to his words, he was not over her.

Finally, I felt myself getting sleepy and knew it was time to leave.

He walked us outside with a huge grin on his face. It felt good to see my father happy. He could be a cantankerous old bastard most of the time, so I cherished this brief episode of his happiness.

We left and drove to Angelica's new apartment. I was impressed at how classy it was and wondered how she could afford the rent, let alone the designer furniture that filled it.

She gave me the grand tour, so I had to ask her. "How can you afford this place? It must cost a small fortune."

She looked at me and smiled. "Not a small fortune, but a pretty penny. My last year's bonus and this year's promotion to senior sales rep paid for all of this. My career is really taking off, with even better things to come. Okay, you need to remember a few rules. Number one rule: pick up after yourself. I am not your house cleaner. Rule number two: only eat at the kitchen table, not on the couch or bed. Now, tell me what rule number three is?" She looked pointedly at me with her arms crossed. I turned around and looked at the bed behind me.

"Uh, make up the bed after I get up?" I asked.

"No silly! Leave the toilet seat down! Making up the bed is rule number four." She laughed and pushed me backward onto the bed. I let her pin me down by my arms and maul me until our faces were only a few inches apart. We both stopped and stared at each other. The room went quiet.

"I missed you Todd. Don't leave me anymore."

"I love you Angie. I won't ever leave you again babe."

She smiled and laid her head on my chest as we closed our eyes and melted together in the moment. It had been a long day and it was late in the evening, so we decided to go to bed. The excitement of spending my first night back in the country with the woman I loved was mind-blowing.

A few minutes later, we were lying in bed under the covers together in the dark. Everything was peaceful and still as her head lay on my chest. I slowly ran my fingers through her soft hair. I felt her breath tickling the hairs of my chest every time she exhaled. It was rhythmic and relaxing and soon we were asleep.

• • •

"No! Wait! No! No!" I screamed, breaking the dead silence of the night. "Wait!"

The light came on and my eyes flew open.

Angie was yelling. "Todd! What's wrong? You're scaring me!"

I looked at her, standing at the end of the bed with her arms folded and trembling. I was confused and sweat ran down my face as I tried to control my breathing.

"I had a bad dream. Sorry, I didn't mean to scare you."

My chest was tight, as if some invisible person was squeezing the shit out of me. I felt ashamed for letting this happen in front of Angie. I jumped out of bed and went into the bathroom. I heard her footsteps behind me, so I closed the door behind me and locked it. A few seconds later, I heard Angie trying to turn the knob.

"Why are you locking the door, Todd? Are you taking a crap?" She was noticeably irritated.

"No, I just want to take a shower." It was a lie. I wanted some privacy. I needed some time to get my head straight, my thoughts together.

"Todd! Open this damn door right now!" she yelled.

I opened the door and stripped down in front of her, then turned on the shower.

"Where do you keep your towels and washcloths?" I asked.

She stared at me without saying a word. Angie was unpredictable and I didn't know what she would say or how she would react. She unfolded her arms and handed me the items from a cabinet.

"Here," she said. "My body wash is in the shower beside my hair conditioner and shampoo. Only use my body wash, not my hair products."

"Not a problem. Thanks."

I stepped inside the shower and noticed that the tightness in my chest was easing a bit. Maybe she would just go back to bed and forget about the entire episode, as if it never happened.

"Todd, we need to talk about this," she said.

I winced and shook my head, just my luck. Why couldn't she let it go? She is so damn nosey! I remained calm, even though this was my personal business. She had no right to know about this side of me. I was the one dealing with these nightmares, not her. There was no way she could understand any of it.

"All right, what's up? What do you want to say?" I asked.

"How often does that happen to you? Where you wake up like that?"

"It happens at different times. It's not every night; more like every other day. Sometimes it will be a couple of weeks between dreams," I replied. I was becoming irritated. "Shit! Why are you making me explain this to you? I'm not some kind of freak for you to evaluate."

She was furious and she snapped back. "I didn't call you a freak and I am not making you explain anything! I asked you a simple question and you started yelling at me. I'm your girlfriend dammit!

We are living together now and you just scared the living hell out of me! That's bullshit!"

I regretted my defensiveness and yelling at Angie. I knew I appeared unstable and reeked of anger issues. I tried to answer but she stormed out of the bathroom and slammed the door behind her. I got inside the shower turned up the hot water while I thought of what I should say or do to make things right with her. After I finished drying off, I silently rehearsed different versions of my apology in the mirror. Then I opened the door to a dark room. Angie was lying on her side, facing away from me. I got into bed and touched her shoulder.

"Angie, I apologize for yelling. I was wrong and it won't happen again. I promise."

She rolled over and faced me. "It won't happen again? You're right. Because if it does, you can pack your bags and go live somewhere else. I am not putting up with any of that," she said.

"It won't happen again, but it's not as if you don't yell at me when you get pissed off. I will never yell again when you ask me a question, but in everyday life, people have disagreements and arguments. Every couple does," I replied.

Her cold expression was unyielding. "As far as me yelling at you, you're a guy and have a hard head. I don't just yell at you for no reason; there's always a reason. I only wanted to know about your screaming out and scaring the shit out of me, that's all. Don't you believe I have the right to know about that?" she asked.

"You're right, I was completely out of line. I was embarrassed and defensive because it happened with you here."

I hoped that she would give up soon and forget about it, so we could go back to sleep.

"Maybe you should go and talk to someone about it." she replied.

"All of us coming back home had to do that already. They gave us information on PTSD over there and before I came home. Some of the guys had serious mental issues and needed medication. I'm sure it helped them, but I don't need any of that. I'm in good shape. I have bad dreams sometimes, that's all."

Instead of responding to what I said, she caressed my cheek and then ran her fingers through my hair.

"Kiss me," she whispered.

I pulled her against my body and kissed her.

"Now, take me," she moaned.

So, I did just that for the next hour, before we fell asleep together again.

• • •

I woke up the next morning to a bright and sunlit bedroom, squinting as I looked at the clock. It was 9:18 AM. She must have opened all the drapes before she left for work, because I remembered them being closed. I stood up and stretched before hobbling into the kitchen and opening the refrigerator. There was a container of orange juice, which I filled a glass from and devoured. I looked around the kitchen and was still amazed at how she could afford this place. I spotted a note on the counter.

Good Morning Todd!

Today's to-do list!
Car keys are on the wall.

1) Go to the market and pick up steak, asparagus, and 2% milk.
2) Vacuum the apartment.
3) Wash any dishes that you use.
4) Complete New York State Police Trooper application online. My laptop is on the coffee table.
5) Go to the State unemployment office and file for your unemployment benefits. I researched it and veterans have at least 3 months of benefits after discharge.

I will see you around 7.
Hugs, Angie.
P.S. Do not wreck my car!

Well, it was considerate of her to plan out the whole day for me. What would I do without her? I crumbled the note and tossed it in the garbage, showered, and grabbed an apple on the way out the door.

By three o'clock, I had completed the list and was ready to sit down and watch some television. I popped the cap off my beer and kicked up my feet. I needed something to take the edge off while adjusting to civilian life. It felt strange to be out in public for some reason, but I couldn't put my finger on it. I expected some weirdness after being out of the country for years, but the sense of waiting for something to feel familiar was smothering me. It made me anxious.

Back at the hospital, the doc gave me plenty of Xanax to help my anxiety, but that gravy train ran out the day I was discharged. If I wanted more of that prescription, I would need to make a trip to the local veterans hospital, see a shrink, and cry to him about my problems. Screw that! I wasn't going to pretend to be weak just to get meds. I knew plenty of crybabies who played that game, with the sole intent on getting high on the government's expense. Besides, good old alcohol worked fine and did the trick for me.

I clicked through the endless cable channels while trying to filter out all the junk, until I found the Military Channel. I was now in heaven. I finished my beer and grabbed another, wondering if the six-pack would last me to the next hour, or if I should run out and grab a case. While trying to decide, a film documentary on the war in Afghanistan began and I was mesmerized.

I felt relief at being stateside in my own skin, as the battle I had just left raged on before my eyes. I was perfectly content to sit here and watch this channel for the next few months. With a future unemployment check coming from the State of New York and my application submitted to the NYSP, I only needed to relax and hang loose until I got my appointment to take the exam. The only thing left on my own "to-do list," was to get ahold of Tucker by the end of the week. That was my number one priority.

• • •

"The total is $194.13. Cash or credit?" the cashier asked me.

"Cash, ma'am," I replied while rifling through my wallet. She finished up and gave me my change. I pushed the cart through the sliding doors and rolled towards Angie's car. The ceiling fan I had just purchased needed to be installed today. Orders from the officer ranks had come in. I had asked Angie why today? Her answer was, "Just do it, please!" That patented response was nothing new to me, Nike had been using it for decades. The only difference between her orders and the Corps was that Angie always said please. I repeated a military mantra to myself, "Mine is not to question why? Mine is just to do or die." Luckily, I was halfway finished with this mission by purchasing the fan. Now I only needed to install it. I opened the trunk and attempted to fit the oversized box inside.

"No, that can't be Todd!"

I heard the voice behind me and turned to look. I was shocked to see one of my best friends from high school, Reggie Huggins.

"Reggie? Damn man! What's up!" We shook hands and gave a chest bump, just like we did years ago. He was like I remembered, but older and his dreadlocks were longer.

"Damn man! My homeboy! It must be at least six years since we last talked, bro. I remember the last thing you told me was that you were going to become a Marine. You look like a Marine, no doubt!"

"I served over six years man. In fact, I just got back Stateside last week with my duffle bags and my honorable discharge in hand. I'm staying with my girl now. You remember Angie?" I asked.

He raised his eyebrows. "Yeah of course, I remember her bro. Fine as wine. I didn't get the vibe back in those days that she approved of you hanging out with me."

I laughed. "There's not too much she does approve of these days. Back then, she probably thought you were a player and leading me astray. She hadn't changed much, still jealous as hell and still with the bitchy attitude, but I love her anyway, straight up," I replied.

"That's what's up Todd. What are you planning on doing for work now that you're home? Going back to college?"

"I'm waiting on a testing date from the NYSP. I'm going for state trooper and expect to test within the month, but I'm not sure when my appointment to the academy will be. Could be anywhere from a couple of months up to a year, so I'll just have to wait and see."

He nodded. "Sounds good. I like your plan but check this out— I took the two years we spent in technical college and started my own HVAC business. I have two employees and all the work we can handle.

In fact, I was about to open a job position and post it online because we really need some more help during this season. Here, take my business card. If you want to work with me until your other plans come through, then hit me up and you got yourself a job."

His offer was unexpected but appreciated.

"I appreciate that Reggie, but I don't remember a lot from tech school. It was so long ago. I've been infantry for the past six years and using a whole other skillset. I wouldn't be much good to you," I replied, pocketing his card.

"Shit, you can do the helper work while I refresh your memory, nothing fancy. I pay weekly. Everything would be above board, though I don't have any health benefits right now since I'm a small business. The other employees are using Obamacare, but that shouldn't be an issue for you being a military veteran. It would be something for you to do until you are called up. Think about it bro."

I looked at his card again and shook his hand. "Thanks, I'll think about it for sure."

"Cool! Call me anyway so we can meet up at a bar and have some drinks."

"Roger that. Take it easy, Reg."

He walked into the store while I finished loading the fan. I started the car and shook my head, still in disbelief at seeing Reggie. He had been a true friend during the worst times in my life, especially when my mom left my dad and me. I lost contact with him back then but didn't remember why. I was glad we crossed paths, but I needed to get to the apartment right away and install the fan. I still planned to call Tucker before six o'clock tonight.

• • •

A few hours later, I had completed the installation and tested the fan. Everything was working properly. I felt good having wired it correctly on the first attempt, which let me know that some of my technical skills were still there. I might have to take Reggie up on his job offer after all. This was a job well done and now it was time to call Tucker. I grabbed my phone and dialed his number. A few seconds passed before I heard the call connect and begin ringing.

Suddenly, my chest began to tighten. I ended the call and put the phone down. What was happening to me? I couldn't get enough oxygen and soon became flush and dizzy. I sat down and tried to relax and control my breathing. I picked up the phone and stared at it as guilt overwhelmed me. I fought back my tears and attempted to call him again, but I couldn't do it. How could I talk to him? How could I stand here as a whole man and face him? How could I not speak to him? I owed him.

I blew my nose and cleared my throat, then dialed. On the fourth ring, Tucker answered. "Hey, Todd. What the hell took you so long to call bro? I've been waiting for you."

I choked up with tears streaming down my face, barely able to talk.

"Hey Tuck. I'm sorry man." I couldn't hold myself together, but I was trying my best. I put the phone on the table and walked away, sobbing quietly, trying to keep my shit together. I paced back and forth a few times and sat back down before picking up the phone. "Sorry Tuck, I'm all emotional right now and had to put the phone down. I didn't hear if you answered back."

Tucker's voice sounded relaxed, even confident. "I can tell that you're upset, buddy. Tom and Jay are gone. I know what you're feeling, I feel it too. You're not alone," he replied.

I stood up with the phone to my ear and began pacing again. "Tuck, I feel like shit. I don't deserve to be the only one walking around. I'd rather be a dead man, goddamn me! I'm sorry Tuck!"

"You stow that shit right now, Marine! I mean it! Don't you ever feel guilty about surviving! Shit happens, remember that. We all did our duty and the chips fell where they did. Tom and Jay won't ever be forgotten. I miss both of them, but where they exist now in glory, they are untouchable! So give thanks to God for having the honor and privilege of serving with them and for saving you. Do you copy me, Corporal?"

Tucker spoke the truth, and I needed to hear it, not from just anyone, but from his own mouth.

"Rah, I copy. Thanks for setting me straight. Tell me what I can do for you buddy. When can I come down and visit?"

"Thanks, but there's not a whole lot you can do for me. My little sister let me know that she told you about my injuries. I've got shrapnel inside me that they want to remove later this year or early next. I've been learning how to get around and do things for myself. I'll look at getting some prosthetics for my arm and leg after my final surgery. It sucks, but they don't want me to try to stand or walk until they remove the shrapnel. They say it's too close to my heart. Besides my physical therapy and counseling, I'm not doing too much. You're welcome to come down here anytime. You can stay with us at my folk's house in the spare bedroom. Don't worry about renting a room. You're like family and my folks and sister know all about you. Other than that, I've just been watching a lot of TV."

"How about the Military Channel, bro? I've been watching that all week!"

"Hell yeah! I can't get enough of it!" Tucker laughed.

We spoke for another fifteen minutes until Tuck had to take his meds and get some sleep. I told him I would call him every few days and he promised to do the same. We decided I would make the trip down there to see him right after the NYSP called me in for testing.

I set my phone down on the counter and walked outside on the balcony.

It was as if a giant weight had been lifted off my shoulders and the negative emotions drained out of me. Tucker's words had eased my guilt. He didn't blame me for anything and understood exactly what I was feeling. That meant everything to me. His attitude was positive, as always, in spite of his condition. I tried putting myself in his situation for a moment, but knew I wouldn't have been as strong as him.

I looked out across the city and daydreamed. After looking at my watch, I realized that Angie would be coming home shortly. A nervous vibe started to rise up inside my stomach. There was still a half bottle of Wild Turkey whiskey left in the kitchen cabinet. I rapid-fired four consecutive shots and shivered momentarily, closing my eyes, as I felt the warm liquor heating up my chest as it went down. Those four shots were the secret remedy for keeping my anxiety at bay nowadays. They were quick and gave immediate results.

I grabbed another beer out of the fridge and sat down on the couch, turning on the television to my new all-time favorite channel. This was the best time of the day for me since no one was around to bother me. I turned up the volume and waited in anticipation to see the smile on Angie's face once she saw the new fan I installed.

• • •

"What the hell, Todd! That's not the fan I wanted!" Angie yelled.

"I swear this is the fan you picked out, remember?" I replied while trying to control my anger. She walked underneath the fan and threw her purse on the couch.

"Look at it! Those blades are oak. I picked cherry. That's not cherry, dammit!" she yelled and then stormed off to the bathroom.

I heard the door slam. I hated when she slammed doors or cabinets, and she did it all the time. I walked to the fridge, grabbed a beer, and sat down on the couch. I know she chose the oak, but it didn't matter because she was always right. I heard the toilet flush and the door open. I prepared myself for the inevitable onslaught that was to follow. She stomped back into the room.

"I know what I wanted and this is not it!" she yelled and shook her head while I remained quiet. "I asked you to do one simple thing and you screwed it up," she said with her hand on her hips.

That was enough. I had to mount some defense. I wasn't going to listen to her bark at me all night. My heart beat faster and my neck tightened.

"All right, it was my mistake. I apologize. I'll return this fan and buy the other one. It's a hundred dollars more but right now I'm low on cash. When my unemployment check comes next week, I'll take care of it first thing," I said calmly.

Her eyes widened. Evidently, my solution was somehow offensive.

"There are a few other issues I want to address," she said. "You're barely coming up with your half of the bills. You sit here all day, drinking and watching that stupid war channel. Also, I can't even get a good night's sleep because I don't know when you'll wake up screaming like a freaking madman. Our sex life is nothing to be proud of either...what is wrong with you?"

I kept my mouth shut. I couldn't believe she would cut me down like this. It hurt and made me angry, but I knew I couldn't give in to the rage inside; that uncontrollable destructive force which slept just below the surface of my sanity.

"Say something dammit!" she screamed.

"What do you want from me!" I shouted. I stood up and put my beer on the coffee table. This time she was the silent one. "Huh? You've been on my ass for weeks! I've been doing whatever you ask me to do, but during my downtime I watch whatever damn channel I want! I don't tell you what to watch, do I?" Still no response from her, but she was taking it all in, and I knew that she would return fire shortly. "About me waking up, well I can't help it right now. It is what it is. I can sleep on the couch if you'd rather."

I attempted to rein in my emotions.

"No, I don't want you to sleep on the couch. I never said that."

I continued, "And sex is a two-way street. Half the time, when I come to you, all I get is excuses. You're tired, not in the mood, have a headache, whatever…"

"Wait, one minute, mister! That might be true, but the other half of the time you can't get it up because you're drunk! You can't blame me for that." She walked into the kitchen shaking her head. I followed behind her and sat down at the counter. She took down a bottle of wine from the rack and poured herself a glass before directing her attention back to me.

"Todd, I think you need to see a doctor or something. Waking up like you do is not normal. I know they have psychologists at the VA who can prescribe you something, or give you counseling. At this point, anything would help. They should be able to give you Viagra or some kind of medication for your impotence. I've never seen you like this before."

"Listen Angie, this is only temporary. I have it under control. Trust me. I don't want to start going to a shrink like I'm some kind of nut, and I definitely don't want something like that to get back to the NYSP and have my application denied because of it. They might require me to have some kind of waiver before proceeding, so I'm not going to the VA."

She sipped her wine slowly while staring at me. I could sense that this episode was nearly defused, and my breathing returned to normal.

"Well," she said, "you need to find a part-time job or something else to occupy your time. Ease up with the drinking and hopefully, we should be able to have some sort of normal sex life. And please watch something else on television besides all that war and killing. I don't understand why you would want to see that stuff after all you've been through."

"You couldn't understand unless you were there, so let's leave that alone. The Military Channel stays, but I'll cut back on my drinking. I can agree to that."

She walked out of the kitchen, sat on the couch, and turned on the television. I hoped it meant this conversation was the last negotiation of a peace agreement, at least for today. I was so relieved I almost forgot to tell her about the job offer from Reggie, and that I had spoken with Tucker.

"Hey, Angie, guess who I saw today?"

"Who?"

"My old buddy Reggie—from school."

She looked puzzled. "The black guy with the dreads?"

"Yep. He's doing good for himself. He started his own HVAC service company and has some building contracts." I walked over to her, took his business card out my wallet, and handed it to her. She looked at it and gave it back.

"Okay, great," she said while changing the channels. I had expected more of a response from her, maybe I shouldn't have. I put the card back in my wallet.

"So, he offered me a job working with him. He knows I'm waiting for the call for the NYSP testing, but he didn't mind. This sounds like an opportunity to get out of the apartment and stay busy while making some extra cash on the side. I'm thinking about giving him a call."

She slammed her glass on the table. "Why the hell would you want to go work with him? Are you serious! You are a decorated war veteran, a Marine for Christ's sake! You're on your way to become a New York State Trooper and are considering working as some two-bit helper for some wannabe Bob Marley?"

"What are you talking about, Angie? It's Reggie!"

She stood. "You know that I never cared for that boy. Whenever you were with him you played that jungle ass rap, that noise they call music. You should've outgrown all that by now. As a matter of fact, you should've learned by now to associate with your own kind. You're a man now, Todd, start acting like one."

I couldn't take it anymore. I had to leave.

"You know what, Angie? I'm done with this. I'm going out." I replied.

I grabbed my jacket and headed toward the door. She trailed after me.

"Oh! So, you're going to tuck your tail between your legs and run? Go ahead then, you coward!" she screamed at me.

I turned and pointed my finger at her, causing her to step back.

"Don't you ever call me a coward again!" I yelled.

At that moment, I could see that she was scared. She realized she had gone too far.

I left, slamming the door behind me and feeling terrible. I hated myself for making her fear me. I wanted to protect her and make her happy, but instead I was making her miserable. As I ventured off to bar hop, my gut was churning with that familiar sick feeling. I couldn't shake the feeling of being alone, out of control, and unsure of myself. I knew picking a fight at a bar and causing damage to someone wasn't the right way to deal with my issues, but it was something that could give me back a sense of control. I hoped I wouldn't regret it later.

• • •

A month had passed since me and Angie's last argument, and things seemed to be getting better. I slept on the couch for the first week, so as not to wake her up at night. I cut my alcohol consumption by half and made sure not to watch my favorite channel while she was around. The sex department was still suffering, mostly from the tension of walking around on eggshells.

Two weeks earlier, I was contacted by the NYSP to complete the entrance exam. I thought I scored well.

I woke up late today. I stumbled into the kitchen and made some coffee. Nothing was more valuable in the morning than my coffee. Then I booted up the computer to check my emails. I began deleting all the junk spam in my inbox, and then stopped. I mistakenly checked one email from the NYSP but caught my mistake and opened it.

"Mr. Todd Goodson, we are pleased to inform you…"

"Oorah!" I shouted at the top of my lungs. I had passed the exam! I stood up and clenched my fists over my head. "Oorah! Yes! Hell yes!"

I paced back and forth before sitting back down and finishing the letter. My report date for the academy was nearly eleven months away. Damn. Why couldn't it be sooner? Oh well, why was I complaining? I just passed the exam!

I called my Dad first and let him know. By the sound of his reaction, he was happier than I was. I told him I would schedule time later in the week to go out and celebrate. Next, I told Tucker, who was totally stoked for me. Since I had eleven months before I could report, I had plenty of time to visit him in Tennessee.

I walked onto the balcony and leaned on the railing. Life was positively changing for me. My goals and dreams were now one step closer. I walked back inside and texted Angie to give me a call. I was surprised when she called me back a few minutes later.

"Hey Todd. What's wrong now?" she asked, sounding tired.

"Nothing's wrong, everything is right! I just received notice I passed the exam."

"That's awesome! It's about time! When do you leave?"

"They estimate eleven months lead time but said to wait for a letter from them with the final reporting date. So, I have a little while yet. Anyway, I'm all set."

"Eleven months? That's almost a year," she replied.

"I told my Dad already, so let's plan to go out and celebrate. I'll call him back with the when and where," I said.

There was a moment of silence on her end.

"So, you told your Dad before you told me? You live with me; I'm your woman, but you tell him first. Thanks a lot."

Could she be any more negative? The answer was yes, but I was determined to avoid all her attempts to bring me down and rain on my parade.

"I apologize babe. I didn't think. Let's celebrate tonight, my treat. I can wait for you to get home and then we can pick up Dad together, or he and I can meet you somewhere."

"Hold on for a second." She put me on hold. She picked back up a minute later. "Today is really not a good day for me. I have to work late and won't get off until seven. You guys can meet me after seven thirty at Triple J's Bar and Grille. It's only two blocks from my job."

"Sounds good. I'll let Dad know. We'll see you tonight."

"All right. Bye."

"Angie?"

"Yes?"

"I love you," I said. I hadn't told her that in over a month.

"You too," she replied before ending the call.

• • •

I got to my Dad's apartment around four and after a few beers, we were beside ourselves. I would be the third generation of law enforcement in my family, and my father had told most of his friends by the time I arrived. Three other retirees from the NYPD came by and congratulated me. We drank and laughed for a while before they left, but by six o'clock, I was restless and needed a change of scenery. My dad and I decided to leave early for Triple J's and continue our drinking at the bar.

We took a cab down to Broadway and got out across the street from the bar. It was drizzling while we rode, but now a steady rain fell as we walked across the street. Dad began to cuss.

"It doesn't rain for two months and decides to rain today! What the hell is wrong with Mother Nature? She's a bitch today!" he complained while I laughed.

"What else do you expect from her? She's a woman!" I replied. We walked past the front window of the bar, laughing, when something caught my eye. I stopped walking.

"What's wrong, Todd? Come on, we're getting soaked."

I leaned closer to the glass window, which was slightly foggy, and saw Angie sitting at the bar. Which was strange, because she wasn't supposed to meet us for another hour. I shrugged, assuming she must have gotten off early and came here. No problem, cool.

I began to turn away and walk inside when I saw a man walk up and hand her a drink. I stopped again, though my dad was getting antsy.

"What's wrong?" he asked.

The dude stood next to her chair, laughing, his hand resting on her shoulder. She was all smiles, flinging her hair to the side in that sexy way she does.

"Angie's in there already. I think some dude is bothering her," I said.

I went inside, directly to the bar, unsure if my dad was behind me. Her back was to me and the guy saw me approach. Surprisingly, he knew my name and called out to me.

"Here he is now! Hello Todd, I finally get a chance to meet you. How are you doing? My name is—"

"I don't give a rat's ass what your name is. You better keep your hands off my damn girlfriend before you get yourself hurt," I said, now standing a foot away from him. His eyes widened while giving me a look of disgust, maybe even contempt.

Angie stood up. "Oh, my god, don't act like a fool, Todd. This is Martin; he works with me. He's not some random guy trying to pick me up at a bar, so just relax," she said calmly.

I looked from her to him.

"I saw the two of you before I came inside. I saw your hands on her shoulder. In fact, you were standing so close to her, you could have laid your cock on her thigh. I'm not buying the innocent co-worker excuse. Like I said, keep your hands off my woman. I won't tell you again."

I sized him up already and was ready for the bell to start the fight. He pretended to be an alpha male and showed no fear, only arrogance, as he stared back at me without saying a word.

"Stop it!" she yelled. Her shout drew the attention of the bartender, who walked over to our side of the bar.

"Is everything all right Angie?" he asked while wiping down the counter. Angie changed her sneer to a smile.

"Yeah, everything is fine, Dave. No problem over here, thanks," she replied. He walked away, and she turned back to me.

"Martin and I got off early, so we came down here. I didn't call you because what would be the point? We already made our plans. I'm here early trying to de-stress from a long day at work, but you can't let that happen, oh no! You have to start some shit with my friend who is here to help you celebrate. If you can't relax and act normal, then why don't you just leave? We'll talk about this when I get home."

She sat back down in her seat and sipped her drink as if the conversation was over. I turned and noticed my dad behind me, looking unsure of himself and the situation. He tapped me on the shoulder and whispered in my ear. "Come on. Let's go, Todd, before something happens you might regret."

I looked at him and knew he was right. I needed to leave before I did something stupid.

"All right Angie, I'll leave. We'll talk about this tonight, before bed," I said while looking at Martin. I turned to walk away until I felt Martin's hand pat my back.

"Good decision Todd, that's the best thing to do," he said.

I turned and caught his arm, locking his elbow and tripped him. Angie gasped, as she looked at Martin face down on the floor. His arm was on the verge of breaking, and I held my foot on his back.

My dad grabbed me. "Let him go, Todd! Don't do it! Don't break his arm!" he pleaded. Angie covered her mouth with both hands in shock, as the bartender rushed back.

"I'm calling the police!" the bartender shouted.

My father interrupted him. "For what? This man assaulted my son; he put his hands on him first! I'm a witness, and your cameras will verify it. This is pure self-defense."

Martin was on the floor grunting in pain, and I could have made him beg me to stop, but I released him.

"Let's go, Dad," I said, and looked at Angie one more time.

I hailed a taxi as the rain came down harder. Once inside, my inebriated father began to ramble.

"So, you think your woman is two-timing you with her co-worker, eh?" he asked. I didn't answer. I was too angry to respond and I felt a splitting headache coming on. My silence didn't stop him from rambling on.

"At least you happened in on them and got a preview of her cheating. I didn't have that opportunity with your mother. I got blindsided," he slurred.

I couldn't handle him talking trash about my mom again, not tonight.

"Don't start about mom. I'm not in the mood to listen to any of that shit right now."

He slid across the seat to the other side of the cab.

"Yeah, I know it hurts to be reminded of what she did to us. That guy in there, he's not all that bad. At least Angie cheating with a white man is better than what your mom did. Imagine what you would feel like if that had been a black guy; you would feel ten times worse." He looked out his window.

"Please, quit talking!" I snapped.

He was quiet from then on, but his words echoed in my mind. I couldn't help but try to imagine the scenario he described. How *would* I feel if Angie left me for a black guy, just like mom? I concluded I'd feel like my father did. I never wanted to find out.

• • •

Within an hour, my dad was in bed fast asleep. I finished my beer before I put on my coat and got ready to go home. I stopped and decided to call Angie to see if she was already there. I was depressed about what I had done, and the reality of my actions at the bar was clear to me. I screwed up in a major way and realized I was in the wrong. I dialed her number. She answered on the second ring.

"Hi Todd. Don't say anything, please, just listen. I don't want to argue with you; I want you to respect what I have to say. I am afraid of you. What you did tonight showed me how unstable you are. You have some serious issues with your anger, and I feel you should stay with your father for a few weeks. I really believe that would be the best thing for both of us. Now, we are still in a relationship, and this is not an opportunity for you to go out and sleep around. Everything's the same with us, but I think we need a break from living together."

Her voice was firm and hoarse, as if she had been crying. My heart sank. I knew this might happen.

"Okay Angie, whatever you want. I want to tell you that I am sorry and—"

She stopped me. "You can get your things tomorrow while I'm at work. Listen, I am not saying we won't still see each other while you are over there. We just aren't living together right now," she said.

"I'll be over to get my stuff tomorrow, that's not a problem. Just to clarify; when am I moving back in? You said three weeks?"

"I said three weeks, maybe more. It's up to you and how you are acting."

"Then I can go visit Tucker in Tennessee," I replied.

"That sounds like a great idea. It will be good for you. Sweetie, I'm tired and need to go to sleep. I'll talk to you later, good night."

"Good night," I said. I was relieved she didn't break up with me completely. I was only in the doghouse.

I sat down on the couch. My eyes wandered across the array of photos on my dad's wall. The latest addition was my Marine Corps graduation photo. I looked so young back then.

It was still early, so I called Tucker. It rang and went to his voicemail, but I didn't bother to leave a message. I would call him in the morning.

My phone rang. It was Tucker.

"Hey Tuck! I just tried to call you, man!"

"I know, that's why I called you back. What's up brother?" he replied.

"Do you still have that spare room you talked about? I was thinking about coming down there ASAP if the offer still stands."

He responded without hesitation.

"Man, hurry up and bring your sorry tail down here. I want you on the next plane, bus, donkey, or tricycle. Whatever it takes, Marine. Rendezvous at the rally point: Nashville, Tennessee."

"Roger that! I'm Oscar Mike. Goodson, over and out!"

CHAPTER THREE

THE REUNION

The flight to Nashville International was fast and definitely better than driving. I had butterflies in my stomach as I stepped off the plane with one carry-on bag. I shuffled along behind the other passengers exiting the tunnel. I was ready to see Tucker, but thought it might be strange seeing him in a wheelchair. I had never seen him wounded in the past. The last memory seared into my mind was when he turned to me before the blast, within arm's reach.

I saw the light at the end of the tunnel and a minute later, we spilled out into the terminal. I looked around through the crowd for Tucker, but didn't see him.

"Todd?" a female voice called out. "Todd Goodson?"

I looked around and saw a young woman standing next to an older man. They had to be Tuck's little sister and father, but I didn't see him anywhere. I waved as we walked toward each other. Tuck's father shook my hand.

"Hello, Todd. I'm Henry Pearson, Tucker's father. He's back home waiting for us and didn't feel physically up to making the trip here, but he sure is excited. We all are."

"It's good to meet you sir!" I replied.

He gestured at his daughter. "This is Tracy, Todd's sister. I believe you've spoken to each other on the phone," he said. She stepped forward and hugged me unexpectedly. I put my arms around her and could tell she was crying. Mr. Pearson smiled.

"I see you're not used to that. Not the crying part, the hugging. You'll get used to it," he said with a grin.

I looked up at him. "Not a problem sir," I replied. Tracy was sniffling and then let me go.

"I'm sorry for wetting up your shirt with my dumb tears. I promised myself I wasn't going to cry, but just couldn't help it! You're the only person besides family that's come to visit Tucker. Even his girlfriend broke up with him after he came home. You're going to make him very happy by being here," she said while wiping her eyes.

Mr. Pearson rubbed her back and put his hand on my shoulder.

"You are family to us, Todd. Tucker shared everything about you with us. Saving each other's lives makes you more than brothers. That's another reason why she's crying. It's like a second big brother has come home," he said.

His words resonated with me and I resisted the impulse to cry, but couldn't help myself and began tearing up.

"My dad is absolutely right," Tracy said.

We stood in the terminal locked in a group embrace, and although none of us had expected this to happen, we were glad for it and needed this healing moment.

• • •

We all climbed into Mr. Pearson's pickup truck for the ride to their house, with Tracy sitting in the middle. Once we left the cityscape and made our way to the interstate, the beauty of the Tennessee landscape overshadowed the highway. Terms like "God's country" came to my mind as the rolling green pastures and thickly wooded hills drifted past. Everyone was quiet and I wasn't sure why.

"It's beautiful down here, Mr. Pearson," I said.

He looked over at me and smiled.

"Amen Todd. You're not the only one to think so. Everybody from up North who comes down here thinks the same. Now this isn't directed at you, but we have Yankees coming down here by the millions to live, and who can blame them? The cost of living up North has gone out of control because of the ridiculous tax rate applied to everything under the sun. The average American can't prosper up there. Most of the major industries have left too because companies can't make a decent profit. So, they relocate down here and their employees follow...with their Yankee ways," he said, with a grimace on his face.

"Yankee ways?" I asked.

Tracy looked at me and nodded her head.

"Yeah, they come down here driving all crazy like they're trying to put out a fire or something. And they put down the South like we're backward hillbillies. We must be doing something right since they're all flocking down here," she said laughing.

Mr. Pearson jumped back in.

"Yes sir, it's like they are leaving the *Titanic*." He laughed. I didn't find it very funny but laughed anyway, out of respect. "We're not talking about you Todd, remember that. It boils down to the states taxing the hell out the working person. It gets downright criminal when you really look at it," he said.

"Yes sir, I understand," I replied.

Tracy turned on the radio. "Daddy, may I play your radio?" she asked him.

"You're already playing it, but yes, you may. Don't play none of that rap music. You know my rules," Mr. Pearson said.

"Yes sir," she replied and turned it to a station playing rhythm and blues. She looked at me and giggled. "Daddy doesn't like rap music He's from the old school, but I do. How about you? Who's your favorite rapper?" she asked.

I shook my head. "I don't listen to that. It's not for me."

Mr. Pearson nodded his head in approval.

"That's right Tracy, Todd has got taste. He doesn't listen to that mumble-jumble. For the life of me, I can't understand what in the world they're saying."

She didn't respond, instead moving her head and shoulders to the rhythm of the music.

I found myself lost again within the panorama of the landscape, unfolding a new scene for every mile we traveled. Mr. Pearson turned off the main road onto a rural two-lane highway. I noticed he waved to the oncoming cars as they waved to him.

"You know a lot of people sir. This must be a close-knit community."

He looked over and smiled.

"I don't know any of those folks, Todd. That's how we do things around here. When they wave, you wave back. It's part of our culture, our ways. For instance, you might see a funeral procession where all the other cars will pull over to the side of the road until the procession passes by. We call it respect, and there's nothing wrong with it."

"Yes sir," I nodded as Tracy turned to me.

"We have a room ready for you. You have a TV in there with cable hooked up, and it's right across from Tucker's room," she said.

"Thank you, I really appreciate it. Not having to pay for a motel room while I'm here really helps me out. My unemployment is about to run out, and I have almost ten months before reporting to the police academy," I replied.

Mr. Pearson grunted.

"The government rarely gives our returning troops their just due. When veterans come back home, Uncle Sam throws them out into the world. They should be giving them ample time to get their bearings. There ain't a lot of time for a soldier to job hunt when he's behind enemy lines. At least it was like that for us in Vietnam. Damn politicians will vote to spend money for a man to go to Mars, but won't spend half that on taking care of the problems we've got right here on this planet. It ain't right!" he shouted, and Tracy rubbed his arm.

"Daddy! Calm down before you give yourself a heart attack," she said and leaned her head against his shoulder. An uncomfortable silence followed. I was surprised at how angry Mr. Pearson became, but understood the amount of stress he must be under, as well as the cause of it.

My chest began to tighten, and I tried to block out the guilty thoughts rambling through my mind. I needed to make myself numb, to cope with the reality of seeing my best friend sitting in a wheelchair with his arm and leg missing. Worst of all, nobody blamed me. Instead, everyone who knew I had served in the military was thanking me for my service. They shook my hand like I was someone special, while the real heroes were either dead or disabled.

"I apologize Todd. I get worked up about the treatment of veterans. Don't you worry about nothing son, your room and board are taken care of. You can stay as long as you like and I mean that sincerely," he said.

"Thank you sir, I appreciate you and your family showing me this hospitality. I'll earn my keep. Give me a list of chores and consider them done," I replied.

"You can keep Tucker occupied. Believe me, that is a full-time chore." He laughed as Tracy looked over at me.

"We have to keep Tucker from trying to do too much, but he's so hard-headed. He still has a few more surgeries before he's even allowed to try to walk. Right now, I bet you he is playing either *Call of Duty* or *Battlefield*. Do you know those video games, like on Xbox?" she asked.

"Yeah, we used to play both of those whenever we got the chance back at the base."

I was wondering how he could play the game, holding the controller with only one hand since one of his arms was gone from the elbow. Maybe he had a prosthetic. I wanted to ask, but it seemed disrespectful. I decided to wait, I'd see him soon enough.

We pulled up to the house twenty minutes later. It was a beautiful raised ranch-style home with a large oak tree in front. As we walked to the front door, I imagined Tucker and Tracy as children, playing in the yard, probably trying to climb that big oak, with Mr. and Mrs. Pearson fussing at them to get down. Tuck would have a hard time trying to climb it now, even if he wanted to. Why was I thinking about this now, just before going inside?

The door opened and Tucker's mom stood there, smiling.

"Hello Todd, I'm Maureen, Tucker's mother, but you can call me Reen," she said and then reached out and hugged me while Mr. Pearson chuckled.

"Like I told you in the truck, you'll get used to it," he said.

I actually didn't mind the hugs, they just caught me off guard— I would have liked to know they were coming.

"It's nice to meet you Mrs. Pearson," I replied.

"How was your flight? Are you hungry?" she asked.

"The flight was good and yes ma'am, I'm hungry."

"Good. I'll have supper ready soon, so after you and Tucker catch up, we'll all sit down and eat," she said. "Come on inside. Tucker's in the family room playing his video games."

She led me to the family room and let me enter alone. Tucker was in his wheelchair playing video games just like his mom said. He didn't notice me at the doorway. The dimly lit room would brighten and flicker from the video game action, with Tucker wholly immersed in it. It was a surreal moment that I wasn't prepared for. My emotions were at odds. I had mixed feelings of joy, guilt, and disbelief. Tucker didn't have any prosthetics and was manipulating the game controller like it was second nature. He turned his head and looked at me, dropping his controller in his lap.

"It's about time Todd! Mama said I couldn't eat until you got here, and I see you took your sweet time. You're such a punk. Now get your ass over here!"

I dropped my bag and walked over to him and got down on one knee. I looked at him with watery eyes. I didn't know what to say, but I had so much I wanted to say. I didn't want to smile, but I was happy to see him.

The smirk on his face was gone, replaced by concern. It was the look of my former squad leader and my best friend sensing trouble in the ranks. He put his hand behind my neck and pulled me close.

"What's wrong? We made it brother. We made it," he whispered.

The dam holding back my emotions finally broke as I sobbed.

"I'm sorry Tuck. Forgive me man. I'm sorry," I pleaded as we embraced.

He squeezed me. "You ain't got nothing to be sorry for Todd. Not a damn thing. You need to let that go. Just let it go and move on. We're home now." He pushed me back and stared. "And whatever you do, don't you ever feel sorry for me. You don't owe me that, and I don't want it. I got your back and I want you to be there for me when I need you, like always. That's it. You got it?"

I wiped my eyes with both my hands.

"I'll always be there for you bro, but I can't help feeling like shit. You took the hits and I didn't. I'll try to move past it, but it's difficult Tuck. But I'll sincerely try."

He sat back in his wheelchair and shook his head, with a look of disgust on his face.

"Either do or do not. There is no try! That's a quote by Yoda, or did you forget that in the desert?" he replied. He lurched forward quickly and lightly smacked my face.

"What the hell, man?" I asked, rubbing my cheek as he laughed.

"What? Do you still feel sorry for the guy in a wheelchair who just smacked you before you could blink? Shut your mouth and pick up the other controller over there. Let's get one game in before we eat supper," he said and reset the game.

I picked up the other controller and pulled up a chair next to his. As the game loaded, we looked at each other without cracking a smile. Our poker faces didn't last long as we both lost our composure and laughed out loud. I snarled at him.

"Okay Tuck, wheelchair or not, I'm kicking your ass this game. You're gonna pay for that sneaky sucker punch."

"Whatever, that was no sucker punch, it was a sucker *slap*. You got caught, young grasshopper. You just weren't ready. Anytime you feel froggy, go ahead and jump. You know where I am. Come and try to get some payback anytime. I'm ready for you."

Tucker won the game convincingly, regardless of my efforts to stop him. Even though injured in a wheelchair, his reaction time was better than mine. I shook my head in disbelief and smiled.

• • •

It was the first game out of hundreds we played during my two-week stay. It took me a couple of days to get used to seeing Tuck as he was now, but it would never erase the memories of what he had always been to me and the others who depended on him for their very lives. I was just happy to be hanging out with him again.

Two weeks seemed more like two months, but in a positive way. We talked about everything, even things we never discussed while in the desert. I thought I was a crybaby because of all my tears, but it wasn't so. When we talked about Tom and Jay, Tucker showed the first signs of sorrow since I arrived. He wasn't immune from the grief either.

Tucker let me drive his car whenever I wanted, which was mostly to run to the store to pick up beer and such, which was great. Even though I had my own bed, I slept on the floor in his room for the first week. It felt normal since we had bunked next to each other when we were deployed. I also noticed I hadn't woken up screaming and sweating from the nightmares since I got to Tennessee. I had a few bad dreams, but they were nothing like what I was used to. This allowed me to get some much-needed quality sleep. I didn't know how tired I actually was until I slept through the entire night without waking up.

Tuck's biggest issue was his restriction on his activity. He had a surgery scheduled to remove the shrapnel lodged between his heart and spine, and they didn't want him to overexert himself and cause more complications. Tuck, with his can do, will do attitude, couldn't be still. He was constantly trying to stand up and hop around. We even caught him trying to do yard work with his electric wheelchair and a rake. I couldn't blame him for wanting to move around more and would probably be doing the same thing if it were me.

After the first week, he finally mentioned his ex-girlfriend and talked about how she had left him when he came home. That situation appeared to bother him more than his physical condition. The feeling of being caught between what you want and what reality dictates was best expressed through his words.

"I wanted to hate her for deserting me, but I understood. I loved her too much to hate her. Some people just can't handle being with a disabled person. When someone declares their love to another person, sometimes they don't necessarily know what love is, they're ignorant of it. They only know what love is supposed to look like, but when it comes time to prove that love through their actions, they fall short. They didn't add up what those words cost, so when the bill comes, the heart can't pay."

I agreed with him. It felt like the truth.

After we talked, I thought about Angela and decided to give her a call to let her know that I was returning in a couple of days. I finished my beer and went into the family room.

"Hey man, give me ten minutes. I'm going to call Angie," I said.

He looked up. "Cool, I'll set up another game. And don't come back crying because you found out that she's dumped you," he said while tipping his head back and laughing.

"She can dump me bro, but she's not the only woman in the world. She doesn't want to let this dog out," I replied.

"Who are you kidding? If that girl breaks up with you, you'll be sulking around here ready to put a gun to your head. You are totally whipped! That poon tang got your nose so wide open you look like a camel," he replied.

"Whatever dude!" I gave him the middle finger, then went to my room and dialed her. It was eight o' clock on a Thursday night, so she definitely should be home.

After a few rings, she answered.

"Hello. How are you?" she asked. Her tone was formal.

"Hey babe! I'm good, how about you?"

"I'm doing well. I'm drained tonight. Today was so long. I think I'm getting a sinus headache," she replied.

I figured that was why she sounded so cold with me. I never could tell if she was really sick or just in one of her moods.

"I'm sorry to hear that. I called to let you know that I'm planning on coming home in two days. I was calling to see if you can pick me up from the airport…and to see if we are still good. You know, are you good for me to move back in?"

I hoped she was ready for me to come home now, but after I heard her sigh, I reconsidered that idea.

"I don't think now is a good time. It really is too soon. You haven't said if you've spoken to someone about your anger problems or the sleeping problems."

"Since I've been down here, I haven't been waking up like I used to. My sleep has gotten much better. I really don't think I need to talk to anyone about that. As far as the anger…there was only that one incident, and even though I may have gone over-the-top, I know I can control myself in that type of situation in the future. I'm good to go Angie. Honestly, come on now."

I hoped that she wouldn't drag this out, and only wanted to come back home. Her tone changed drastically.

"So let me get this straight. Since you've been visiting your friend, the violent outbursts and crazy nightmares are gone, and you don't think you have any anger issues. Does that cover it?" she asked sarcastically.

"Yeah, that's what I'm saying," I replied, knowing that I was being drawn into an ambush.

"I don't agree with you. We talked about this before you left and you agreed you could come back when you had everything under control, but that included getting some help. You haven't done that. So the answer is no, we are not good. We are not where we need to be yet and it's your fault, not mine."

"What the hell am I supposed to do, Angie? My unemployment runs out this week. Where am I supposed to stay? My dad's apartment?" I asked.

"I thought your unemployment ran out next month! Oh, you really are in a world of shit now. Rent is due, along with the utilities. You better think of something, and fast. You're not going to ruin my credit by having me pay late rent!"

"Rent? You expect me to continue paying rent when I don't even live there? What kind of shit is that?" I asked. My blood pressure was rising and my chest began to tighten.

"Yes I do, because we are still a couple. First, you got yourself put out of here, but that doesn't absolve you of your responsibility to maintain our home, no matter where you're living temporarily. I reminded you before that this is a temporary arrangement. Secondly, you need to go to therapy for your anger and make sure your sleep episodes are completely over with. I'm sick and tired of living and sleeping in fear."

I threw the phone on the bed and clenched my fists. I wanted to call her a bitch at the top of my lungs! I really wanted to, but I understood it would only make a bad situation worse. I took a few deep breaths and picked up the phone.

"I don't know what to do, I really don't. Shit." I was confused and sincere, but had no answers.

"Do you want to hear my advice?" she asked.

I had no other choice, as she held the upper hand. "Yes, what do I need to do? I'm all ears."

"My advice is to stay there with your friend until it's time to report to the academy. During that time, we can set a definite date for you to move back home, maybe a couple of weeks before you're supposed to report. In the meantime, while you are down there, you should look for a job. You have a much better chance of finding work down there than in New York. You've already tried to find work up here, but for some reason, you weren't able to get hired anywhere. I'm sure the Southern states' wages will be lower, but so is the cost of living. And you *need* to get some counseling for your issues. It's obvious that you are suffering from PDST—"

"You mean PTSD. Post-Traumatic Stress Disorder," I said, correcting her.

"Dammit, you know what I mean. Yes, PTSD. You need to see someone at the VA or somewhere, and I need to know you're doing that. That's my advice. I suggest you take it if we're going to make this relationship work. If you don't think that I'm worth it, just tell me. Then I'll move on with my life and you can move on with yours."

"Okay, fine. I'll have to talk with Tucker's family and see if they can help me with all of this. Mr. Pearson has already said that I can stay as long as I want. He knows this area and can probably help me find some type of work in a hurry."

"And…?"

"Yeah, I'll go to the VA here and make an appointment for counseling, therapy, or whatever they say I need. How does that sound? Is there anything else you want me to do?" I asked.

"No, that's all. It's not some impossible task Todd. Or do you think I'm wrong?" she asked, baiting me.

"No, you're right about everything. I promise you, I'm gonna get my shit together and keep it together. I love you. I don't want to lose you over some bullshit."

"The bullshit part was when you failed to follow through with what we agreed on, just remember that. I'm going to sleep now; my head is killing me. Have a good night, sweetie," she said, her tone switching back to happy mode.

"Okay babe, I'll let you go. I love you," I said.

"You too!" she replied as we ended the call.

I returned to the family room and sat next to Tucker as he handed me a game controller.

"The expression on your face tells me that I was right, the backdoor man has struck. Your girl is now soiled by another man's touch," he joked.

I started the game.

"Nah bro, nothing like that, but I'm in a tight spot now. She's not ready for me to come back yet. She wants me to talk to a shrink about my anger issues and get help with my nightmares. The biggest thing is that she wants me to continue paying half of the bills, even though I'm not living there. I need to ask your folks if they wouldn't mind me staying here a little while longer until I find a job. Then I can rent a room somewhere until I leave for the academy." I scratched my head. "This has got me messed up bro. I'm so sorry about all this."

I hated the thought of imposing on Tucker's family and bringing my own personal baggage with me. Good times had now turned to bad. Tucker paused the game.

"Are you serious? Man, you staying here would be awesome! I'm telling you right now that my folks will feel the same way, so no worries there. Also, about seeing a shrink, that counselor I told you about from the VA makes house calls for me. I'm sure he can talk to you, too, or set you up with someone else. He's cool, not like what you would expect. You just talk and he helps you work things out. Anyway, wipe the frown off your mug and lose the duck lips. It'll all work out in the end. Now game on!"

Just like that, within thirty seconds, Tucker had changed my outlook and attitude.

"Thanks bro, I appreciate—"

"Shut up and play!" he replied, and we did exactly that until the early hours of the morning.

• • •

A week had passed since that night. My days were filled with job hunting and completing online applications, while the nights were spent with drinking, watching the Military Channel, and playing video games.

Tuck had called it; his parents were happy to let me stay with them as long as I needed. They told me I didn't have to pay them any type of rent, even if I found a job, which was a huge relief. I didn't want to take advantage of their kindness; I needed to pay my own way, so I planned to give them money every week I stayed. Most of my pay would be wired to Angie for bills, but I believed that was the cost of love.

I completed eleven applications but didn't receive a call back from anyone. I was primarily looking for blue-collar jobs. I specifically stayed away from security guard positions. It would be difficult to sit around all day. I wanted a job where I could move around and stay active.

Tucker and I were sitting in the family room and watching videos online when my cell phone rang.

"Hello."

"Hello, I am trying to reach Todd Goodson," said a female voice.

"This is Todd."

"Great! My name is Sherika Jones, and I am calling on behalf of Barry Thomas, the District Manager for Pyramid Prime Properties. You recently completed a job application for a position at one of our commercial properties."

I was caught off guard, unable to remember all the positions I applied for.

"Yes, I did," I replied.

"Mr. Thomas has selected your application and asked me to call you in for an interview. Are you still interested in the Building Maintenance Technician position?" she asked.

I didn't remember that one.

"Yes I am."

"Wonderful! Let me give you the property address and schedule a date and time for your interview. Do you have something to write with?"

I grabbed a pen and wrote down the information on the top of a pizza box. I ended the call and looked at Tuck.

"Got a job interview tomorrow baby!" I shouted.

"Give me some skin brother!" he hollered back.

We slapped hands, then I put the address in my phone and searched for directions.

"Hey Tuck, the address is in Nashville, about thirty minutes from here. I need to use your car. Is that cool?"

"No dumbass, it's not cool. Of course you can! Stop talking crazy. I can't drive that car right now anyway and when I'm finally able, we'll just share it. What's mine is yours and vice-versa. You know how we roll."

"You're right, my bad," I replied.

He smirked. "Great, now I want you to share Angie with me. We'll have a love triangle. Thanks for being a man of your word!"

I smacked him in the head and we both laughed.

"Sorry bro, but we can't share that. You'll have to get your own!" I replied.

• • •

The next day, I arrived early for my interview. I inspected my face in the rear-view mirror to make sure I didn't have anything on it, with a quick nose check for loose boogers. I dreaded the thought of being interviewed with a booger hanging out of my nose. Most people wouldn't tell you about it, they'd just let you go on talking.

I walked into the office. An African American woman sat behind the front desk.

"Hello, I'm Todd Goodson. I'm here for an interview."

She stood, and we shook hands. "Hello Todd, I spoke with you yesterday. I'm Sherika. It's nice to meet you. I'll let Mr. Thomas know you are here. He'll like that you arrived early."

She left and came back a minute later, followed by an older African American gentleman. We shook hands.

"Mr. Goodson! Hello, I'm Barry Thomas. Let's go back to my office."

"Yes sir."

I followed him to his office where he closed the door. I began to feel uneasy. I hadn't envisioned having a boss who was black and it threw me for a loop. I started writing the interview off before it began.

I expected to receive other employment phone calls sooner or later and was eager for this interview to be over.

"Please, have a seat sir," he said.

Another curveball. He called me sir, but he was the boss. He was in control of the interview, so why give me that respect? I sat down while he rifled through papers on his desk, coming up with my application. He thumbed through the three-page printed out form.

"So, you're fresh out of the military?" he asked.

"Yes sir. I've been out for nearly three months. I'm down here from New York, visiting my best friend who was severely injured in combat," I replied.

It occurred to me that I had a way to get out of this interview quickly. Maybe he wouldn't hire me after learning I would be quitting and returning to New York in ten months.

"I see. It must feel good to be reunited with your best friend. I'm sure he appreciates that. Looking through your application, I notice that you have a technical school certificate for HVAC repair. You have applied for a position with us as a building maintenance technician, for which you are definitely overqualified. Your certificate is a huge bonus because this job description is basically for the lowest-tier position in maintenance. You would be painting, removing carpet, cleaning the apartment grounds, and basically acting as a helper to the senior maintenance staff. Is this something that you really want to do?" he asked, bluntly. This was my chance to get out egress out of here.

"Mr. Thomas, I apologize sir, but I believe there may have been a mistake. I plan on reporting to the New York State Police Academy in ten months. I must have misread the job posting. I'm not interested in this position now that you've described it to me. I apologize for wasting your time." I stood up and reached out to shake his hand. Although he seemed surprised, he smiled and shook my hand.

"Mr. Goodson, I like your honesty. In fact, I admire and respect it. Would you please sit down and hear me out for two minutes? I have a special offer I'd like you to consider." He was still gripping my hand. It almost felt like a non-verbal challenge. I wanted to leave, but he piqued my curiosity, so I sat down.

"Okay Mr. Thomas."

He leaned back in his chair. "You have an associate degree, a technical certificate, and are a decorated military combat veteran. In my book, you can do anything you set your mind to. I have a problem and I need help. I manage fourteen apartment communities across the state of Tennessee. They range from high-end luxury, gated communities to low-end Section Eight subsidized communities. The low-end communities are what used to be called 'the projects.' One of these projects has been a thorn in my side for the past few years. Basically, it never turns a profit and has become a money pit. The residents are constantly tearing up the place and running off every property manager that I hire to clean it up.

"Now, I know you don't have any experience running an apartment community like this, but you do have experience in keeping law and order. In fact, you have a doctorate in imposing your will and completing the missions set before you. I can also tell that you won't scare easily. Would you be willing to accept a position as the property manager at this particular location?"

I didn't expect this offer from him and I didn't know anything about property management.

"Mr. Thomas, I appreciate the offer, but I don't know much about this business. Like I said, I plan on leaving in ten months. Offering me a higher position which I know nothing about won't get me to stay."

"Let me finish Todd. You don't have to know the business end. I will have Sherika come in and train you on the fundamentals and basics of daily operations. I will pay you and get you started on the courses for your state property manager's license. She will do your books, budgeting, and most of the administrative tasks. You would be able to live in the manager's apartment, if you choose, which has been fully renovated. You'd also have a maintenance staff at your disposal. When, or if, you are ready to leave, just give me your two-week notice. If you don't, then I'll know you've decided to keep the position. It's that simple."

The deal kept getting sweeter by the minute.

"How much does this position pay?" I asked.

"The position is salaried exempt at thirty-nine thousand annually, with rent-free living on-site. We also offer medical, dental, and 401k; a truly competitive benefits package," he replied confidently.

I sat forward in my seat.

"What exactly do you want me to do?" I asked.

He leaned forward on his desk.

"Officially, I need a manager at the site who won't be afraid of these people. Some of them have a loud bark, but no bite. I have to provide a financial report weekly, monthly, and quarterly to the property owners, and they expect certain numbers to be consistently met. At the same time, we have requirements to fulfill for HUD. We'll take care of the numbers; you just need to be the manager. Unofficially, I want you to be a zookeeper and keep these animals in their cages, fed, quiet, and under control. After meeting you in person and speaking with you, I don't believe you're the type of young man who will allow them to run roughshod over you."

"So I would be in charge and able to operate at my own discretion?" I asked.

"Mr. Goodson, you will be the boss and in charge. You do whatever you feel is needed, under company guidelines of course, to avoid any violations or civil liability. You will learn all of that soon enough, if you accept the position."

It sounded too good to be true. I needed to recon the spot before making any commitments.

"I'd like to see the property first, by myself, before I give you an answer," I replied.

His raised his eyebrows.

"Of course!" He wrote down the address for me. "Call me as soon as possible."

"I plan on driving there after dark tonight and recon the site."

He stood up and walked around his desk.

"That's what I want to hear. I like that military jargon. Call me tonight after you take a look and let me know your decision."

We shook hands and I drove back to Tucker's house.

• • •

"Damn! That's a rough place over there, Todd. You might want to hold up on accepting that job." Tucker said after I told him about the property location. "Shady Meadows ain't no joke. I've never been over there, but they've been in the news for years. Shootings, robbing, drugs…all of that. Might want to rethink that one, seriously."

"You make the place sound worse than Falluja. It sounds like the ghetto to me, no big deal. I'm on my way over there now. You want to roll with me?" I asked.

He shook his head.

"What? Are you crazy? I'm not trying to get my other arm and leg shot off, no thanks." Then he laughed. "I'm just messing with your head. I've heard of the place before, but there's nothing special about it, just another apartment in the hood; rough living and hard times.

"Cool. I'll be back in a few hours. You know I don't scare easily, especially not by any of the brothers." I reached to give him a fist bump, but he left me hanging and turned away. "Really?" I asked him and walked out.

I followed my phone's GPS to the property. The driveway entrance was dark, though the sign was lit up, *Shady Meadows*, appearing in good condition. My first impression wasn't bad. The apartment units had a partial brick-and-wood exterior and looked decent from the outside. The property landscaping had been kept up. This place looked nothing like the projects in New York. I began to wonder if I had the correct property address. I expected to see a run down and ragged housing project, but I saw no signs of anything resembling that.

Then I noticed the trash, it was everywhere. There were dozens of walkways and building lights that were burned out, and as I drove forward, my headlights caught the actual filth scattered across the grounds. I made a loop around the property and then made a right turn toward what looked like a playground. I pulled into an empty space, parked, and turned off my lights.

Then I waited. I slumped down in my seat, so I wouldn't look too suspicious. A few minutes later, I was startled by a knock on my window. A young white man stood next to my car. My natural reflex was to grab my pistol, but I left it in my bag at Tucker's house. I wouldn't make that mistake again. I rolled down my window a few inches but prepared to roll out quickly.

"What?" I asked.

"What you need, player?" he replied.

"What do I need? I don't need anything. I'm waiting for someone."

He seemed puzzled. "Who you waitin' for?" he asked.

"None of your damn business. You need to step away from my car now."

I was in a vulnerable position. He might have had a weapon, though I could still see his hands for the moment. I moved my hand from the window switch to the door handle. I mentally prepared my next actions: open the door, egress, advance, close the distance, then subdue with direct aggressive action, or whatever the situation dictated.

He quickly stepped back from the car.

"Damn man, it's cool. You got it, homey," he said walking away. I watched him stroll to the entrance of an unlit building, where he joined a group of shadowy figures in the dark. My adrenaline was flowing, but it was time for me to leave. The guy might come back strapped and it was too dark. I couldn't risk getting shot, so I made my decision: I didn't need this shit or this job. I started the car and turned my lights back on, then dialed Mr. Thomas to let him know my decision. I drove away from the playground and headed toward the apartment complex entrance.

"Hello?"

"Hello, Mr. Thomas, this is Todd Goodson. I'm over here at Shady Meadows. I've taken a look around the property and I'm about to leave."

Suddenly, my headlights shined on a white female. She was sitting on top of a picnic table, kissing and making out with a young black man. I stopped the car.

"Thanks for giving me a call. So, now that you have had a look, what's your decision," he asked.

My attention was on the couple. They stopped kissing and tried to see who was spotlighting them, but both were blinded by my headlights. I felt numb but wasn't sure why.

"Hello? Todd, are you still there?" he asked.

The couple went back to making out while the young man raised his hand and exposed his middle finger to me, waking me out of my daze.

"Mr. Thomas, I'm ready to be your manager and your zookeeper. When should I report for duty?"

CHAPTER FOUR

CHERRY'S FIRST DAY

I woke up the next morning to the smell of bacon. I rolled over on my back and stretched out the morning tightness, then sat at the edge of my bed. It was seven o'clock and I needed to meet Sherika Jones at Shady Meadows in one hour. I began my morning workout and kicked out two sets of sixty sit-ups and push-ups, and since I overslept, there was no time for my five-mile run. I heard a knock at my bedroom door, followed by Tuck's voice.

"Sleepyhead! It's chow time!" Tuck yelled.

I opened the door. "Morning... I overslept for sure. I need to get going," I replied.

"Come on to the table and scarf down some vittles. Mama has got your coffee and lunch ready," he replied as I began to put on my clothes.

"Your mom is the best. Let me go wash up and brush my choppers first, I'll be right in."

Tuck watched me with a smirk and shook his head.

"You got it made in the shade. Got my mom treating you like she gave birth to you, my lil' sis loving on you like a big brother, my dad's about to put you in his will, and I'm acting as your personal servant and alarm clock." He shook his head and rolled down the hallway. I put my shoes on and headed to the bathroom.

"You better get used to it punk!" I yelled. He stopped and held up his middle finger. That kept me laughing as I finished up in the bathroom.

I came into the kitchen and took my seat at the table.

"Good morning," I said to everyone, and everyone said the same back to me. Mrs. Pearson set a full breakfast plate in front of me.

I would never get tired of eating her cooking. Hell, all her meals were amazing. She even brought me coffee just the way I liked it. She was a mother to me in many ways. It was her true nature. She was naturally a motherly person to anyone and everyone it seemed. Being around her often led me to daydream about my own mother when I was younger, and the times we shared. Sometimes, Mrs. Pearson seemed to have the same scent as my mother, which was weird. Childhood memories would surface from the days before my mom left us to be with Herman.

Whoever heard of a black guy being named Herman anyway? Apparently, he was worth breaking my dad's heart over. My heart wasn't broken, but it hurt me bad, really bad. It turned my world upside down and I honestly still believe it affected me until this day.

"Are you excited about your first day at work?" Tracy asked. Her eyes were beaming with excitement. She was always full of energy and enthusiasm. The epitome of a vibrant young college freshman; optimistic, energetic, and ready for the world.

"I am. I've got a few butterflies floating around in my belly," I replied with a smile.

Mr. Pearson patted me on the back as he stood up to leave.

"You'll do fine. Just remember these two things I'm gonna tell you. Down here in the South, a little bit of courtesy goes a long way, and always answer with ma'am or sir. You got it?"

"Yes sir. I got it."

"Good." He ruffled the top of my crew cut, then walked over and kissed his wife on her cheek, bent down and kissed his daughter, then looked at Tucker. "Hold down the fort son. I might have to work a few hours of overtime today. Call me if you need me."

"Yes sir, have a good day. Don't work too hard," Tucker replied.

"Hard work never hurt anybody," Mr. Pearson said with a wink and left.

We finished our meals and left the kitchen, except for Mrs. Pearson. She couldn't stand to have a dirty dish in the sink or a crumb left on the table. I picked up the car keys from my nightstand and met Tucker in the family room.

"All right Tuck, I'm Oscar Mike. What are you gonna do today?" I asked.

"Same ole. Watch the judge shows, *Family Feud*, Military Channel, and play video games. The physical therapist will be here at one o'clock and my therapist at three o'clock. Hey, I can get him to come one day when you're here, so you could meet. You know, if you need someone to talk to."

I gave him a fist pump. "Thanks, but I'm good."

The bright morning sun hit me in the face, and I caught the last hint of the morning dew evaporating. I thought to myself, *"Today is going to be a good day."*

• • •

I made a right-hand turn into the Shady Meadows entrance, passing a group of children standing by the corner, apparently waiting for a school bus. I pulled into the parking spot marked PROPERTY MANAGER, right next to a sweet, brand new Lexus sedan. I thought to myself that Mr. Thomas must be here for my first day. By the look of his car, he had impressive taste for an older guy.

I was fifteen minutes early, which was right on time to me. I got out and went inside. I passed by the water fountain and restrooms. The office was to the right and I was surprised to see Sherika sitting there instead of Mr. Thomas. She looked up and smiled at me.

"Good morning Todd."

"Good morning Sherika. How are you this morning?"

"I'm doing well, thank you. It's Monday, which means we will be swamped today. I have a status report to give at nine o'clock you'll be doing in the future. We will be training all day and for most of the week but first, we need to fill out your new employee paperwork, direct deposit, etc. If you don't mind, I'll be using your desk while I'm here. Please work from the other side of the desk today. It will just be more convenient for me. In a minute, I'll start getting the Monday report ready."

I threw my hands up.

"No problem at all, Ms. Jones. I am here to be trained and do whatever you need me to do," I replied with a nod, pulled up a chair, and sat down.

"Let me explain some of the property manager's responsibilities briefly now and what you'll be learning during the next week. We maintain the integrity of all buildings, landscaping, driveways, and parking lots, either through established contracts, or by our own on-site maintenance personnel. We lease apartments based on the region's fair market value, as well as federal subsidies. What that means is we adhere to HUD Section Eight guidelines and offer subsidized housing to qualified applicants. This property is also mortgaged through Farmers Home, so we have to collect income and status verifications for Section Eight tenants on an annual basis. Eviction of tenants has to go through the local magistrate. We also provide the necessary paperwork to Farmers Home, as well as to the Pyramid Prime Management group, our employers. It sounds like a lot of paperwork, and it is."

After listening to her introduction to the position, it sounded to me like Ms. Jones hadn't gotten the memo on what I was truly here to do. She needed to be set straight.

"Mr. Thomas told me that you were going to do the majority of the paperwork. I have zero experience in business and I think he wanted to utilize some of my other skills. He knows that I plan to resign and fly back to New York in ten months, so this is sort of a temporary contract position for me," I said calmly, trying not to sound like a smart ass. "This is what Mr. Thomas told me."

Sherika raised her eyebrows in surprise.

"Yes, he informed me your role would be limited as it pertains dealing with contractor's bids, quotes, submitting the annual budget, and tenant verifications, but I still plan to train you in every aspect, whether or not you are tasked with those particular responsibilities. You need to know what to do, especially if I am out sick or at another property. Our group manages over a dozen properties which I visit regularly. Also, I'm getting married later this year and will be on vacation for a week. So, you need to let me know right now if this is going to be a problem for you. I don't want to spend a lot of time and effort training you, and then have you decide to leave next month. Do you have a problem with any of what I said?"

"No problem at all, Sherika, we are clear. I'm ready to start whenever you are," I replied.

She patted the desk and smiled. "We've already started. Oh, before I forget, here are the master keys for all the locks. I've already filled out the receipt form, you just need to sign it. Don't lose this key please. It will be more paperwork for us to fill out."

I took the keys from her and put them on my keychain. "No worries."

I heard the front door to the building open and someone walked inside. A very tall black man came into the office.

"Good morning," he said to Sherika.

She stood up and shook his hand.

"Good morning William. I want you to meet the new property manager in training, Todd." She turned to me. "Todd, William is the senior maintenance technician here. He also repairs most of the HVAC units."

I stood up and then had to look up to face this imposing man who stood at least six foot six inches. I shook his hand.

"Todd Goodson."

"William Reed."

It was clear this man was strictly business. He looked to be mid-fifties, had a steel handshake, and wore a serious expression. Along with the wrinkles and lines in his weathered face, I could tell he was either a combat war veteran or had been through brutally hard times. His presence alone commanded respect. Sherika walked to the front window and opened the blinds which faced the front office parking lot.

"William, where is Eugene?" she asked.

William glanced out the window. "Running late. I reckon he'll be here soon," he replied. Sherika sat back down at my desk.

"Todd, Eugene Gladney is the other maintenance technician. He's also a resident and lives on the property with his family," she said.

The front door opened, followed by shuffling footsteps. A short and stocky black man stepped inside the office. His eyes widened when he noticed me.

"Morning, y'all. Sorry 'bout being late," he said nervously.

William gestured to me, smirking. "Good day you picked to be late. Meet the new manager," Eugene shook my hand.

"Yes sir, I'm Eugene Gladney. It got me looking bad today, but I'm not usually late for work, it won't happen again," he said, smiling.

I looked him in the eyes and shook his hand.

"I'm Todd Goodson. Don't let it happen again Eugene. Tardiness won't be tolerated and it will be dealt with. You get a break this time," I said, releasing his hand. He stepped behind William. I needed to immediately exert control on these two subordinates. I didn't care who they had worked for in the past, they worked for me now. There was an uncomfortable silence, which Sherika broke by changing the subject.

"Well! William, what do you and Eugene have on your agenda for today?" she asked.

"There are two open work orders that we didn't finish last Friday. After that, we can start installing the last pallet of the sheetrock and start painting unit two twenty-eight. You can start showing that other unit by Wednesday at the latest," he replied.

"Great!" she replied and looked at me.

"Todd, why don't you let William and Eugene show you around the property and get you familiar with the maintenance procedures and the work order system? That will give me time to send out the nine-thirty report."

"Sounds good." I looked at William. "Lead the way." He nodded and led me outside. We began to walk and talk, with Eugene following behind. I needed information from these guys. They were the only boots on the ground that I had access to. I decided to be direct and go in hard.

"Okay William, let's cut through the bullshit. What are the two biggest problems here at this property? Don't sugarcoat it, just tell me," I said.

He looked off into the distance, as if deep in thought.

"You want it straight? No bull jive?" he asked.

"Ten-four, give it to me straight up."

"This complex looks all right on the outside, except for the trash, but on the inside they're garbage. Most of the units need new carpet, linoleum, paint, appliances, and fixtures, but management won't give us the money to do the upgrades; that's number one. Two? We got this group of punks that try to be thugs—a small-time clique they call a gang. They sell dope and all that, mostly at the playground. From time to time, they like to play 'cowboys and Indians' with their rivals, and that makes it dangerous for anybody living or working here," he said.

I thought about what Mr. Thomas had told me.

"This gang situation needs to be dealt with, but the condition of a person's home is their own responsibility. If you keep your place clean, you won't have much disrepair. I was told by upper management that the tenants have destroyed this place, and that's why I'm here, at least for the next few months. I plan to put a stop to all of this crap."

"You asked me and I told you," he replied.

I looked at Eugene. "Do you have anything to add?"

"No sir. I'm with William on this," he replied.

"Of course you are, but you are also a resident here. I bet you want your unit renovated as well, right?"

"I wouldn't mind that at all sir," he said, smiling, but unaware of my sarcasm.

"Wow, what a surprise," I answered.

Over the next hour, we walked around the entire property and perimeter of the grounds. Shady Meadows was surrounded by trees and nestled beside a small valley just off the highway. The whole complex was separated from the main road by a long driveway and was similar to other apartment complexes I had seen throughout the city and suburbs of Nashville. It was entirely the opposite of my experiences and ideas of low-income housing in New York.

At Shady Meadows, the rent for many tenants was not subsidized at all. The majority of the tenants were working, middle-class people, and even a few professionals, from different walks of life. While African Americans were the predominant group residing here, there were also Caucasian, Hispanic, Asian, and East Asian residents.

William and I left Eugene at Shady Meadows to continue working and drove into the city, where he showed me the police station, the magistrate's office, and the Department of Social Services.

"You'll get fed up with coming down here," he said.

I believed him. He was telling me everything that needed to know, but I still didn't trust him or Eugene. They both had a vested interest in keeping their jobs and could even be responsible for some of the disarray.

"Let's head on back. I need to start my employee paperwork and get some office training knocked out before lunch," I said.

"All right, but speaking of lunch, sometimes we're so busy that we don't even have time to take a lunch break. If it's a plumbing, heating-cooling, or electrical problem, we usually work on through," he said.

"Really? Good! I expect both of you to do whatever it takes and finish the job. I can't really sympathize with you on that. It's the nature of the work. Besides, what do you want me to do about it?"

He was silent for a few moments.

"You don't have to do anything. I was just letting you know boss," he said, turning the corner and heading back to the Meadows.

· · ·

A few hours later, I was halfway through completing my benefits paperwork as the clock approached noon. Sherika stood up and stretched.

"It's lunchtime Todd. I brought mine and plan to eat here. We have an hour, what are you going to do?" She asked.

I tucked the rest of the forms into the folder and capped my pen.

"I'm not sure. I'll probably grab a burger and fries. I never knew paperwork could make me so hungry." It was my turn to stand and stretch, as Sherika set her lunch cooler on the desk and began to sort out the contents. "I'll be back by one."

The front door opened and Eugene walked inside, out of breath and his shirt soaked with sweat.

"Mr. Todd, I need to show you something if you got a minute. For the second time this month, unit 115 has backed up their toilet, and I'm catching the devil trying to unstop it. We need to use the electric snake to break the trash free in the line, but that piece of equipment has been broken for a long while now," he said.

I first looked to Sherika, then back to Eugene.

"What do you want me to do about it? Do we need to buy another electric snake or get the broken one fixed? Why do you need to show me when you just told me? I don't get it." I said.

"Sir, because you might want to see what caused the blockage, since this is the second time for the same thing. Being the manager, you might choose to have them pay the plumber's fee for our service call. That's the policy, as far as I know. I'm not sure about fixing the rooter. You need to get with William about that, but he did try to fix it plenty of times," Eugene replied nervously.

Sherika stopped eating and wiped her mouth. "Todd, we haven't gone over any of that yet, but if a resident causes damage to the property, then they are responsible for the charges. For example, if a sink or toilet is stopped up because the resident put unauthorized items in the system, or too much food down the drain instead of the trash or garbage disposal, then they are usually charged a nominal maintenance fee for the repair." She looked at Eugene. "Eugene, what stopped up the toilet?"

Eugene hung his head. "Ms. Sherika, I'd rather not say it in front of you, ma'am."

I was confused, hungry, and losing my patience.

"Come on. Show me, Eugene!" I barked.

We walked to unit 115 and knocked on the door. A young lady holding a baby let us inside. Behind her were two small children sitting on the couch.

"Mr. Todd, this is Tina Browne," Eugene said. "Tina, this is Mr. Todd, the new manager."

"Hey," she said and led us to the master bathroom. I noticed the carpet in the room was soaked with water as Eugene pointed to the bathroom floor.

"Look at all the women's pads!" he snarled.

I looked closely at the white pads, which appeared unused.

"It looks like someone opened up each one and stuffed them in the toilet," I replied.

Eugene shook his head.

"William just unstopped this same toilet two weeks ago. We stay busy around here, and we've got a lot more important work to do besides coming down here for some nonsense," Eugene said.

I heard wet footsteps approaching from behind us.

"No Eugene! That ain't true! The last time wasn't our fault. Mr. William replaced something in the tank and fixed it!" She looked up and sighed. "Listen, I know my little boy did this shit right here, and I have done cut his ass already. I got him and my sister's boy sitting on the couch right now. But this here is the first time," she said, clearly upset and rocking her baby feverishly.

"Ma'am, from what I just saw, this is unacceptable and this is your second offense, so you're going to have to pay the service fee. I don't know what else to tell you except to be careful in the future and watch your children more closely." I walked past her to leave the apartment.

She followed me out, now furious.

"Wait a damn minute mister manager! I watch my kids just fine! Don't tell me a child can't get into devilment sometimes!" I ignored her and opened the front door. "Please Mr. Todd! I can't afford no fee for this right now. I declare I can't! Just ask William, he'll tell you that it wasn't our fault last time!" she pleaded. I looked back at her as I walked away.

"You need to pay the service fee ma'am," I replied, and walked back to the office.

I was burning up. I bent over the water fountain to get a drink. Sherika looked up from the book she was reading and put down her sandwich.

"Sherika, I verified that feminine products caused the stoppage, so we need to charge unit one-fifteen a service fee," I said.

"Okay. After lunch I'll explain the procedure and how to complete the form yourself," she replied.

"Cool, then I'm leaving for lunch now."

I walked out of the office and was met by a middle-aged man wearing an undershirt, shorts, and flip-flops.

"Are you the new manager?" he asked.

"Yeah. I'm Todd Goodson."

My name is Clarence Tuthill. I live in unit 320. I work third shift road construction for the highway department and I need my damn sleep! That young fool upstairs from me has got his music blasting with the bass cranked up! I should be an asshole and call the police, but I know his mama, and she's at work right now. It's early in the day, but the music is still too loud. This is the last time I'm putting up with this shit. Somebody needs to do something today!"

"Show me where he is." I answered, irritated and ill-tempered.

As he led me closer to his building, I could barely hear any music. I couldn't see why this man was livid. We stopped at his front door.

"I'll leave it to you, thanks," he said.

"I know this might sound like a stupid question, but have you ever asked him to turn it down?" I asked.

"Of course I have, and my car window was busted out the next day. I can't prove who did it, but it doesn't take a genius to figure that one out."

I walked up the stairs to the unit above Tuthill's and knocked on the door. Anyone who was inside should have heard me, the music wasn't loud at all. After a minute, my patience had worn through and I began beating on the door as hard as possible. Finally, a young black man opened the door.

"What do you want?" he asked.

"I'm the new manager, Mr. Goodson, and I got a complaint your music is too loud. I need you to turn it down."

He looked surprised. "Seriously? Okay, my bad, hold up a second," he said and closed the door. The music went from barely audible to silent. He opened the door again. "All right? We straight now?"

"Straight? That's up to you. The other tenants have complained about the loud music coming from up here and I just witnessed it for myself. Is the lease in your name?"

"Nah, the lease is in my mom's name, Felicia Jackson. She's at work," he replied.

"I see. What's your name?"

"Andre Jackson."

"Well, consider this to be your final warning from management. I'm going to have to write your mother a warning since she's the leaseholder. Keep the music low and don't disturb the neighbors anymore. If not, your mother will be given a violation resulting in fees, which eventually will be followed by an eviction notice," I said, proudly. I was learning the job and becoming a quick study.

He nodded. "Yes sir. I'll keep it turned down even lower. There won't be any more complaints. I didn't realize it was that loud. Goodbye," he replied.

He began to close the door and I saw a young white woman pass by. She was the woman I had seen in the park last night making out with this very guy. I hadn't gotten a close look at him, but after seeing her I recognized him.

"Wait." I put my hand on the door and he opened it back up. "Were you and that young lady at the park last night?" I asked.

He seemed bewildered. "Why?"

"It's just a question," I replied.

"No sir," he answered.

I smirked to cover up my loathing, realizing he was lying to my face. Not only did he treat the young woman like she was white trash by groping her on a park bench, but he wasn't man enough to admit he was there with her. I was tired of seeing black guys mistreat white women. Just because most of them came from broken homes didn't give them the license to violate females and break up families. But they did that all the time. Half of the soldiers who got dumped while I was deployed found out that the backdoor man was a black guy! It was time to draw a line and start returning fire. Call it payback.

"Doesn't matter, just asking. On another subject, back to the fees. I changed my mind. Your mom is going to be charged, and that's a shame because it isn't her fault, it's yours," I said.

His demeanor changed.

"Man, that's some bull! Nah! That ain't right. You said we were cool," he shouted.

I walked to the stairs and looked at him. "I never said we were cool. I don't talk like that, you do. I'll be waiting for your mother to come by the office so I can explain the fees in detail to her."

I didn't bother waiting for around for his comments but could hear him cursing as he slammed the door shut. I paused at the ground-floor landing for a few minutes, waiting to hear if he would turn the music back up, but he didn't bite on the little trap I had set for him.

I smiled as I walked back to the office. I could see my future here and the need to make a list of these problem tenants. This guy was already at the top of it.

I felt lightheaded and was fighting off hunger pangs while walking back to the office. When I opened the front door, three tenants were standing around in the hallway. I walked past them into the office, where another tenant sat with her baby. Sherika looked at me and smiled.

"Todd, this is Mrs. Sanchez from unit eighty-seven. Her ceiling is leaking again. The other two residents are waiting for you as well. They all need assistance."

I breathed deeply and looked at Mrs. Sanchez.

"Mrs. Sanchez, I'll be with you in a moment," I told her before heading toward the bathroom.

One of the tenants stepped in front of me.

"Excuse me sir, I live in unit 404 and want to report them badass boys who are pissing behind the breezeway. The smell fills up the entire area, I can't even open my bedroom window without that piss smell coming inside. They've been doing this mess for a long time and I am tired of it. It's disgusting," she stated.

"Yes ma'am, I'll be right with you. Just give me a few minutes," I replied and went into the bathroom. I stepped up to the urinal, shaking my head and wondering what I had signed up for here. "Shit," I whispered. Just then, I heard the commode flush inside the toilet stall next to me. I had assumed the bathroom was empty.

William stepped out and walked around me to wash his hands. He dried them and looked at me via the mirror.

"What's the matter boss?" he asked.

I shook my head. "People are pulling me left and right and I haven't even had lunch yet. Shit, I'm dying here."

"Sounds familiar," he said and walked out.

I knew what he was getting at. I washed my hands and looked at myself in the mirror. I wasn't feeling good, but I had to push through and remember the job was only temporary. It should be a cakewalk for me. I walked out and began the rest of my day, being continuously pulled in different directions.

• • •

I finally left the office at 6:55 PM and arrived at Tucker's house thirty minutes later, mentally and physically drained. In the past, I'd spent weeks in the field on deployments, busting my hump, but I never felt this tired.

That night, everyone at the supper table wanted to hear about my day, so I told them everything I could remember. Later, I realized that by merely recounting those events caused me to feel even more tired.

They all encouraged me. Except for Tucker, whose job it was to bust my balls whenever possible, and this was no exception. After he was satisfied doing that, I had to laugh at the day and I began to de-stress. That was the point of his harassment, to make things seem worse than they were until I realized things were actually better than they appeared to be.

By midnight, everyone but Tucker and I were sleep. He was playing video games with his headset on, so as not to disturb the rest of the house. I walked back to my room and fell onto my bed. I thought it had never felt so good as my body sank into the deep, memory-foam topper. It was quiet in the house, but I could hear crickets outside. For me, they were a natural source of white noise, which helped me to sleep better. I quickly dozed off.

• • •

"No! No!" I woke up yelling.

I tried to catch my breath, but it felt like I was suffocating. I searched for the lamp and turned it on.

Not again, please, no.

The nightmares had stopped since I got to Tennessee, and now they were back. I sat up on the edge of the bed and heard a knock at the door.

"Hey, buddy, are you all right in there?" Tucker asked from the other side.

I ran my fingers through my wet hair, ashamed to let him know the nightmares were back. He was the wounded one and had earned the right to wake up screaming, not me.

"Ten-four Tuck, I'm good to go. I hit my toe on the dresser, that's all. Sorry I hollered out." I hoped he would buy my excuse.

There was a long pause.

"All right then. Good night brother. Sweet dreams," he said.

"Good night Tuck."

I turned off the light and laid there with eyes open. I desperately needed to sleep but was too proud to admit that I was afraid to.

CHAPTER FIVE

SCORCHED EARTH

Two weeks had passed since I started my job, and I had started to make my mark. I learned the policies and procedures and began to implement the necessary measures to establish proper control over the community. Warnings, violations, and fees were the main tools that I used to bring order to the chaos. Several tenants made a concerted effort to continually complain and nag to Sherika and me daily about repairs or upgrades to their units. I'm sure she was glad to finally get a break from Shady Meadows.

Thankfully, the once-steady flow of complainers trickled to a halt. Within the past couple of weeks, I handed out nearly $800 in fees for various violations. I was tired of hearing the same old excuses they tried to con me with. One single mother told me her boyfriend, who wasn't on the lease, came over unannounced and found another man in the apartment. His answer was to kick open the locked door and beat up boyfriend number two. Afterward, boyfriend number one left, but she didn't call the police. She actually expected the management to fix the door for free! Not on my watch.

William and I walked around the grounds of the property, doing what I called the ghetto recon. It was mid-morning and the pigeons were picking through the trash in the southern parking lot. There was a lot of waste, too much. Eugene did trash pick up every morning, but the wind continued to blow debris right back from hidden corners and crevices. That was frustrating because Eugene and William were backed up on work orders and trash was a never-ending battle.

We walked by the park and I remembered about the white guy who had approached me that first night.

"Hey William. I came out here one night before I took the job and parked right over there." I pointed. "A white guy, about my height, dark hair with a trimmed beard, came out of nowhere and asked me if I needed something. Do you have any idea who he might be or what he was talking about? My first guess was that he was trying to sell me some crack or meth, but I don't know."

He smirked and answered in his deep raspy voice, "That sounds like a guy that calls himself Lil Rob. He's supposed to be a small-time pimp and meth dealer, so he was probably trying to sell you some booty, some meth, or both."

"What? You're kidding me, right? I didn't see any prostitutes, so he must have been pushing the meth."

William shook his head. "Na, you won't see the women, they'd be in his car. You pay, then they get in and play. That's how that works," he replied as we walked through a building breezeway.

"That's a pretty tough white boy to be doing business like that in this hood, right?" I asked.

"Well, I don't know how tough he is, but he follows the same rules as the tricks…I mean to say, the customers, meaning that if he wants to play, he has to pay too. It's the way it is," he replied.

"Who would he have to pay? And how do you know all of this? Don't mess around and tell on yourself William. I don't have time to be firing you and looking for a replacement. Not with all these damn open work orders," I said.

William stopped walking and turned to me, putting his hands in his pockets.

"All right now Todd. If I tell you what you want to know, I don't ever want to hear my name attached to none of it, you understand? Don't let my name come up about nothing, because I don't have time for it. Are we clear on that?"

The pitch of his voice intensified and rose higher, which made me wonder if he was afraid. We stood face to face.

"I promise you Will. I won't repeat whatever you tell me. I haven't seen any signs of drug dealers, hookers, or anything like that. I haven't even seen any type of gang activity. Shit, I'd like to know what's going on though, so just tell me. Quiet is kept, you have my word on that."

He looked me up and down for a moment, as if sizing me up for a fight, and then resumed walking.

"This is the hood, but we all grew up together. Everybody knows who is who and what is what, even me. I grew up with half of these knuckleheads' mommas and daddies. Their kids went to school with my kids, played ball, went to the same prom, and everything. The reason you don't see anything is that everybody is laying low right now because you're the new manager. But as soon as you drive off the property, the freaks come out. Mostly at night, just like vampires. When we leave, this whole apartment complex changes," he said.

I heard him but was having a hard time imagining what he was saying was true.

"One family runs this place at night, the Stevens, in unit 515. I went to school with their mama, Minnie. There are four boys and a younger sister. The leader is the oldest brother, Derek, and behind him are his brothers Leonard, Jeff, and Tyrone. They've got gang members and recruits spread around town. They call themselves the D.H.S, I believe—stands for the Dread Head Shottas—and this whole apartment complex is part of their so-called territory."

He stopped and pulled out a small bag of chewing tobacco and put a pinch under his lip. I waited, wanting to hear every detail he divulged to me without slowing him down. "Lil Rob pays them, and in return, he can shop his women here. Since Derek and them only sell crack, there's no conflict of interest, so they let Lil Rob sell his meth, again for a cut of what he makes. So, everybody is making money and happy. That's it, end of the story. Again, don't let me hear my name attached to anything I just said."

I processed everything that he had told me and tried to wrap my head around it and make it fit. I looked like a fool. How could all of that be going on right under my nose and I not see any sign of it?

"Damn, I had no idea," I replied. "Let's get back to the office. I need to get a few things done and you need to get to work. Do me a favor and grab a chair out of the community room. I couldn't get past all the supplies and crap you have stored in there; it's a junkyard."

"All right, no problem," he replied.

We were walking back through the breezeway and across the front parking lot when I caught sight of Barry Thomas turning into the front entrance. I turned to William.

"When you find that chair, just put it in my office. The big boss is coming, so let's look alive and get busy. Buttholes and elbows are what he needs to see."

I stopped at the edge of the sidewalk in front of the office parking lot. Mr. Thomas pulled up and parked the car. He hopped out of his BMW with the ease of a young man, equipped with a full smile, or should I say it looked more like a cheese-eating grin. Either way, he seemed to be in a happy mood as he strutted toward me and shook my hand.

"Todd! How are you doing today?" he asked.

He reminded me so much of a particular type of military brass, the disingenuous types, not the true leaders of men.

"I'm doing fine Mr. Thomas, how about yourself?" I replied.

"I can't complain, can't complain. I read your last weekly report and noticed that your tenant fees have risen over $800. Excellent! Just keep pushing and be consistent. Don't get lazy on me," he said as he looked around with his hands on his hips. "You've got to stay on these people Todd, don't let them breathe for one second."

I nodded. "No worries, I've got everything covered. For example, I have a list of undesirables that need to go, and they will soon be gone."

He looked back at me and nodded. We shook hands again.

"I'm on my way to a regional meeting in Nashville and wanted to stop by and tell you that you are doing a great job. If you need anything from me, you just call." He got back into his car.

"Yes sir. Will do. Have a good day," I replied.

I walked into the office and sat down at my desk, grabbed the armrests, and leaned back. Barry wasn't such a bad guy to work for. At least he left me alone and didn't micromanage me. It felt good to get my first pat on the back from him. We were alike in some ways, especially the method needed to handle these people. I liked the fact he didn't show favoritism for the black tenants just because he was black. I had to respect that.

It was almost lunchtime and I debated what I wanted to eat today. I had been going to the Waffle House consistently for the last week. It was the first Waffle House I had ever been to that had attractive waitresses. I would never cheat on Angie, but there was nothing wrong with looking. There was one waitress in particular named Lisa, a beautiful black woman, who served me regularly. In fact, she was super-hot! Thinking about her made me relax and daydream. If she wanted, I'm sure she could become a model or an actress. My guess was that she was probably a former stripper that decided to reform and change her wicked ways, but I wasn't sure.

I snapped out of my daze as I heard the front door open, and I began to straighten up my desk. A black woman whose beauty rivaled Lisa's walked inside. I stood and introduced myself.

"Hello, I'm Todd Goodson. How can I help you?"

"Hi, I'm Stephanie Harris in unit 262. I'm here to report that my A/C unit is not working. I know you're the new manager and wanted to give you some background on this issue. It hasn't been cooling properly for the last three weeks and your maintenance technician, William, has been working on it every few days. He keeps charging it with refrigerant which lasts only a few days and then there is absolutely no cooling at all," she said. She was holding her car keys and her hands were on her hips. I got the feeling she was holding back some frustration. That takes discipline, which made me wonder why the restraint? Most tenants didn't seem to care how they sounded or acted when getting their fee notices. What made her so different?

"I'm sorry it hasn't been fixed yet. I'll have William look at it again."

She frowned and the lines in her forehead told me she didn't like my answer.

"Evidently, there is a leak in the refrigerant system, Mr. Goodson, that's obvious; either in the condenser or evaporator coils. He leak-checked it once, and I saw him trying to apply some type of stop-leak from a plastic bottle. The defective component needs to be replaced," she said confidently.

I sat back down and laughed to myself. Who did this woman think that she was? She'd probably heard some technical terms from

William and now she thought she was an expert. Nope, I didn't think so. She needed to be put in her place.

"Miss Harris, you don't know what's wrong with the system. Leave the technical work to us. I'll ask William about the job and might even look into it myself. By the way, I have an advanced HVAC certification from a well-known technical school in New York. I'm not just a property manager or pencil pusher just so you know," I replied.

She appeared surprised by my answer, and then pulled her wallet from her purse and handed me her business card.

"I appreciate you sharing your credentials. You have mine in your hand. Can you read it to me?" she asked sarcastically.

"Stephanie Harris, Technical Forensic Consultants. P.E., Professional Engineer; B.S. Mechanical Engineering B.S., Electrical Engineering M.S...." I said, before she interrupted me.

"My alma mater is Purdue University, Mr. Goodson. I believe I know how to troubleshoot a simple A/C unit. You are testing my patience, so I am going to give you an ultimatum. If my unit is not repaired and operating normally by the end of this week, then I will do three things. First I will contact the Housing Authority, then HUD, and lastly, I will file a suit against your management company in small claims court. Don't get it twisted, I live here because it's close to my job, my church, and I have good neighbors. I pay full market rent for my apartment and I'm not going to allow you to neglect your legal responsibilities. That is all I have to say to you. Good day." She turned on her heels and walked out. I watched her leave and get into her car.

"William!" I shouted. "Come in here, we need to talk!"

• • •

I walked into the Waffle House and found an empty booth. It was crowded as usual and the table hadn't been wiped down yet. There was no need to see a menu. I had a routine of eating steak and eggs for lunch and today wouldn't be any different. I looked around to see if Lisa might be working and saw her behind the counter. It was hot inside and outside, which made me wonder if their A/C unit was working at all.

I thought back to the conversation I had with William about Ms. Harris's unit. He filled in all the blanks and explained that she was, in fact, correct. The evaporator was leaking and needed to be replaced. The reason it hadn't been removed and replaced already was simple; no manager ever signed off for the purchase of the parts. He explained the parts requisition had been shown to Barry Thomas, but he refused to authorize the purchase, telling William instead, "I'm not spending seven hundred dollars for that! Be creative and fix it another way, that's what we pay you for."

According to William, this was Mr. Thomas's automatic response to spending anything over a hundred dollars for repairs. I knew Mr. Thomas wanted to cut spending, but I don't think he understood who the tenant was or what they appeared to be capable of. This woman wasn't full of hollow threats, she meant what she said. I decided to head off the potential firestorm of trouble and signed the purchase requisition.

I gave William three days to get her unit operating as if it was brand new. I could see in her eyes she wasn't bluffing. A professional engineer, double degrees in mechanical and electrical engineering from Purdue University, for God's sake. I had no choice but to respect her. However she got there, she had done the work.

Lisa walked up behind me.

"Hey there! What would you like to drink today?" she asked with a demure smile.

"Hey Lisa. I'll have a tea…I mean to say sweet tea. I keep forgetting I'm in the South."

She wrote it down.

"One sweet tea, all right. Would you like to order now or do you still need time?"

"Lisa, you know I get the same plate for lunch every day. Medium steak and two eggs over easy. I can't believe you haven't caught on yet. You probably don't even remember my name, huh?" I asked playfully.

She took my order and wiped down my table, still smiling.

"Of course I know your name, *Todd*. I needed to make sure your order was right. What if you wanted something different? I would have to pay for that mistake and I'm struggling enough as it is," she replied.

I was listening but became distracted by her natural scent.

"I'm just giving you a hard time Lisa. Why are you struggling? With your looks, you can make a ton of money. I was curious, have you ever worked in a strip club? I mean, as an exotic dancer?"

My sudden question triggered an ill expression and her smile was replaced by a frown.

"I'll bring the sweet tea and your order will be right up," she replied and walked away.

I thought I must have touched a nerve and got too close to the truth of her past. I hadn't meant any harm though. Suddenly, I felt increasingly bad about prying. She was a good waitress and a nice person and once again, I did something stupid, I think.

Soon, she brought my drink and food but didn't stop for any of our usual small talk. Maybe all her small talk had just been a show so I would give her a good tip? Hell, maybe she was menstruating and had cramps. Either way, I didn't have time for her mood changes, especially over a dumb question.

I scarfed down my order and signaled her for the tab. She came over and put the bill on the table.

"Thanks for coming, have a great day," she said and turned to walk away.

I touched her arm. "Lisa, wait for a second."

She crossed her arms. "You can talk without touching me, thank you."

I turned both my palms over. "You're right, I should keep my hands to myself. I apologize for asking that question and I don't blame you for being pissed off. I know that you're a nice person and sometimes I can be a jerk. I hate to have you mad at me. We were cool with each other, you know. Can you forgive me?"

She sighed and shook her head. "I appreciate your apology and I accept it. It hurts when the first thing someone asks about you is if you've been a stripper. Why me? Out of all the things you could have asked me, what would make you ask me that question?"

Her voice wavered for the first time. I was at a loss for words and honestly didn't know what to say. She was hurt and I was embarrassed.

"I don't know Lisa. I must confess, you are stunning and extremely attractive, but you work here at the Waffle House? I just assumed that…well…I'm just an idiot. I shouldn't have asked, and I apologize again. Sincerely."

I was truly sincere, feeling the need to hopefully make this right. I stood up and laid a twenty-dollar bill on the table, which always included her tip.

"Okay Todd, I understand. But quickly, I'm a very private person and keep my business to myself. It's considered unprofessional to talk about my life or my past to any customer, but you and I have always had great conversations when you come in here. I'm going to share a little about myself, so hopefully you will know the type of person that I am. No, I have never been a stripper or exotic dancer. I have never been a prostitute either, just in case you were going to ask me that, too. I'm a single mom of a beautiful three-year-old girl. I work two jobs, here and at a clothing store during the day, and I go to college. I'm studying for my bachelor's degree in nursing. That's why I told you that I'm struggling, and that's why I got so angry."

Once again, I had read her totally wrong, just like I misread Stephanie Harris. A waitress studying to become a nurse. I was impressed.

"That's awesome! I mean that. You'll make a great nurse."

"Thanks. I only have one more year to go, and I'll be starting my clinical internship next month. I say I'm doing it alone, but I get a lot of prayers and support from my immediate family and my church. It all helps!"

Her sweet demeanor had returned, which made me feel better.

"Does the baby's father help out any? I know that's a big deal. Hopefully, he isn't a deadbeat dad."

Her expression went blank, and I didn't know why. What had I said this time? Her eyes began to water, as she explained, "Her father and I were planning to get married whenever he next came back home on leave, but he died before she was born. He was in the Army and was killed in Iraq," she said in a broken voice. "I have to get back to work. Be safe driving. Take care."

I watched her walk to the bathroom before I left, and as I drove back to Shady Meadows, thoughts of the war rushed through my mind. I had been deployed to both Iraq and Afghanistan, and although they were two totally different places, they both gave me the same sick feeling in my gut. Even now, I could smell the stench of both countries. I thought about her fiancé and what a shitty deal he got to be snuffed out like that, but it happened all the time. You have one of two outcomes in war, survive or be killed.

Sometimes, surviving isn't the best outcome for everyone. Every soldier has their own opinion about that. Some think it would be better to bite it over there, rather than come back to the world all messed up. Others just want to survive and come back home in any condition. The prospect of being severely injured didn't change their minds at all. They were hard choices to make

• • •

The rest of the day was filled with angry tenants coming to the office and arguing their cases. Everyone had received their fee notices and I was reaping their fury. The line to the office seemed never-ending, as angry folk stood by, talking about their problems while waiting to have their grievances heard. But I didn't break from the pressure and gave them no pardon or quarter. They all were given the same response.

"The decision is yours. Don't pay and I'll report it to the credit bureaus. After six months, I'll begin eviction proceedings. It's your choice. Have a good day."

If they were looking for sympathy, they were looking in the wrong place. Still, it began to wear on me. Some of them were extremely aggressive and confrontational, and I frequently had to restrain myself from violence.

Since I started the job, my nightmares were worse than before. That sucked for me, but I learned that if I drank hard during the night, I could pass out and skip the nightmares altogether. But I felt the downside of that every morning. My stomach would feel raw and nauseated, besides dealing with a massive headache. Despite those side effects, the tradeoff was preferable to me.

Tucker confessed his experience was different. Even though he had some nightmares, they weren't as extreme as mine. He didn't drink like me either, and the medication prescribed by his doctor worked well for him. He also had the therapist visiting him and tried to get me on board with that program, but I laughed when he suggested it. I didn't need a mobile shrink telling me what I already knew about myself. Plus, I wasn't disabled or crazy.

It was close to the end of the workday and I was ready for it to be over with, when I saw a short woman peeking around the door.

"Hello, are you busy?" she asked.

I wondered who she was. I hadn't seen her before.

"No, come on in. I'm Todd Goodson, but you probably already figured that out,"

She walked in and stood in front of my desk.

"I'm Felicia Jackson in 324. I came here to talk to you about a fee notice I received, and to see if you would consider removing it. My son Andre told me that he was playing music and that you had words with him. Sir, I can assure you that it will not happen again and actually this is the first time he has done that." She was clearly nervous.

"Ms. Jackson, that's hard to believe. One of your neighbors told me that your son always plays his music loud. I won't mention the neighbor specifically, but they reported that after asking him to turn it down, their car window was mysteriously smashed in. So, I can't remove the fee for the violation. It wouldn't be right or fair. Don't you agree?"

She nodded her head and grinned.

"Did this neighbor tell you he and I were in a relationship for several years, and that one of his crazy ex-girlfriends admitted to smashing his window, not Andre? I mean, you are talking about Clarence Tuthill, right?"

"Ms. Jackson, I can't divulge who exactly complained, and I don't want to get in a he said, she said situation. I personally witnessed the loud music after I received the complaint. I went to your apartment and talked to your son, who took forever answering the door. Possibly, because he had a young woman inside and was a bit distracted," I replied and grinned back.

"That young woman would have been Kim, his girlfriend since junior high school. They have a baby together. Her mother or sister had to be babysitting my grandson that day. She lives with her family in Kingston Springs," she said.

I didn't see how all that was important, and I really didn't care where she was from, but I needed to make a point.

"Maybe they should be more concerned with finding jobs than hanging out during the day blasting music and doing what we know teenagers usually do behind closed doors. Just some advice," I replied.

Her eyes widened. "Sir, Andre and Kim are both nineteen years old and have graduated from high school. Kim works full-time and Andre consistently applies for employment every week. I know because I stay on him and verify his applications. He is a hard-working young man and not choosy about work either. The only thing limiting him is transportation. He was working as an apprentice for a bricklayer and carpooling to work when the co-worker he rode with quit the job. I don't want you to get the wrong impression of my son."

She defended him without hesitation, but I wasn't impressed, and besides that, it was time for me to get off work.

"Ms. Jackson, I can't help you. Pay the $75 fee and keep the music down. I need to leave now, so is there anything else I can do for you?"

She smiled and shook her head.

"No, thank you sir. I'll pay the fee. Thank you for your time."

I followed her out of the office and was locking up, when I saw William and Eugene walking across the parking lot.

"See you guys later!" I shouted. They looked at me and slowly raised their hands in acknowledgment, then kept walking.

Hmm...If they had attitude problems, I could definitely give them attitude adjustments. I cranked up the car and headed home to Tucker's house. It was a thirty-minute drive to Watertown, but first I needed to pick up another bottle of bourbon at the package store. There was a store, caddy-corner to Shady Meadows, that the tenants would frequent. I went to it twice before, but to me, it was a dump in the ghetto part of town. The next closest store was a block from Shady

Meadows and had reasonable prices, as well as a convenience store attached to it.

I pulled up and parked. To one side of the package store was an awning which covered a picnic table. There were always a few good old boys hanging out there drinking after work. I went in and bought two bottles that were on sale and walked back to the car.

"Hey buddy!"

I heard someone call out and saw one of the regulars under the awning waving at me. I waved back and he gestured for me to come over. I put my bottles in the car and walked toward the group. There were two other men with him on the bench, drinking. He extended his hand.

"Hey man, I'm Cody. I see you stop by here a lot and wanted to let you know about the football pool we got going, you know squares… to bet on. Do you want to get in on it?" he asked as we shook hands.

"I'm Todd. Thanks, but I don't gamble. I appreciate the heads-up, though."

He nodded and stepped back.

"That's cool, man, just thought I would check. By the way, that's Toby and Pete over there. We're co-workers. We install siding and gutters. Where do you work?" he asked, speaking with loud country tone and country grammar.

"I'm the property manager at Shady Meadows, one block down from here."

He smirked. "I know where it is. That's the hood! I'm surprised them coons ain't run you outta there."

"Man, I served three tours between Iraq and Afghanistan. They can't run me off," I replied.

He saluted me and shook my hand again.

"Hell yeah! Thank you for your service. I could tell by your haircut and the way you walk that you were a vet."

He looked back at his friends. "You hear that? This man has been three tours in the desert! Smoking them Arabs!" The one he called Pete looked at me.

"My Pop was in the Navy," he said.

I nodded, and the one named Cody turned back to me.

"Look here, brother, if you ever need any work done at your plantation, just let me know. I can guarantee—"

He was interrupted by Toby shouting at someone.

"What the hell you lookin' at, sissy boy?"

I turned around to see who he was addressing, and the only person walking past was a young black man who looked to be in his early twenties. He seemed to be looking at me, but I couldn't tell for sure with the others standing nearby. He was walking toward Shady Meadows. I could see why Toby called him a sissy. His braided hair, with pink barrettes hanging from the ends, and walking like a woman were clear indications.

Toby stepped out from under the awning and continued to shout.

"You better go to the other store down the road! I done warned your ass before, boy!" he yelled, nearly foaming at the mouth.

The young man turned away, clearly unaffected by the threats.

Cody turned to me. "I don't know what's wrong with that boy. You'd figure being colored is bad enough but being queer and colored ain't no way to go through life!" He laughed.

"Amen to that," Pete chimed in. "They need to shoot every last one of them gay bastards."

"He's one of yours. Looks like he's heading back to the plantation!" Cody said to me.

I shook my head. "Just when I thought I had seen everything," I replied. "Well, I got to run boys. See you later."

"Later man!" Cody shouted. I started the car and drove away. It was Friday, and I had my mind set on a relaxing weekend of drinking whiskey and playing video games with Tucker.

• • •

As I approached the house, I noticed a car pulling out of the driveway, and Tucker was at the bottom of the wheelchair ramp. The woman driving looked familiar.

I pulled in, parked the car, and got out with the liquor.

"Who was that? I didn't get a good look, but she seemed familiar," I said.

Tuck was still watching the car as it sped off.

"That was Amy, my ex-girlfriend. You saw pictures of her before when we were deployed. I put all her photos away after she dumped me."

"What did she want? She broke up with you."

He wheeled around beside me.

"She wants to get back together. Can you believe that shit?"

"Cool. So you two are back together now?"

He shook his head.

"I told her I needed time to think about it first. I asked her why the change of heart. She said she was miserable without me, that she made a huge mistake. I told her how much it hurt me, but I understood and forgave her."

"Right. You think she's wishy-washy and might break up with you again at any time?" I asked.

"Not really. I just think she might be coming back because of the guilt of deserting me. She's the loving caretaker type of personality, you know. I simply want her to be happy and don't want her to be with me because she feels guilty. I need some time to think about it."

"I can understand that," I answered and changed the subject by holding up the two bottles. "Look what I found. It's Friday and time to party bro!"

"Awesome, well done young Jedi, but we'll start after supper. Don't turn into a drunk...punk. Hey, that rhymed! I might begin studying to be a rapper. I only need to find the right name for myself. Hmm...maybe something like Rolling Tucker P!" he mocked.

"Don't forget about me your partner, Toddy G!"

We both laughed and went inside. The aroma from the kitchen crept outside, and we knew supper was almost ready.

Within the hour we were half-finished with dinner. I enjoyed dinner with a family. I had missed out on a lot of that after my mom left us, but the Pearson's treated me as one of their own and I appreciated them for that.

"Todd, how do you like your job? I'm sure it's exciting," Tracy asked.

She was so young and innocent that I couldn't tell her what I actually thought, so I gave her the kindergarten version.

"I like the job, but it's challenging. I basically work at a zoo, with every kind of animal you can imagine," I replied, smiling.

Mr. Pearson stopped short of finishing his glass of water.

"What do you mean a zoo? Like a zoo with animals? Please, make it plain for me young man," Mr. Pearson said.

I was sure Mr. Pearson knew exactly what I meant, but I was confused why he wanted me to elaborate in front of his daughter. I tried to choose my words tactfully.

Tucker spoke up, always the instigator. "Yeah Todd, what do you mean?" he asked.

He knew precisely how I felt about black guys and remembered all the heated debates we got into overseas, but I hadn't used the N-word since coming back to the states. I looked at Mr. Pearson.

"Sir, I mean to say that a lot of the people living there act like animals. I don't know if it's the culture, the economics, or what, but they are just different. It's not so much the women, but most of the black men, they don't seem to respect themselves, that's all," I replied and continued to eat.

Mr. Pearson looked at his wife and then back to me.

"Todd, maybe you should consider going to church with us someday? We don't believe in pushing our beliefs on anyone and I am not doing that, but the bible explains how the good Lord made us all. There is only one heaven and there ain't no segregation there. It's not divided into parts where white folks are over here, African Americans there, Spanish folk over yonder, or Asians hanging around up there somewhere. No sir, there's none of that. Just one heaven, for all people," he replied.

I looked around the table. Everyone was looking at me quietly and waiting for my reply. This was the first time I felt like an outsider in their home. They obviously had different beliefs than me about race.

"Mr. Pearson, I respect you and your beliefs, I do. But on some things, we will have to agree to disagree. I just believe that people of different races get along better with their own kind. Yes, we can live and work with each other, after all this is America, but at Shady Meadows, I see things differently. I mostly see black men who act like animals. They walk, talk, and act differently. I'm not sure what you want me to say sir."

I felt exposed in a strange way and out of place, but I hadn't asked for this conflict. Mr. Pearson slid his chair back from the table.

"I never knew you were prejudiced. I know you served with soldiers of different races while in the military and should know better than most." He shook his head in dissatisfaction. "That's disappointing Todd, honestly. Whenever I get the chance, I tell loudmouth racists and bigots my secret. Did you know that I'm part African American?" he asked.

"No sir," I replied, confused and dumbfounded.

"You know I was in Vietnam, but what you probably never knew, unless Tucker told you, was that I was wounded at Khe Sanh in '68. I needed a blood transfusion immediately or I would have died within the hour. An African American gunnery sergeant volunteered on the spot. At that time, I held different beliefs, similar to yours right now, and I'll admit that I had some fear. But the fear of death forced me to put my small-minded and foolish prejudices aside. To make a long story short, that black man saved my life that day and now I sit here, alive with my family and you. I learned that day, the color of a man's skin is not what makes him different; it is what's inside his heart and his deeds that make him different. There's good and evil in every race of folk around the planet. Colors? That don't make a hill of beans," he said.

I didn't know how to respond at first and found it hard to argue with what he was saying, so I answered with what I knew from experience.

"Sometimes color does make a difference sir," I replied.

"How so?" he asked.

"The day we got ambushed, there was a new squad going out with us for the first time, an all-black squad that should have been on point. We had to pull them back and swap positions."

Tucker slammed his glass down on the table. "What does that have to do with anything? You're telling it wrong! I pulled them back! Me! Not *we*! It was my decision and my responsibility!"

Tracy got upset at the commotion and stood up to clear her plate from the table.

"Please don't yell Tucker, and would everyone please stop arguing!" she said, her eyes beginning to tear.

Tucker turned to me. "We need to talk right now. Come on." He rolled away from the table toward his room.

I stood up and placed my plate and glass in the sink. Mrs. Pearson sat silently looking down at her plate. I walked to Tucker's room but felt the need to stop and explain.

"I apologize Mr. and Mrs. Pearson. I didn't mean to cause any problems or ruin dinner."

Mr. Pearson looked up at me.

"Everything is fine, Todd. I might not agree with you, but I still love you son," he replied.

Mrs. Pearson stood up and smiled.

"We are just having a family conversation. Go talk to your brother and you two work it out," she said, smiling.

"Yes ma'am," I replied and walked out.

I entered Tucker's room and closed the door.

"Sit down Todd. I want to talk to you eye to eye."

I sat with him again, just as we had done many times before during deployments, ready to receive my verbal reprimand.

"I don't know what you were implying about the ambush, but it sounded like you were blaming Charlie team. Let's go back down memory lane. That day, you were bitching about them, remember? The all-black fireteam, bad luck, yadda-yadda, is what I remember you talking about. What part about the debrief from that day did you not understand? When I was healthy enough, I read the report and all the events were clear to me."

"I don't remember getting an official debrief, but some guys from the battalion visited me and gave me all details," I answered, wondering where Tuck was going with all this.

"After the blast, we were out of the fight. Charlie and Bravo team flanked and returned fire. It lasted two minutes, and they scored two confirmed kills. They secured the area, extracted us from the vehicles, and performed combat first aid en route back to base camp. If they hadn't applied tourniquets to me, I would have died back there. So, they saved both of our lives and that is the plain truth."

I processed what he was saying in my mind. It was hard to believe, but Tucker wouldn't lie to me. I ran my fingers through my hair, struggling to imagine the scenario which he had described. Tucker put his hand on my shoulder. "Bro, you can't blame them for what happened. If you need to blame someone...then blame me," he said. He began to cry and I put my hand behind his head.

"No Tuck, don't cry. I would never blame you," I said.

He pulled back and wiped his eyes. "Yes you should, you stupid son of a bitch! You can try and deny it all you want, but I decided to pull them back and for us to take the point, but you can't bring yourself to admit that. Do you realize how guilty I feel? Tom and Jay might be alive today if I had followed standard operating procedures. Now I have to live with that decision. Me! Don't lay the blame at someone else's feet," he said, rolling backward.

I slowly remembered that day's events more clearly.

"I kept complaining. You pulled them back because of me! Don't you see now? It's *my* fault!"

I stood up as my chest tightened. My heart beat ferociously as the air became thick and suffocating. Tucker shook his head and wiped his eyes.

"Nope, sorry. It was my decision alone, and you have no responsibility whatsoever. The bottom line is that one of our vehicles would've been hit by that I.E.D. that day. If it hadn't been us, it would have been them. The sooner you accept that fact, the closer you be to moving on with your life. You need to talk to the therapist, man! There's too much trauma for you to hold inside. All these issues need to be worked on and fixed, trust me. Therapy has helped me a lot. Bro. No bullshit."

I became infuriated and frustrated.

"Tuck, man I need to be alone. I need to leave right now."

He looked at me curiously.

"Where are you going?" he asked.

I wondered about that myself and then remembered the empty property manager's apartment.

"I'll grab a few things and crash at the manager's apartment."

"You don't even have any furniture over there man. Where are you gonna sleep?"

"Let me borrow a sleeping bag. All this shit is coming down on me hard. I'm trying to process everything, but I feel like I can't breathe."

He nodded.

"I understand. No worries. There's a sleeping bag rolled up in the top of my closet; I haven't used it since the Scouts. Take anything else you want. Just remember to go easy and don't do anything stupid," he said.

"Stupid like what? What do you mean?" I replied.

"Like hurt yourself. Duh," he replied. "Also, leave one of those bottles here if you don't mind, sir. I think I might invite Amy over this weekend."

"Okay."

I grabbed his sleeping bag, my pillow, and packed an overnight travel bag. I let Mr. and Mrs. Pearson know that I would be sleeping at Shady Meadows. Mrs. Pearson wouldn't let me leave the house empty-handed and prepared a picnic basket for me, filled with snacks and water. Tracy met me at the front door with watery eyes.

"Are you ever coming back?" she asked.

I hugged her.

"For sure, don't worry little sister. There's no problem, I just have some things to do at work tonight, but I'll be back." I replied.

"You promise?" she asked.

"Yes, I promise."

I kissed the top of her head and walked to the car as the sun began to set.

Chapter Six

Reluctant Revelations

I t was dark when I arrived at Shady Meadows, and I turned into the main entrance. What William had told me was true—the freaks came out at night. I heard ridiculously loud music playing from all directions. People stood in groups all along the driveways and I noticed figures milling around in the shadows, their identities masked by darkness from the burnt-out building lights.

I drove to building number six, a three-story building where the manager's apartment was located on the third floor. The buildings were arranged in a figure-eight pattern, with the main drive leading to the two intersecting cul-de-sacs in front of the office complex. I was forced to go around parked cars that were stopped along the driveway. I watched people I didn't recognize walk to and from various vehicles.

I was no fool to the fact that drug deals and prostitution was being conducted on an epidemic level right before my eyes. I moved through the traffic quickly, wondering if anyone would recognize my car, or me. After parking, I grabbed my bag and basket and walked into the breezeway between the buildings. I heard someone call out from the other side of the parking lot and I stopped to look.

"Coo-caw! Coo-caw!"

It was a figure standing next to building number five, behind the shrubbery. I reasoned they were probably high on some drug. I walked up the stairs and I heard the same kind of call from a different direction.

Now I knew what was really going on. They were sending out a message, an alarm to each other. My arrival was noted, and now I had eyes on me. I shook my head and chuckled, reminded of the same tactic being employed overseas. I stepped onto the top landing and was nearly at the front door when I noticed a scrawny cat sitting on my doormat.

"What the hell?" I mumbled. "Get! Go!"

The cat flinched in surprise and darted past me down the stairs.

I wondered what the condition of the apartment was as I opened the door and went inside.

All the blinds were closed, and it was pitch black. I tried turning on the interior light switches, but there was no power. I opened the flashlight app on my cell phone and walked through the unit until I located the circuit breaker panel. They probably kept the breakers off to save electricity on the empty unit. I turned them on. A few ceiling lights turned on, and I could hear the refrigerator start-up and begin to hum. I pulled out a few snacks from the basket Mrs. Pearson had prepared for me and put the rest inside the fridge.

It was hot and humid in the apartment. I never noticed this stagnant heat during the night at Tuck's house because the air conditioner was always running. I turned the A/C on and looked through the apartment, turning on every light and looking in the closets. There was an empty five-gallon bucket sitting on the floor in the kitchen pantry closet that I placed bottom-up on the floor in front of the living room windows. I turned off all the ceiling lights except for the bathroom hallway light, so it was still dark in the living room and kitchen.

I opened the bottle of bourbon whiskey, connected my phone to my favorite internet radio rock station, and sat down on my improvised bar stool. After taking a few shots, thoughts about my last conversation with Tucker filled my head. What he told me about Charlie team had affected me in some way that I couldn't fully comprehend. I knew Tucker was telling me the truth, but I still didn't want to accept it. I felt like I was riding a seesaw, going up and down about it. I took another drink and began to feel a strong buzz taking hold of me, while in the back of my mind I knew that I had no choice but to accept the truth about the fateful events of that day.

Why *did* I dislike black men so much? What was it about them that could change my mood instantly? Once upon a time, Reggie had been my best friend. Hell, we were like brothers. He had my back in any fight and I had his. Most importantly, we trusted each other. Even though Mr. Pearson chastised me like I was some closet racist, I knew that I wasn't. How could I be? To this day, I still respected Reggie and when I thought about it, I knew I respected William also. I was no damn skinhead or Klansman; I was just me!

After a few more shots of bourbon, I went to the bathroom, wiped my mouth, and looked at myself in the mirror. As I became drunk, it was harder to focus. I had grown a goatee and my face looked aged and more weathered than a 27-year-old man should, but I had been fighting a war for the past six years. Still, why would I have deep lines under my eyes and in my forehead?

The noise from the activity outside caught my attention, so I sat down again and cracked open the blinds. I could sit here and look out without being seen and recon the savages to see precisely what was going on in the jungle. It was past time for all their deeds done in the dark to come to light.

• • •

Two hours later, I was stone cold drunk and had seen all there was to see. The drug dealing and prostitution continued without fail, which demonstrated to me that those people could care less that I was here. That was fine with me because I wasn't going to make a fool of myself and chase down every car or go to every apartment that was playing loud music tonight. Why should I care? I was leaving next year or sooner and going back home to New York and be with my family.

I closed the blinds, unrolled Tuck's sleeping bag, and laid down. I turned the music off and tried to get comfortable, but realized I that left the pillow in the car. I wanted it but couldn't muster the sobriety to fetch it, and the room was spinning. This became my nightly goal for me to have nightmare-free sleep.

The chaotic sounds outside transformed into white noise as I drifted off.

My cell phone rang. I couldn't tell how long I had been asleep, or if I had even slept because the noise outside hadn't changed. I wanted to look, but I felt nauseous. Maybe it was Angie? If I answered, she would definitely know I was drunk, and I didn't need to give her any more ammunition to use against me. I kept my eyes closed and searched for the phone until I found it, then cracked my eyes to look at the caller ID. It was difficult to focus on the name. Mom? Why would she be calling this late? Our time zones are three hours apart, so it was still early in California. I hadn't spoken to her since I got back and I was too drunk to talk to her now. Then I wondered if she needed my help. The room continued to spin, so I closed my eyes and answered.

"Mom. Hey, what's wrong?"

"Hello sweetheart. Nothing is wrong at all. I hadn't spoken to you for a few months and wanted to see how you are doing. So, how *are* you doing?" she asked.

"I'm working in Nashville. Tennessee. Going to the academy in April," I slurred, trying my best to speak clearly and coherently.

"You sound like I woke you from sleeping. I'm sorry, dear! But what are you doing in Nashville? Are you with Angie?"

"Angie's in New York. I manage apartments. Going back in April," I replied, mustering all my brain cells to communicate, but I was beginning to fade.

"All right, I understand. You sound so tired. I'm going to let you go back to sleep sweetie, but I'm going to call you again tomorrow so we can finish talking," she said. I was relieved. "Oh, by the way, Herman says hello and is hoping we can plan to meet soon."

I opened my eyes.

"Why mom?" I asked.

"Why? Because Herman is your stepfather and you've never met him, and I haven't seen you in years. Are those reasons good enough for you?" she asked.

Her voice was elevated, which was a rarity for my mother. She was always naturally quiet and demure.

"No it's not. Why did you do it? Why did you abandon Dad and me? Why did you leave us for that black guy?" I asked. "What kind of mother would do that? What kind of wife?"

I had never spoken to her like this before, or about this.

"Todd, you are my son and I love you with everything I have inside me. I never abandoned you! I divorced your father but I did not divorce you!"

"Then why not take me with you?" I shouted. "Dad told me everything, so don't lie to me!"

"Enough! Todd Allen Goodson, you be quiet and listen to me! I was never going to share what I am about to tell you, out of respect for your father, but don't ever insinuate that I would ever lie to you! I was a faithful wife to your father and took care of his every need in this world; I treated him like a king. But eventually he decided I wasn't enough for him. When you were about five years old, he began having extramarital affairs.

"Over time, I gained the strength to confront him about it, but his response was to become extremely abusive to me. He never hit me physically, but sometimes I wished that he would have, instead of destroying me on the inside. I'm still trying to recover from the damage he inflicted on my soul, okay? He broke me down until I felt like nothing more than a bag of dirt. Through fear and intimidation, he terrified me into accepting these affairs, so I shut my mouth and accepted the situation.

"I did that for nearly a decade. One day I prayed to a God that I thought I knew but really didn't know. I asked for help, as well as deliverance for you and myself. I secretly made plans to leave your father and take you with me, but somehow he found out. That was the worst day of my life Todd. Your father knew a lot of important and influential people, some good and some very bad. It was your father who kicked me out."

Her words penetrated my heart like a bayonet. I couldn't believe what she was telling me.

"What?" It was the only word I could get out of my mouth.

"Let me finish. He made sure I didn't seek full custody in the divorce. Had I petitioned for that I was convinced I wouldn't live to see your next birthday as a free woman. I believed I would be writing you letters from behind prison walls, an innocent woman, convicted for crimes I did not commit.

"Now concerning Herman; I met him two years after the divorce was finalized. You seem to have a problem with him being African American. I don't see why that is because you've had African American friends all your life and I never raised you to discriminate against anyone, ever! I want you to know that Herman has treated me with more respect, consideration, and love than any other man has in my life, including your father.

"That's not a vengeful attack on your father either, it's the honest truth. Herman just so happens to be African American, but it wouldn't matter to me if he were Hispanic, Asian, or any other race, and it shouldn't matter to you. What should matter is that he loves your mother every second of the day and he shows it."

I was at a loss for words, but not for emotions, and I couldn't move or escape her words. My mother never lied, but the story she just described shook my reality.

"Todd, you don't have to say anything, I can't let this tension continue to separate us because of the lies your father has evidently filled your head with. I want my son back! I want you back, Todd!" she cried.

I couldn't tolerate hearing my mother cry. Her weeping ignited a filial link of fire that raged inside of me.

"I'm sorry Mom," I replied and felt tears streaming down my cheeks and into my ears. "I never knew. I thought Dad still loved you. He still has your picture on a wall in his place. I know you don't lie Mom. It's hard to imagine Dad out with another woman, cheating on you. But I believe you. It's gonna take some time to process all this."

"Thank you son, for believing me. Go back to sleep now. I love you," she said. "But there is something you just said that I need to clarify: your father didn't cheat on me with women."

"Huh? I don't get it. You just told me he cheated on you. What do you mean he didn't cheat on you with women? What else is there for him to cheat with?" I asked.

She was silent for a few moments, then I heard her sigh and I realized what she was trying to tell me.

"Good night, Todd," she said.

I don't remember responding to her or ending the call and wanted to forget the secret that I had just learned. I closed my eyes and prayed for one of my horrible nightmares to come, so I could escape the one I was having.

• • •

Knock knock…knock.

I heard someone at the front door. I opened my eyes and immediately shut them against a ray of sunlight which had escaped through the window blind. My mouth was parched and my bottom lip was split as if from a paper cut. I must have slept with my mouth open all night. My head pounded with each heartbeat, like a hammer on an iron anvil, radiating from between my eyes. This was one of the worst hangovers I could remember.

"Who is it?" I mumbled. There was no answer. "Who is it?" I croaked again, feeling the pressure in my head increase with every syllable uttered.

"Mr. Todd, it's Eugene!" he shouted from the other side. Eugene? I didn't want him to see me looking like a drunk. I shouldn't have answered when he knocked.

"Hang on a minute," I said, rolling over on my stomach and making it to my knees.

I looked at my watch and was surprised to see it was 11:53. I stood and stumbled into the bathroom. I splashed cold water on my face and drank from the faucet, desperately gulping down water, then dried my face off with my shirt and looked in the mirror. My eyes were bloodshot, and I looked like crap. I opened the door to reveal a smiling Eugene.

"Good afternoon, Mr. Todd. I saw your car and checked the office, but when I didn't see you there, I figured you were up here. How long you been here?" he asked.

"I came last night. I spent the night," I replied.

I felt weak and hungry. I needed something to eat soon or I might pass out. "Come inside."

I moved away from the door and headed to Mrs. Pearson's snack basket. Eugene came inside and closed the door while I rummaged through the empty wrappers, finally retrieving that last packet of salted peanuts.

"I know your back must be hurting from sleeping on that hard floor," he said, looking at my sleeping bag. "And by the look at that empty bottle, I know your head must be hurting too."

"Yeah, I'm in bad shape Eugene. I had a hard night, in every way." I sat down on the bucket. I was a bit shaky and low blood sugar made it difficult to keep my balance.

Eugene walked over and put his hand on my shoulder.

"Mr. Todd, you don't look so good. You need to eat something more than peanuts. You need something to give you some getup," he said, seemingly concerned.

"You're right. I just need some time to get my bearings straight. I'll be fine."

"Give me fifteen minutes boss, don't you fret. I got you covered," he said and walked to the front door.

"No Eugene, thanks anyway. I'll be up and around soon."

My hand started to tremble as I lifted the open bag of peanuts to my mouth.

"No sir. You wait here and I'll be right back. My wife is gonna hook you up!" He left in a rush.

As the door closed, I dropped off the bucket, facedown onto the sleeping bag. My hangover wasn't only physical but mental as well. I shoved all the questions inside my mind into the brink of unconsciousness, right beside the cusp of willful ignorance, knowing one day I would have to face the truth that followed. I loved my dad, but now I felt a new resentment, almost a hatred for the things he had kept from me and the lies he had told me, which had alienated me from my mother. Instantly, my world was turned upside down; just like the day my mom left and the day of the ambush. I was tired of dealing with all the sudden new developments and was exhausted by it all. No matter how I dealt with these life-changing situations, the ending was always the same: I had to accept, but I don't agree.

A short time later, I heard a soft knock at the door, then Eugene used his keys to unlock and open it. He came inside with a covered tray and was accompanied by his twin sons. One was carrying a fold-up tray and the other had a thermos. He directed one son to unfold the stand in front of the bucket, where he set the plate of food and thermos.

"These are my two crumb snatchers, Morris and Norris. Say hello to daddy's boss, Mr. Todd," Eugene said.

His sons weren't any older than five or six years and they stared at me as if they were terrified. They both slowly waved and spoke, their mouth's barely moving with no sound coming out. Despite being extremely hungover, their mannerisms were likable and I couldn't help smiling.

"You have to excuse them sir. They're powerfully shy. They get it from their mama," Eugene added.

I shook their little hands.

"Nice to meet you both. You look just like your father," I said.

They both smiled in unison before running to their father and grabbing ahold of each one of his thighs. Eugene looked down at them and laughed. As he did, I was struck by the brief snapshot of the love between a father and his child. I related to the way they looked at him. He could do no wrong in their eyes.

"Y'all go on now," he told them and escorted them out the door before turning around. "Now, them vittles right there, that's made with love. Go on and enjoy all of that!" he said proudly.

I removed the cloth napkin and revealed an enormous breakfast plate of freshly cooked southern goodness.

"Oh man...Eugene, you're a lifesaver. Tell your wife, thank you. You didn't have to do all this, but I appreciate it," I said while unwrapping the silverware.

"You got bacon, sausage, eggs, cheese grits, and biscuits with grape jam. That'll get you going. Oh, and that coffee is instant, hope you don't mind. It ain't no decaf though!" he said, laughing.

I began to eat voraciously and didn't respond verbally, but nodded my head in agreement.

"Great day! You sure are hungry!" Eugene said, smiling. I looked at him and rolled my eyes in breakfast ecstasy while sipping the coffee. "I'll come back after a while and get everything."

"Thanks Eugene, give me fifteen minutes and I'll be finished sir," I replied.

He stared curiously at me.

"Yes sir, I'll be back," he replied and left.

I walked to the living room windows and fully opened the blinds. The landscape was completely opposite from the night before.

Children were playing everywhere. Patios were peppered with residents enjoying the shade on a Saturday afternoon, but the smell of breakfast pulled me back to my stool to finish what I had started.

• • •

Eugene came back thirty minutes later with the twins, who he recruited to take back everything which was brought.

"How was the food?" Eugene asked.

"Eugene, you saw how clean the plate was. Everything was delicious. Gordon Ramsay would be proud, no doubt," I replied. "But I couldn't really enjoy the coffee because it got cold quick. Let's walk to the office and make a small pot before I leave. Unless you're busy. I know it's your day off, and I won't blame you for not wanting to tag along with me."

"Let's go, I ain't doing nothing. I'll probably watch a football game at three o' clock, but that's about it."

"All right then," I replied.

I gathered my things, grabbed the basket, and we left. I stopped at the car to put everything in the trunk.

This was the first weekend that I had been on ground level at Shady Meadows, so I stopped and surveyed the surroundings. It was uncanny to see the transformation from a chaotic night into a typical, peaceful day, with only the sound of children laughing and playing. The sounds resonated with me, reminding me of my own childhood in New York. The sight of the kids getting along together and mimicking their elders like miniature adults made me think of a simpler time. But, unlike their grown-up counterparts, these children didn't have a care in the world. I wondered, when did I lose my innocence and why?

There were a group of teenagers skipping rope, but they had two of them. Two kids were each holding a line and there was a young man in the middle jumping. It was the same guy I had seen with the pink barrettes in his hair walking past the liquor store.

"Who's that guy over there? The one jumping the rope, doing the Double Ditch?" I asked Eugene.

"Double Ditch? You mean to say Double Dutch!" Eugene laughed. "That's Chavis. He's been living here most of his life. I went to school with his mama."

I thought about telling him about what happened at the liquor store and wanted to profess my opinion about gays, but then remembered my father's secret. How could I condemn this gay man when my father was evidently gay? I was having a difficult time accepting it, but I refused to become a hypocrite and bash this kid for who he was. I'd have to figure it all out one day.

We walked to the office and went inside. I grabbed the coffee pot, filled it up enough for two cups, and prepared the brew while Eugene sat down and began playing with his cell phone.

"Those games are addictive," I said.

I sat down behind my desk as Eugene looked up.

"Nah, I'm texting this hard-headed woman," he replied.

"That's no way to talk about your wife. On your wedding night, I bet you weren't complaining."

I smiled and thought of Angie. She was strong-willed too, or hard-headed, to Eugene's point.

"It's not my old lady, just a side chick. I keep telling her not to text me; let me text you. She doesn't listen! I'm gonna have to cut her loose if she won't quit. She's putting me at risk."

His incoming message notifications continued to chime as he continued to send his responses.

"Not your wife? You're playing with fire. If you already have a wife and family, why risk it all for another woman?"

I was surprised by him sharing this with me. Eugene seemed like a happily married man, always smiling and upbeat. I wouldn't have suspected him of being a cheater. But then again, a smile can hide a lot of secrets.

Pop-pop, pop! Pop-pop! The sound of small arms gunfire erupted.

I dropped to my knees, taking cover behind my desk and instinctively drew my .380 semi-auto pistol from my ankle holster. There was a pause. I moved to the side of the front window and peeked out.

Children were running everywhere, but primarily from behind building five, away from the playground. I turned to Eugene.

"Call 911, right now! Tell them shots fired at Shady Meadows! The manager is engaging! Do it!" I yelled and ran out of the office and across the parking lot.

In mid-stride, I felt the same rush of adrenaline when breaching and clearing during the war. Dammit! I was revived! As groups of children ran past me on both sides, I caught glimpses of their wide-eyed and terror-filled expressions. I wasn't sure if they were reacting to the gunfire or seeing me running past them with a gun. These innocent children were now unknowing participants and experiencers of the fog of war. It didn't matter how many people were around you, you always felt alone.

The sound of skidding tires came from the front entrance and I saw a small red car speeding off the premises. I approached the park with caution and saw a group of guys milling around the park bench. No one was running anymore and everything went quiet. They saw me and quickly huddled together for a few moments before dispersing in separate directions, while four of them stayed. The biggest of the bunch, probably the oldest, was the only one sitting, while the others stood around him.

I perceived that the imminent threat was over. I didn't hear any screaming or see anyone shot. Parents and children were now looking at me and witnessing the new situation that was unfolding. There had to be some conflict between the red car and these thugs. All stereotypes aside, they were hardcore thugs in appearance, but I knew looks could be deceiving, more often than not. I slipped the .380 into my left pocket and stood down. It was time for a confrontation, so I walked confidently but not aggressively toward the four.

I thought they must be affiliated with the gang that William reported to me, the Dread Head Shottas? They all had dreadlocks, some long, others short, some pulled back and tied up. I smelled the odor of spent gunpowder in the air. The shots had definitely been fired in this area. I reasoned that one of them had carried away the weapon when the group scattered, which was probably still warm from being discharged. I wasn't worried about being shot, but I wanted to know who was responsible for endangering the lives of innocent civilians. I could handle being in this element, but I didn't have a warrant or the authority to conduct the operations which were needed. I was alone with a 7-shot .380 pistol, no extra ammo, and no reinforcements. Had they been enemies, I would have already killed them and had three bullets to spare. Instead, I had to stand down.

I stopped a few feet from the leader or whatever he considered himself.

"Did any of you see who was shooting?" I asked.

The young man looked puzzled.

"Shooting? We ain't heard no shooting. You're the only one running out here with a pop gun. Sure it wasn't you?" he replied.

He wanted to play games. Okay.

"I haven't been shooting, but if there's a question about it, the police are on their way, and I'm sure they have a gunpowder test kit with them to test for residue. I'll let them find out who was shooting. I don't mind waiting, how about you? By the way, I'm Todd Goodson, the manager."

"We know who you are," he replied.

"Who are you?" I asked.

He laughed. "You don't know? Everybody else around here knows who I am. Go run and ask them."

He stood up, spit on the ground, and walked off, followed by the other three.

I turned back toward the office and saw Eugene standing by the corner of the building. We met up and began walking.

"Did you get the call off?" I asked.

"Yes sir, I called them. They'll probably be here in twenty, thirty minutes."

"What! Did you tell them that shots were fired?"

"Yes, I did. I'm telling you they are slow to come out this way," he replied.

"Okay. Those four guys…who are they?" I asked.

"That's Derek Stephens and his brothers," he answered while looking down. I didn't want to press him for more information. He lived here and might suffer repercussions if anybody saw him running his mouth to me. Besides, William had painted an accurate picture, so I had an idea of what type of threat I was dealing with.

"Let's go sit down in the office and wait for the police," I said.

We both stepped inside, sweating, and we each got a drink from the water fountain. Every swallow helped me ramp down my adrenaline and finally plateau to where I wouldn't tremble from being still. I sat in my chair with my fingers interlocked behind my head and inhaled, trying to regain my mental focus.

"Mr. Todd, I ain't had no idea you that you were strapped like that. You came out of the chute like James Bond! Damn!"

I looked at him and explained.

"I have a concealed weapon permit from New York State. Tennessee reciprocates my rights so I can legally conceal and carry here. Usually, you would've never known, but this was an emergency situation. I wasn't trained to run from gunfire. I was trained to run toward it and then silence it."

I wasn't trying to be cool, just honest. There was no cool feeling about what had just happened. Simply, I had been continuously trained and that repetition was always present, ready to initiate at any time. I didn't believe I overreacted, but responded appropriately without any bullshit ego and the like. This was no Hollywood movie and I absolutely felt no joy in it.

"That's cool. I might need to check into getting something like that," he said while looking out the window behind him.

"How often does something like this happen? I'm sure this isn't the first time," I asked.

Eugene scratched his chin while trying to recollect.

"It's been a good long while, come to think of it. Those boys used to shoot every week, once upon a time, but never on a Saturday afternoon," he replied.

We waited inside the office for half an hour for the police before my patience ran out and my anxiety began to build again.

"I can't let this shit happen again. Kids were everywhere! It's a wonder that none of 'em were hit!" I stood up and saw a police cruiser turning into the complex. Their lights were on, but there were no sirens. "You've got to be kidding. Really?" I said as Eugene and I walked out to meet them.

After a short discussion, the officers walked around the immediate area and questioned tenants about what they might have witnessed. With no one seeing anything, the officers made a report and gave me a copy before leaving. That was the end of it as far as they were concerned, but it wasn't the end for me, it was only the beginning. I locked up the office and left for Tucker's house, feeling exhausted and worn out.

• • •

I walked inside the house and followed the sounds of the television to the family room. Tuck and Amy were cuddled up on the couch watching a movie.

"Hey love birds, how is everything going?" I asked.

"There he is. We're just relaxing. Todd, meet Amy. Amy, meet Todd," Tucker said.

Amy stood up and shook my hand.

"Nice to meet you Todd. I feel like I already know you. Every other letter from Tucker over the years had your name written in it somewhere," she said.

"Roger that, I feel the same way." I looked at Tucker. "I am going to my room and lay down for a bit. My back is killing me from sleeping on the floor last night. Plus, some idiots decided they wanted to start shooting guns this afternoon at Shady Meadows."

Tucker sat up on the couch.

"Say what? Anybody get hurt?" he asked.

"No, thankfully," I replied and walked towards my room.

Tucker yelled after me. "Pa will probably come in there and talk to you in a minute. He thinks he ran you off last night and feels bad about it. I told him that wasn't the case, but you'll have to convince him yourself."

"Ten-four," I replied.

I went inside and shut the door behind me, leaving the lights off. I laid down and closed my eyes. Finally, peace and quiet. The only noise was in my mind and unless I was drinking or sleeping, it wasn't going to stop. I could turn it down sometimes if I were in a good mood, but I had learned to live with it. Thoughts darted through the dark spaces of my mind...my father...my dad. I was devastated to know my own father had discredited my mother for all those years. I would have preferred that he come out of the closet and accept his homosexual lifestyle publicly. I would have still loved him, how could I not? I loved him right now, but I also hated him for putting a fence between us.

I heard a knock on the door. "Hey Todd, can I come in for a minute?" It was Mr. Pearson.

I sat up on the edge of the bed. "Yes sir."

He walked in and shook my hand.

"Todd, I want to apologize for yesterday at the table. I had no right challenging you about your beliefs and making you feel uncomfortable. You are more than a guest here. Like I said before, you are like a son. I feel like I drove you off last night. Can you find it in your heart to forgive me?" he asked.

"Mr. Pearson, you have nothing to apologize for. I didn't leave because of the things said. You were right about a lot, and a lot of things changed for me since last night. Today, I see some of those things differently, though I'm not sure why or how. My mother told me some things last night on the phone, family issues, that shook me up. Then, this afternoon there was shooting at Shady Meadows. No one was hurt, but it opened my eyes,"

"How so? Make it plain," he said.

"It's like…I've been judging people for what they look like, what group they fit in, but I haven't been looking at myself. When I do look in the mirror, I see a sorry son of a bitch—excuse my language sir. I've been a hypocrite; a self-righteous, homophobic, racist jerk. But that's not really me. I wasn't always like that, I swear.

"Today, I realized that something needs to be done at Shady Meadows. I see everything crystal now, Mr. Pearson. First, I need to come up with a strategy, a plan to deal with all the different issues. The units are deplorable and need to be renovated. Drug dealing and prostitution goes on daily, no doubt bringing the violence I saw today. So, I've decided to move into the manager's unit permanently. It has nothing to do with you. I have to get in the fight somehow and help make a change. Maybe I can get the place turned around before leaving for the Academy. At least I can try to make it safer and improve the conditions."

He nodded his head smiling and patted my knee.

"Reen and I prayed last night that you would find peace in your heart, and that the Lord would guide you in the direction you need to go. I believe our prayers have been answered and I'm happy you chose to answer the call. You just wait until I tell the missus!"

"I'm glad you understand. I haven't really been able to talk to anyone about these things, but it was easy with you. I'm planning on staying here tonight and leaving in the morning."

"I tell you what, why don't you come to church with us tomorrow, and afterward you and I will gather up some furniture from storage. Reen and Tracy can pick up some household items for you at the Dollar King. Then we'll all meet at your apartment and help you move in. Reen is cooking fried chicken tomorrow and we can eat that at your place. How's that sound?" he asked.

"Okay, that sounds good to me. I don't really have any dress clothes for church, but I can go out later and buy something."

"No Todd. The bible says, 'come as you are,'" he said.

"Yes sir. Sneakers and jeans it is then."

• • •

It had been a long time since I stood in church and sung from a hymn book, but the feeling was the same, like everyone was staring at me. I knew they weren't, but I couldn't shake that feeling. Tucker and Amy stayed at the house while the rest of us executed Mr. Pearson's plan by the numbers.

We were the main attraction of the day at Shady Meadows as the residents watched us walk up and down the stairs as the Pearsons helped move me in. I chuckled and declined the offer from a group of small kids who wanted to help us carry some of the load. That was pretty cool.

By five o'clock, the four of us sat down on my new plastic chairs at my small used kitchen table, and after prayer we ate. The family was so very good to me that it became surreal in an odd sort of way. It was hard to comprehend how a family could love an outsider so much, but they did.

My furnishings were simple, spartan to some. I had bought a simple box bed with a memory-foam topper, four plastic chairs, and a small flat-screen television with Wi-Fi capabilities. An old recliner, fold-up card table, and a love seat were given to me, compliments of Mr. Pearson.

After we were finished, I walked them to their car where Reen and Tracy embraced me as if they would never see me again. They finally left around 6:30 PM. I stood on the curb in front of my building and watched them disappear out the front gate.

Before turning around, I caught a glimpse of someone across the parking lot. It was Derek Stephens sitting on the bottom stairwell in the breezeway, looking at me. I stared at him from the corner of my eye as I walked upstairs into my apartment.

Shady Meadows was my new assignment, and I began to draft a list of objectives to complete. After unwrapping a small pack of notepads, I grabbed a pen, sat down in my recliner, and started writing.

Needed:
1) *Security cameras.*
2) *Security gate.*
3) *3rd maintenance assistant position filled.*
4) *Start apartment renovations.*
5) *New roofing on buildings.*
6) *Replace toilets and sinks.*
7) *Paint, new carpet, and linoleum in all units.*
8) *New playground equipment for kids. (Basketball court, tennis court? Maybe?).*

The list was short but contained the essentials, in my opinion. It was apparent to me that Barry Thomas hadn't spent much money on Shady Meadows in the past, but it was long overdue, and it was part of my job to let him know that. Sherika would be at the office tomorrow, and it would be a good idea to have a meeting with her and the staff.

William and Eugene had worked here for years, and it would be absurd to overlook their insight. The last decision I needed to make was whether or not I should get drunk. I decided to risk having nightmares and give my liver a break from the alcohol. I got ready for bed and went to sleep.

CHAPTER SEVEN

HEARTS AND MINDS

The next day, I woke up groggy with my head pounding. I hadn't gotten much sleep and had a splitting headache, but I took a shower and got dressed for work anyway. I opened the office early and made a pot of coffee while I unwrapped a jumbo honey bun and took a bite.

After giving the weekly report, I placed two more chairs inside the office so everyone would have a place to sit. Time was flying by and an hour later, I was ready to host my first staff meeting with Sherika, William, and Eugene sitting around my desk.

"Good morning everybody. I've called this meeting for a few reasons, but the main one is that I need help. All of you have worked here for many years and know the challenges that we face every day. I know I'm the newbie here, but now that I've gotten my feet wet, my eyes are open to the fact that my particular style of management hasn't been practical here. I had a short-sighted outlook and was doing more harm than good. But I don't want that to be the case, and the residents living here don't deserve that. The gunfire which took place here this weekend helped to open my eyes. I'm asking you all for your help and I'm swallowing my bullshit pride, shutting my mouth, and opening my ears.

"We have a responsibility to the residents living here, who also are the same taxpayers who subsidize this community. I have some ideas of my own, but I want to know your thoughts first. What can we do to turn this place around and make it a safer and a more decent place to live?"

They looked surprised and I understood why. My change from a headstrong tyrant to a humble manager was a shock for all of them. They looked at each other and Sherika spoke first.

"First of all, I'm glad to see you have changed your attitude. The approach you've been using was not effective at all. I understand residents must follow the community guidelines, but most of them don't even know what those guidelines are. You've charged a lot of fees for violations, but haven't stated those violations clearly beforehand. At Shady Meadows, managers come and go frequently and because of that, there has never been any consistency in enforcing rules and regulations," she said.

"Agreed. What do you suggest I do?" I asked.

"Rescind all the fees immediately. Print updated copies of all the community rules and distribute them to the residents. Then have a community meeting to explain those rules. Make sure the residents understand the guidelines and that you're serious about enforcing them. A scheduled monthly community meeting would also be a good idea. Give everyone a fresh start. I believe that will go a long way."

It made perfect sense to me.

"Let's do that. Will you take care of printing the updated copies of the community guidelines? The rest of us will deliver them today.

"Yes, I can do that," she replied and began taking notes, as did I.

William spoke up next.

"I need serious inventory to get this place back to the way it was meant to be. Toilets, sinks, and at least twelve refrigerators. Six ovens. Hmm…eight kitchen countertops and five-bathroom countertops. That's just to start, but then there's paint, carpet, and linoleum. The same items that I have been requesting for years," he said.

"Why didn't it get approved?" I asked.

"Ask your boss, Barry Thomas. Every manager gives me the same answer: the district manager won't approve it or the money is not in the budget. I'm tired of asking because he sure doesn't want to spend the money," William replied.

I looked at Sherika.

"Have you witnessed any of what William is talking about?" I asked.

"William is telling the truth. Barry hasn't approved any major repairs or upgrades over the past eight years when recommended by

William, but he has approved a general contractor to come in and complete major renovations of several units," she answered.

William rolled his eyes and stared at her.

"Ms. Sherika, that general contractor comes here once a year, slaps on a coat of paint, plunks a piece of carpet down in a unit, and leaves. I don't know what kind of contract they have, but no real work is being done," he replied.

She appeared bewildered.

"Sherika, when you get a chance, would you find that particular contract for me so I can review the scope of their work. We need to hold these contractors responsible for their work...or lack of," I said.

William nodded and raised his finger. "Oh, and the third maintenance position still needs to be filled. I don't see why that's so difficult. It's only for a helper and we'll be training them, but every year it's the same story, I'm told that it's not in the budget," William said.

Sherika looked at him again.

"I've prepared the budget for this property the past three years, and Barry always has me remove the cost for a third maintenance position. I can verify that, but I don't know how we can get around that issue," Shericka replied while continuing to take notes.

I noticed William appeared uncomfortable and was staring at Sherika.

"I hope you're not going to run back and tell Mr. Thomas I've been complaining or starting trouble. I'm just answering Todd's questions," William said.

Sherika put down her pen. "William, we have worked together for years. When have you ever known me to run back to Barry and tattle? I don't do that, and you should know me better. I'll be honest, I'm sad and tired of watching this place going downhill. It used to be so beautiful here, but over these last few years it has gone down and it seems that no one cares at all, and that's a crying shame."

"You're right," William responded.

Eugene raised his hand. "We sure could use some new uniforms and work shoes. These rags we been wearing for the past four years need to be swapped out. I keep putting silicone on my boots to keep them from falling apart." He raised his right leg to show us, and I shook my head in revulsion. This meeting was starting to remind me of military memories when we requested a re-supply of the essentials, but continuing to get denied, being told to make do with what we had.

"Noted Eugene. I'll give you those funds out of petty cash today. I want you and William shop for some proper work boots. Just bring me the receipt. Give me your uniform sizes later and I'll approve and order them tomorrow."

"Thanks!" Eugene replied.

"You're welcome, and thank you for your patience. I'm sorry it has dragged on for this long, but we're going to get you both taken care of. Does anyone have anything else to add?" I asked.

They all shook their heads.

"Let me share what I came up with last night. Some of these issues we've already covered, which means we are all on the same page." I read my list to them. "We need security cameras, a security gate, a third maintenance assistant position filled, start apartment renovations, new roofing on buildings, replace toilets and sinks, paint, new carpet and linoleum in all units, and new playground equipment. After that's been completed, we need to possibly research the costs for a basketball court or a tennis court. Any comments?"

They stared back at me with blank expressions.

"You have everything covered, but good luck getting any of that approved. Don't get me wrong, I hope you do, but that's going to be a hard hill to climb," William said.

"You're right Will, I can see that, too, but eventually we'll find a path to the top of that hill. I can't do this alone, but we can do this together, as a team. Let's motivate and begin first with printing and handing out the community guidelines to each unit with the first community meeting date. Today, go and get your new work boots and I'll order the uniforms. I'll schedule a meeting with Barry within the next couple of days and present our list to him. We'll see what comes of it, and then we'll have a better idea of how to proceed. Sound good?" I asked.

Everyone agreed and we worked with a renewed, but tempered, sense of purpose.

• • •

It was near the end of the workday and I had left several messages for Barry Thomas, asking him to return my call. William and Eugene distributed the updated community guidelines on every unit door, along with a notice stating that all violation fees had been removed, along with an invitation to a resident meeting on Wednesday.

When I checked my phone, I noticed my dad had called earlier in the day but didn't leave a voice message. It didn't matter to me because I wasn't prepared to talk to him yet, and I wasn't sure I would ever be ready. It was a different situation for Angie and me, and although we texted some throughout the week, she insisted we talk only once or twice a week. When I suggested we speak every day, she said that it made me appear needy and that it wasn't attractive.

It had been over a week since she returned my last call, and even though I knew she was usually busy, I still didn't like the space between us, whether it was physical or verbal. But I trusted her completely and understood that she knew what was best for both of us.

I decided to write Barry Thomas an email and describe my proposal in that format. I wasn't naive and didn't expect him to approve every request on my list, but the essential items shouldn't be an issue. Once the email was sent, I locked up the office and walked to my apartment in the sweltering heat. The climate of the deep South was worse than being in Iraq, mainly because of the humidity. Once inside, I changed into my gym shorts and a T-shirt, then poured myself a triple shot of whiskey. The apartment temperature was a cool 68 degrees, which is what I kept the thermostat set at. As I sat down in the recliner, the cold leather helped to chill my body until I was comfortable. I grabbed the remote to my tiny flat-screen television and began flipping through the channels.

My cell phone rang. It was Barry Thomas, so I muted the television, swallowed the triple shot, and cleared my throat.

"Hello, Mr. Thomas."

"Hello, Todd. I'm driving right now in heavy stop and go traffic, so let me make this brief. I read through your email just now. I want you to listen to me carefully because I'm only going to tell you this once.

"I hired you to do a specific job, and I gave you the scope of that job in detail. At no time did I tell you to go off on a crusade and bring up every issue at Shady Meadows. I know about everything, and in much greater detail than yourself. I explicitly told you not to worry about budgeting or financial issues. I have Sherika handling that part. She is experienced and knows how to conduct the business operations at every one of my properties. Your job is to keep the residents in line and hold them accountable for tearing up the place!" He grew more irritated and more hostile with every sentence he spoke. "Now, I want you to forget about your list—in fact, I want you to tear it up right now. None of what you requested is going to be approved. Don't ask me why or when either! I don't have to justify my reasons to you. Do you understand me?"

Yes, I understood completely, but I didn't like it at all. He was my superior and had made his point with perfect clarity. With my military bearing intact, I responded.

"Yes sir. I understand, but we had gunfire over the weekend. I believe security cameras are really needed," I replied.

"Gunfire? This is the South; gunfire is common down here. You didn't say anyone got shot. Some kids were probably target shooting in the woods. Either way, that doesn't warrant purchasing an expensive security system. I want you to remember what I just told you because the next time I have to address this issue you'll be looking for another job. Are we clear?" he asked.

"We are crystal clear Mr. Thomas."

"Good. Now, if you need something critical done or if you need to buy anything in case of an emergency, you have a $750 limit to make those purchases without my authorization. The requested items in your email easily total over $100,000 or more and would have to be budgeted and approved. Besides, I already have contractors scheduled to come every quarter, and they've already completed most of these repairs and upgrades. These are large-scale capital purchases we are talking about, not small items." He paused and must have sensed my frustration or his own volatility because he began patronizing me. "I don't mean to discourage you, because you are doing a great job, I only want you to understand where your focus should be. Continue the pressure and enforce the community rules, maintain order…Oh, and keep those fees coming in! All right, young man?"

"Yes sir. Will do," I replied, and we ended the call.

He clearly thought he'd straightened me out along with my big ideas. I poured myself another triple shot, but I couldn't sit down. I was pissed off. Not only did he refuse to approve the security cameras, but also the new toilets and new sinks. Barry Thomas was becoming the epitome of a slum lord. Maybe I was angry because he scolded me and I didn't like that, especially coming from a civilian. Regardless, he didn't give a damn about fulfilling our responsibilities at Shady Meadows.

My cell phone rang again. Maybe ole Barry thought about it and reconsidered his decision? No, it was William.

"Hey William. What's up?"

"I wanted to let you know I just finished that job in unit 207. I know you said we shouldn't work overtime, so do you mind if I come to work thirty minutes later tomorrow morning as compensatory time?" he asked.

"That's fine with me. Thanks for finishing the job."

"Okay, I'll see you tomorrow," he said.

"Hey Will, I just talked to Barry Thomas about the list we discussed. He shot everything down, and man, I'm not happy about it. I don't know—"

"Are you in your apartment right now?" he asked, interrupting me.

"Yeah, I'm up here."

"I'm off right now, and usually don't talk about work after I clock out, but if you give me five minutes to run to the store and grab a six-pack of beer, I'll come over off the clock. Then you can finish telling me what's going on."

"I've got a bottle of JW Black just opened if you want to save yourself a trip."

"Be there in five minutes," he replied.

I set another glass on the kitchen table next to the bottle of whiskey. A few minutes later, he knocked, and I let him in. He shook my hand at the door, which I thought was odd since we were officially off the clock. Then I realized I needed to loosen up somewhat. He saw the bottle and the empty glass and sat down.

"Help yourself, but you have to pour your own troubles. Do you need some ice, a chaser? I've got a couple of beers in the fridge," I asked.

He shook his head. "No, this is the way I get down, straight up and neat," he replied as he poured his drink. "You better get some before I finish this bottle off."

"Sure," I replied.

I sat down and poured my drink, then held out my glass for a silent toast. He tapped it, and we both drank. He set his glass down and leaned forward on the table. The cheap table legs began to buckle, and I thought for a second that it might collapse under his weight.

"So, Barry Thomas chapped your ass? Don't feel too bad about it. It figures you ain't the first or likely the last. I have to respect you for a least going to the man and trying to get something done. I already knew he was going to reject whatever you brought him," he said with a straight face.

"I don't understand why he wouldn't approve anything. It makes no sense to me. The money is there, so why won't he spend it? He told me that he has contractors coming in here quarterly to do major repairs and upgrades; I don't see the work being done."

William leaned back in his chair. "Do you want to know my opinion, off the clock? Off the record?"

"Absolutely, go for it," I replied.

"Listen to me young blood, Barry Thomas is full of shit. We ain't seen a contractor come to this property in over three years, but you can bet your ass that an invoice is paid, somewhere by someone."

I leaned back, puzzled.

"What are you saying?" I asked.

William's expression changed from cheerful to foul in an instant. "Wake up and stop acting simple, dammit! How much plainer can I make it, Todd? Close your mouth and think about it for a minute."

I wasn't mad at him for being harsh with me, in fact, I welcomed it. I had known for a while that my head was up my ass, so he was right. I knew exactly what he was talking about but didn't want to confront it. I was working for an embezzler and all the pieces fit together perfectly. I hung my head.

"Ten-four, I got it," I replied while scratching my head.

Once again, I felt like an idiot. Barry Thomas was a white-collar criminal and I knew it. The thought of being manipulated by him infuriated me. "Yes sir," "No sir." I had answered him as if he was my commander. I stood up and walked into the living room to look out the window.

"Look, you're leaving here soon, so just ride out your time and lay low 'til then. Like I said, you're not the first. The average property manager at Shady Meadows lasts around a year, more or less. The man is probably paying you good money and he rarely comes around, so just collect your paycheck and when the time comes, ride off into the sunset. He'll hire another one after you and the scam will go on," he said calmly.

"Damn the paycheck, man! I'm no mercenary; there's no honor in that. No, I didn't sign up for this. Also, I could quit, but then he'll have won. I'd rather just tough it out and try to do the right thing, push my list forward anyway. If he fires me, so what? At least I'll go down fighting, while possibly making a difference here, for the sake of the people."

My course of action was becoming more apparent to me, but William laughed.

"You talk like you're in a battle. This ain't no war," he said.

"You're wrong Will. This is a battle and my life is a war. Ever since I came back home, I've been fighting and getting attacked on all sides. Man, what the hell are you talking about? You're the one that needs to wake the hell up! You know what's going on here, but you just sit on your ass and accept defeat. Well, I haven't been bred and trained for that. I'll find a way to win."

"What can I do? Tell me, since you have all the answers! I need my job and am trying to make it seven more years here before I retire. Hell, you're still young! It's easy to talk shit when you're not married and don't have any children."

"You're right and I don't want to argue with you. We are on the same team, but something has to be done. There has to be a way to procure what we need. Barry told me that I have a $750 petty cash limit to spend without his authorization for 'emergency' expenditures. That's money we can spend some kind of way, but I don't know how to use it. Come on William, help me out here. Think man!"

I sat down, while he tensely plucked at his beard, seemingly deep in thought. The whiskey was affecting both of us and we were on our way to getting drunk. It appeared this was what William and I needed to work together for this common purpose. It was spontaneous and awkward but felt synchronous, like it was meant to happen.

"How about this for the maintenance helper position? You can call a temp job agency and place an ad with them for maintenance helper. Withhold publishing the property address, only disclose it to the approved applicants. Then you can pay the temp service every week by check out of petty cash. That's one way to get our third maintenance position filled," he said.

"If that is the case, then I could buy supplies, security cameras… basically whatever we need in $750 increments," I replied, stumbling from the alcohol.

William smiled and nodded.

"Yes sir, you could do that too. But when Barry Thomas finds out about it, you are going to catch holy hell. He'll fire you without a doubt."

"True, but I want to do something that I can be proud of. Helping out these folks has some kind of honor in it. If he does fire me, oh well… too bad, so sad. But I won't just lay down and let him win," I slurred.

I hadn't eaten anything since lunch and began to feel sick. "I need to get some shut-eye William, but I appreciate your counsel."

He stood up as we shook hands and walked to the front door.

"As long as you shoot straight with me, I'll do the same with you. Just know I got your back covered and expect the same from you," he said.

"Roger that," I replied.

I closed the door and stumbled down the hallway into my bedroom and onto my bed. I chased unconsciousness while running from the seeds of nightmarish thoughts, just before passing out.

• • •

Wednesday arrived, and I stressed about the scheduled resident meeting all day. It was now 6:55 PM and I needed to leave my apartment. I should've already been there. I could have greeted each resident as they came in, but instead anxiety was strangling me. I walked to the bathroom to splash cold water on my face and took several slow and deep breaths.

Images of the residents at the meeting ran through my mind. How hostile would they be to me? I had removed the initial fees I had charged them, but they still had to be bitter over my approach to their situations.

My first impression with the community wasn't a good one, but I couldn't change the past and would have to suck it up.

William called my cell phone.

"Hey Will, I'm leaving now."

"The community room is filled up, standing room only. They are waiting on the governor," he snickered.

"Very funny. Hey, did someone put out the refreshments yet? Tracy was supposed to buy donuts, cookies, sodas, and bottled water."

"She set them out thirty minutes ago, and the folks devoured all of it already. Ain't nothing left but crumbs," he replied.

"Really? Damn! Should someone run out and get some more?"

"No, Todd. They'll demolish anything you set out here. I'm sure folks have wrapped up some to take home anyway. It was a kind gesture, but you need to come start this meeting."

"I'm walking out the door now," I replied.

I grabbed my clipboard and left. Children were playing outside the office while residents stood in the hallway. The entire building was completely full. William wasn't exaggerating; it was literally standing room only. Immediately, my stress and tension levels increased. From the time I stepped through the door, all eyes were on me.

My face was locked into a nervous half-smile but probably looked more like a grimace. I walked tensely through the crowded room and to the front where a small podium stood. I was glad to see Eugene and William standing behind the podium; Tracy was sitting down in the first front aisle chair. I understood they were supporting me, so I used that encouragement as an emotional springboard. After turning on the switch to my military bearing, I was ready.

"Hello everyone and thank you all for coming out to this first community resident meeting."

Immediately, a female voice in the crowd spoke out.

"That's a lie, this ain't the first meeting."

I couldn't see who said it, but I needed to keep control of the meeting and not let it deteriorate into a shouting match.

"Whoever said that, you are correct. Let me re-phrase: thank you all for coming out to this first community resident meeting under my management. I've called this meeting to inform everyone about the future plans the management and staff have in store for the Shady Meadows community, and also to receive your feedback as residents about issues, ideas, or whatever you want to bring to the table. We want to improve the conditions here, so I'm scheduling a community meeting every month."

"Before I begin, I'd like to hear from anyone who has concerns or issues they would like to have addressed which are not currently in our work order system. So, who's first?"

My eyes scanned the room for a volunteer. Again, the same female voice spoke out.

"For what? Ain't nothing gonna change around here," she said.

I looked for her in the general direction of the crowd but still couldn't see her. I thought it best not to call her out, even though her negativity struck me like a slap to the face. Her attitude could become contagious and cause others in the meeting to accept defeat before ever beginning. In my past experience, that type of negativity came from broken promises, hopelessness, or low morale. Sometimes it was a combination of all three, so my gut instinct took control and I detoured from my prepared talking points.

"Ma'am, I'm sorry you feel that way, and to anyone else in this room who feels the same, but I do understand. Let me tell you all how I feel about it. I've been serving in the military stationed throughout the Middle East, fighting for our country these past few years. I wasn't only fighting the enemy, but I was helping to build communities in war-torn areas. Bullets were our currency over there, but that alone wasn't enough to earn trust inside certain communities or to build good relationships and keep them. The most important part of community building was keeping our promises and our commitments. Our word was our bond.

"Shady Meadows can be like a war zone at times, as witnessed by myself just the other week when we all heard the sound of gunfire. This to me is totally unacceptable, and we're going to do something about it.

"What makes this community different than those in Iraq or Afghanistan? I'll tell you: this is America, our homeland. The citizens living here should expect more from me, and I believe that you deserve more from me, too."

The room was silent and everyone quiet, so I continued.

"When I first arrived here, I strayed off course and neglected to give you all the respect and consideration which you deserved. My reason was ignorance and pride, but those can't be used to excuse my conduct. So I sincerely apologize for any disrespect or ill feelings I have earned. I have wiped away the fees incurred from all your accounts, and I hope that you can wipe my slate clean too so that we can start again.

"Thank you for hearing me out. Again, I open the floor for any questions or comments before sharing our ideas and activities going forward."

I had extreme dry mouth and motioned to Eugene for bottled water. He shrugged and shook his head as there weren't anymore.

The community's responses came out slowly and mainly consisted of only minor issues. It seemed very unusual to me that no one mentioned the obvious: gunfire, drug dealing, and prostitution. I knew those issues were the worst on the table and the most significant threat which needed to be combatted. Still, no one mentioned them. From knowledge, this told me that the enemy was in our midst. It was the same scenario I had faced overseas and it was manifest in this very room.

I scanned the room but didn't see any recognizable gang members, but surely, someone was keeping track of everything being said and who was saying it. After a short while, it appeared that anyone who wished to speak had done so. Just before I began to outline my plan for the future, a tiny, elderly woman stood leaning on a cane and raised her finger to speak.

"Yes ma'am, please go ahead," I said.

"Mr. Todd, I'm Ms. Pearl and everybody in here knows who I am. I done raised half these folks in this room at one time or another," she said, turning to her right and left, daring anyone to challenge her. "When this here Shady Meadows was first built, I moved up out of the country and was one of the first people to set foot on this soil. I tell you the truth when I say it was beautiful! Shady Meadows was safe, clean, and it was truly a blessing to live here. Thank you Jesus! I'll repeat it, thank you Jesus!

"But the devil somehow got his foot in the door and made this his home. Something got to be done! I've listened to what you said and I want to tell you something, I am with you! I want you to press on young man, but you can't do it alone, no. But together, all of us can make a change for the better. We don't need no more bickering and fighting or sowing discord." She turned toward the back of the crowd. "Together as one! Do you know that some folks won't even bend over to pick up a piece of trash sitting right outside their door?" She shook her head in disgust. "Well, I'll tell you what needs to stop. That loud music coming from that park and popping them guns off at night. That, and I hear tales about whores and whoremongering, too! No, this has to be put down. Now I have done said my peace," she said and carefully sat back down in her chair.

Her words and her courage inspired me. She was physically the frailest among us all but had the strongest heart and spoke the truth.

"Thank you Ms. Pearl. Know that your concerns, as well as all the others raised here tonight, will be addressed," I replied.

I spent the next twenty minutes outlining my plan for improving the living conditions for the residents, including expanded activities for the children and the community to be involved in. The atmosphere of the room began to change positively as I detailed the innovative repairs for the playground, and the use of the community room as an educational media center during the day where a schedule of science, nature, and historical documentaries would be shown on the new television.

I informed them that during these last hot weeks of summer, we would be providing a fun water slip-and-slide area on the grassy area next to the office. I asked for volunteers to help set up these areas and monitor them and was glad to see that several residents added their name to the list. I let them know that the community room could also be reserved in advance for birthday parties and planned events or meetings.

Also, with approval, car washes and food cookouts could be conducted on the property for community organizations who agreed to donate a portion of their proceeds back to Shady Meadows, and into a community improvement fund. I explained that this fund's primary purpose would be to purchase back-to-school items for the resident children, upkeep, purchase of materials for the media center, and to purchase recreational sports equipment and games, which could then be signed out in intervals.

I concluded the meeting by informing everyone that I had been in contact with the sheriff's department, who committed to provide increased patrols through the property. Furthermore, that the patrol officers would have a key to the main office, which could be used as a satellite location for them to take their breaks, where hot coffee and snacks would be made available to them.

As the meeting ended and the crowd began to file out, the weight from the stress began to drain from my body. Sherika smiled at me while William patted me on the back.

"You did good," he said.

"He did really good," Sherika added.

Eugene walked up to me with a bottle of water.

"I just found this boss. I saw your tongue getting fat up there earlier, but better late than never," he said.

"Thanks Eugene," I replied, and drank half of it.

A dozen residents shook my hand after the meeting and thanked me or said that they enjoyed it and were glad of the new changes coming. That made me feel good, but it was time to get to work and put everything into action. I felt someone tap me on my back.

"Mr. Todd, you're doing a fabulous job. Keep up the good work. I'm with you too," the woman said.

"Thank you ma'am, we're going to do our best."

After everyone left, I locked up the office. Sherika and Eugene were gone and I walked with William to his car.

"It started off a little rocky Will, but I think I recovered nicely. Thanks again for your help."

"No problem. I saw that she was starting in on you and trying to get people riled up, but you handled it," he replied.

"I couldn't see who she was. Did you see her?" I asked. William laughed.

"She was the woman who just tapped you on the back and told you what a fabulous job you are doing. What else did she say? Oh, she's with you. That's Minnie Stephens for you. She'll smile in your face and then put the knife deep in your back. Her boys run that gang and deal the dope, too. Remember I told you about them? Snakes in the grass, Todd. Just watch where you step."

I was correct, the enemy was in our midst.

"I will, thanks for looking out."

We shook hands and he drove off.

It wasn't very late so I called Angie. She didn't answer so I left a message. My mind started to wonder about her and about us. I wasn't as confident about her feelings. Considering we were basically having another long-distance relationship, I had mixed feelings about how we got to this place. In the end, I knew part was all my fault and I wouldn't make excuses for my actions. Yet, I couldn't help feeling uneasy about our future.

As I approached my apartment door, I noticed the skinny cat was sitting on my doormat. I stopped and shook my head, knowing I wasn't a cat person. There was nothing wrong with them, but I didn't want to step over one to get through my front door. The skinny cat was alert and staring intently at me.

"What? Did I disturb you?" I asked, not expecting an answer.

I pulled out my keys and walked to the door, and the feline darted past me toward the stairs. I walked inside and turned around to close the door, when I noticed the cat looking at me from the top of the staircase. The cat kept coming back to my door, so maybe he belonged to one of the former managers and got left behind, but who knows. I thought about it for a few seconds, then closed the door.

I went to the kitchen and poured a glass of bourbon to catch up on my drinking. After going to the bathroom, I came back to the kitchen and opened a can of tuna for my dinner. Tuna fish was great. I could eat it all day. I opened another can, walked to the front door, and opened it. The cat jumped up from my doormat and ran to the top of the staircase. We stared at each other for a moment as I sat the can of tuna next to the doormat.

"You're welcome," I said and went back inside, thinking that I had performed my good deed for the day. Hopefully the charitable act would bring me good karma and tonight would be nightmare-free, unlike the night before.

• • •

A week passed and substantial changes were made and noticed by the residents. The response from the community for all our efforts was exceptional, which even surprised the staff. They hadn't anticipated the amount of support we would receive from the residents, and neither had I.

By the time Friday rolled around, fourteen adults had volunteered to supervise the community room during viewing hours, and the slip-and-slide activity. Sherika designed and printed out release forms for parents whose children would be participating, which she said needed to be done for liability issues, then the volunteers handed them out for us.

The news of our charity car wash had evidently been spread around and resulted in four agreements with local organizations to use our facilities for a car wash with vendor food sales. Two Christian churches, one mosque, and the local VFW signed our agreement and set Saturday dates, which became our designated day for those activities.

The organizers didn't object to the stipulation that 20% of sales would be used to cover the incidental costs for water and electricity use, while the remainder would be donated to a separate petty cash fund designated for the back-to-school supplies and youth-related property improvements. I allotted $250 to William for the purchase of a badminton set, two footballs, one soccer ball, four baseball gloves, and a tube of baseballs, which was all I could spare at this time. Sherika made an equipment sign out log for the office, so we could keep track of the equipment.

William purchased a Wi-Fi-capable television which was also able to play movies from a USB drive, while Sherika downloaded video documentaries about science, history, anthropology, nature, travel, and the like. I expected the children were getting this same information in school, or perhaps not, but for those who wanted to learn and see things outside of their immediate environment, this was their opportunity.

Sherika also created and printed out scheduled times and dates for the programs which went into our weekly newsletter, which we sent out every Monday. We agreed that consistent communication between management and the residents was necessary.

The community room was reserved and paid for nearly every weekend over the next three months. Birthdays, graduation parties, baby showers, sales events, and even a Spanish Quinceañera were on the reserved list. It was refreshing to see how much social activity was just under the surface of this community, which I had previously thought was one dimensional. I had confessed my ignorance, but how could I have not been ignorant if I never saw all these things for myself? The recent advances for the better got me excited, but I still felt anxious. In the back of my mind I still held the belief that when things are going too well, all hell is about to break loose.

William and I contacted a local temporary employment agency, gave them our requirements, and signed an agreement for one worker. They would cover the costs of advertising the position and forward us the applications of qualified personnel. William was optimistic, but Eugene was the happiest of all, knowing he would have an apprentice, or in his words a "young buck," under him to do most of the manual work.

As for my personal life, my relationship with Angie was always on my mind. She continued to insist we only talk once or twice a week, but that our texting had no limits. I didn't agree with that and thought couples who loved each other would want to converse at least once a day. Then I heard Tom's voice in my mind. *"That's what you get for thinking, Jarhead!"* he said. I shut down the war-torn memories of the good times before depression crept up and strangled me. I learned that depression stalked me that way, quietly and deliberately, like a special operator.

William came into the office, followed by Eugene.

"It's about time to clock out. The last video ended, so I locked up the video room. Do you need anything else before we leave?" William asked.

"No thanks, I'm covered," I replied as I locked up my desk.

"Me and Eugene are gonna get a few drinks down the road. You're welcome to join us," William said.

"I would guys, but I'm going over to my buddy Tucker's house for dinner. I haven't seen him or his folks for a while. You two have at it, but no DUI's and stay out of trouble. Be like Batman and Robin!" I barked, clowning around.

Eugene removed the toothpick from his mouth and pointed it at me.

"If we are Batman and Robin, then who you be? Alfred the butler?" He laughed and William snickered. I stood up and ushered them out of the office.

"That's right, I'm Alfred the butler at the manor keeping you two out of trouble. Hell, even saving the day a time or two if I remember the series correctly. Hey, all jokes aside, I want to thank both of you for jobs well done. No shit, I appreciate your help."

We shook hands and I locked the front door. They laughed and waved me on as I got into the car and drove to see Tucker and family.

• • •

I unlocked the front door and went inside, smelling the Southern home cooking, which I sorely missed. I heard voices coming from the kitchen and found Mr. and Mrs. Pearson talking at the kitchen table. They looked up at me and Maureen stood with her arms spread wide.

"Todd! My youngest son, how have you been dear?" she said as we gripped each other. I felt a surge of relief pulse across my body and felt nothing but unconditional love from her. All this love from the mother

136

of my best friend was transcendent, but at the same time I felt unworthy and fraudulent. Her natural-born son was a true hero. Why should she have so much love for me? I didn't merit it.

"I've been doing good ma'am. I missed you all, for sure. Especially your cooking. The food of the gods."

"Reen! Please stop smothering the boy and let him breathe. How're you doing son?" Mr. Pearson asked.

Mrs. Pearson released me as I reached down and shook his hand.

"I'm doing a lot better now that I'm here." I smiled. "How have you been doing sir?"

He leaned back in the chair and clutched his spine. "My backbone is giving me fits. Muscle spasms and such. When you get to be my age, all the foolish decisions of youth come back to haunt you. I've just got to deal with it and call down strength from the Almighty. Kind of like calling in airstrikes to the Air Force."

"Ha! Let me go holler at Tucker. Is he in the back?"

Mrs. Pearson raised her eyebrows and said, "Tucker is in the family room with his therapist from the VA. They're finished with their session, but I think Tucker wants the two of you to meet, so he's staying a bit longer."

I nodded and went to the family room where I found Tucker and the therapist. The therapist stood up while Tucker wheeled over to me and we shook hands.

"Todd, I want you to meet Josh Eshelman, the therapist that I told you about. Josh, this is Todd who you already know about," Tucker said. He rolled back to give us space as Josh extended his hand.

"Todd, I'm thrilled to meet you. As you can imagine, being best friends with Tucker and serving with him, your name has come up more than a few times. I'm happy to finally meet you," he said, upbeat and intense. I was having a hard time reading him.

"Good meeting you too. Are you finished or do you need more time for...whatever you do or talk about?" Tucker rolled closer.

"Nah man, we're finished. I asked him to stay until you got here so you could meet each other. Josh is a good guy. I trust him and can vouch for him. He's helped me out a lot, so if you wanted to talk to someone or needed to get things off your chest, he can definitely help."

Tucker watched me, looking for the slightest reaction. He knew I wasn't on board with the therapy idea, at least not for me. I didn't need it. I felt like this was a setup, and almost betrayed in a peculiar way. I understood why Tuck needed therapy; he had lost a lot, much more than me.

"Cool man, I appreciate that, but I'm good," I replied.

The therapist crossed his arms. "You know something Todd? I hear that same response from seventy-five percent of first-time assessments when considering PTSD therapy. I can understand their reasoning so it's not surprising. All I want to offer you is my contact information and a promise of trust. It will be up to you to make the decision to engage in therapy, assuming you need therapy, and most importantly, that you *want* therapy.

"I know you both served together, and I know how many confirmed kills there are between you. I also understand what was taken from you. Todd, no one can endure that type of fiery vigil and come out untouched. No one. I've helped hundreds of PTSD sufferers. Not only soldiers, but people from all walks of life who have experienced traumatic events. Rape victims, starving children of drug addicts, victims of child abuse, people growing up in crime-infested neighborhoods who are terrified every time they walk out of their front door, because they're afraid of getting shot. The list goes on and on. Trauma comes in many forms Todd, and I want you to know that I am here if you feel the inclination to talk. That's all."

He was bold and seemed sincere enough, but I wasn't ready for any of this. Things were getting better with the job and with my sleep, so why go digging up the past and rock the boat.

He reached into his shirt pocket and handed me his business card. "Calling me is the same as saving a trip to the local VA, except I make deliveries and you're not allowed to tip me," he said jokingly.

I smirked and took his card. "Thanks Doc." I put the card in my pocket and looked at Tucker. "I'm starving bro. Are you ready to eat?"

"You better believe it," he replied.

We walked the therapist to the door and let him out. Tucker swiftly turned and raced me to the kitchen, only winning by blocking me off at the hallway. We settled down at the table and after Mr. Pearson said the blessing, we ate to our heart's content.

Twenty minutes later, Tuck and I were as fat as Potbellied pigs, guilty of Southern cooking gluttony. Mr. Pearson tapped me.

"So how's the job coming along? What's going on over there?" he asked.

I told him about the meetings, the possible embezzlement by my boss, our ongoing progress, and the positive involvement of the community. I let him know things were getting much better, even though we were only at the beginning stages. He smiled and leaned toward me.

"So, now do you understand one of the most important lessons in life about people?" He asked.

"I'm not sure. What?"

"If given a choice, the vast majority of people in this world prefer a hand up rather than a handout," he replied and leaned back in his chair. I nodded and kept my mouth shut and thought about what he'd just said. It was the truth.

That night, I closed the door to my old room and took the therapist's card out of my pocket, crumpled it up, and threw it in the trash can. I laid down to sleep but tossed and turned. I had a longing for home, but where was that? With Angie? That didn't feel like home, but again I felt that was my fault. I fell asleep thinking about the only home I ever knew, with my dad. I was a little kid and ignorant about life, but I felt safe at home. That was a long time ago, and now it seemed as if it was only a faraway dream.

Chapter Eight

Camelot

I locked the door to the storage locker in the back of the community room, and handed a soccer ball to young Marquise and his two friends. He poked out his lips.

"A soccer ball? Are you sure you don't have anything else? We want a football," Marquise asked.

I wrote down his name and added the date and time.

"I told you what all wasn't signed out, and this list keeps an inventory, besides I even checked again for you. Everything else is signed out. What's wrong with the soccer ball? Soccer is the biggest sport in the world. Try something new, kick it around. Just remember the two-hour rule and bring it back on time. You can sign it out again if no one else is on the list. Maybe by then, someone else would have returned something you guys want. You good?" I asked.

He nodded his head and left with his friends trailing. I returned to the office and looked through the applications for today's scheduled interviews. There were five applicants, one of whom lived at the property, Andre Jackson. The name sounded familiar. I thought it might be the young man I had trouble with on the first day. I faintly remembered an exchange of harsh words and threats. I was surprised to see him apply for the position due to the nature of our first meeting. It showed perseverance and determination on his part.

William and Eugene came in and sat down. Eugene began fanning himself with a manila folder.

"Great day! It's hot out there boss," he said.

Will stared at him. "It doesn't help if you eat fish with hot sauce and habaneros. I know you got to be burning up," he said.

I sat down at the desk and handed them notepads and pens.

140

"Here guys, think of a few questions to ask the applicants and I'll have you ask them in turn. Then, write down any notes about each one of them. When it's all over, we'll share our notes and decide who's the best choice. Sound good?" I asked.

They both agreed and we waited for the first interview.

• • •

Three hours later, it was almost time for our last interview. All the prior applicants were more than qualified, and there were some great candidates to choose from. It was a quarter till four and we had fifteen minutes until the next interview.

"So, what do you think? Does anyone stand out?" I asked the guys.

"I don't care for any of them, to be honest," William replied.

"Huh? Why not?" I asked. I was confused as to how we could be polar opposites on this.

"All of these guys can do the job, not a problem. I get that. But none of them *need* this job. It doesn't pay much at all. Every one of those applicants can make top dollar. Hell, any one of them could do my job. They're just waiting on other jobs, that's all. Mark my words, Todd, if you hire one of them, they'll quit after a few weeks and will have moved on to greener pastures. Remember I said it," he said.

I looked at Eugene. "I'm with William on this. We need someone who is gonna stay, not pick up and go down the road by the end of the month. That don't make no sense," he replied.

The front door opened and Andre Jackson walked in.

"Sir, I'm here for my four o'clock interview. I'm a little early but I can come back if you want," Andre said.

He stood tall, clean, and shaved. He was wearing a polo shirt and khaki pants and a worn belt. He looked sharp. I stood up and stretched my hand out to him.

"Hello Andre. We met before, a while back. I'm Todd Goodson, and I'm sure you already know William and Eugene," I said as we shook hands.

He turned and shook hands with William and Eugene.

"Mr. Will, Mr. Eugene," he said respectfully with a nod.

I got the feeling that they all knew each other very well.

"Sit down Andre, and let's get started," I said, motioning toward the chair.

He sat down with his head upright and straight, his hands resting on his legs. His serious demeanor and rigid posture led me to wonder if he had been part of the JR ROTC at his high school. He didn't resemble the young man I met at the door of his mom's apartment that day. His cordiality and mannerisms were so professional, it was as if he was a different person. It was humorous to me because he was probably thinking the exact same thoughts about me.

We started the interview as we had done with all the others, and I allowed William and Eugene to go first with their questions. I found out that Andre did have some experience with carpentry and basic shop mechanics while attending a vocational school, and he did meet the minimum qualifications. His language wasn't as polished as the other older candidates, but he communicated clearly and we understood each other, which was all that mattered. When it was my turn to ask questions, I deviated from the previous format. We needed to cut to the chase and make a decision, so I asked him only one question.

"Andre, if we hire you, tell me what you can offer us?" Then I sat back and listened.

He didn't hesitate and looked directly at me.

"Sir, you should hire me because I will come to work early every day and work hard. I will do whatever y'all need and learn whatever you want to teach me. I won't play around. I give you my word, and that's on my baby."

I was able to read Andre like a book. As much as I knew what a bullshitter sounded like, I knew he wasn't one. He was young, honest, and hungry. I glanced at William and Eugene. They both nodded in approval as I stood up.

"Mr. Jackson, you are hired. Welcome to the staff of Shady Meadows," I said, extending my hand.

His whole demeanor changed from someone who was wound tight and stressed, to a person happy and relieved. We all took turns shaking his hand.

"Thank you, and thank you Jesus!" he blurted out.

I noticed that a lot of folks down here made those types of comments, but I wasn't sure if it was just a saying, or if they were ultra-religious.

"Andre, we want you to report tomorrow morning at 9 AM. I'll call the staffing agency and let them know you've been hired."

"Yes sir, Mr. Todd," he said, and left the office.

I looked at the guys and smiled, while William pointed his finger at me.

"You made the best choice. That young fella will work and he needs the work. He's got a baby to support. You did well," he said.

"No William, we all made the right choice. I would've hired that first dude if it weren't for the feedback you guys shared. So this was a team decision and a team win."

They nodded.

"You said there was something else you wanted me to look at before I left for the day," William said.

"Yeah, thanks for reminding me. Hang on for a second," I replied.

I sat down to check my email when Eugene stopped at the door.

"Mr. Todd, I wanted to ask you, I got up early this morning to go to the bathroom, and when I looked out the window, I saw a man, technician or somebody, on a ladder near building four. He was wearing a white hard hat and was on the side of it messing with some wires. Do you reckon he was from the electric company?" he asked.

I had to think quickly for a moment.

"Oh, that was a contractor from the cable company doing some upgrades on the outside terminals. I forgot to tell you guys about it. They called last week and said someone would be out early in the morning."

"Oh okay. I need to finish the caulking inside a bathroom, then I'm clocking out," Eugene replied.

"All right, see you tomorrow. I need to go over some contracts with William," I said.

I handed William a folder containing the quotes that were received from our request for bids. I definitely wasn't going to renew the agreement with the current contractor.

"Those are the quotes for the contractors you recommended. Their quoted price per unit is fifty percent less than those hustlers who took the money and ran."

William looked through the quotes. "Good prices… you might as well take the middle bid. All of these companies are top shelf and have good reputations, which is what we want," William said as he handed me back the folder.

"It's hard to believe Barry Thomas was scamming like this. I suppose he figured that by changing managers every year, it wouldn't be exposed. If anyone ever questioned him from the corporate office about the contracted work being paid but not completed, he could always plead ignorance. It would all fall back on you, the senior maintenance technician, for not inspecting and reporting work not completed. But by you and Eugene signing those affidavits and stating you both informed him of this issue, you have covered your hind ends from any fallout.

"I now have copies of all the past unsubmitted budgets which Sherika created, as well as the officially submitted budgets. All this data, along with your scanned affidavits, have been put on a flash drive for safekeeping. I'm waiting for the right time to send it to the corporate. I might even find some more dirt to add to it," I said.

He handed me the folder and stood up to stretch.

"I can tell you we were glad to sign those statements. We ain't gonna get caught up in Barry's dirty dealings," he said. "I'm going to clean up the shop and head home. Do you need anything else?"

"No sir, everything is good. I'm going to lock up the office in a few minutes after I file the third noise violation warning for Minnie Stephens. Her sons are going to get her evicted if she doesn't rein them in. One more violation and they're out of here," I said.

"I grew up with that woman, and she doesn't care what those boys do as long as that dope money keeps coming in. She does have one good son out of the bunch, Tyrone, the youngest. He's an outstanding ballplayer, but hanging out with his knucklehead brothers will hurt him in the future," he said.

"Everybody has choices to make. Hopefully everything will work out for the kid. See you later William," I replied as he left.

I put the violation in Ms. Stephen's resident file, straightened up my desk, and left. I was hungry and had my mind on the Waffle House for some reason. I locked up the building and walked to the car. There was a group of kids jumping rope in the empty parking space next to me. I decided to joke with them.

"You girls don't know how to Double Ditch," I said.

"It's Double Dutch!" the three girls yelled out in unison. The girl jumping turned and faced me, without missing a step.

"Do you want to try?" she asked. I thought her name was Dawn.

"I would probably break my ankles trying to keep up with you," I replied, unlocking the car door.

"Come on Mr. Todd! Just try it. Don't be scared!" she shouted, while the other two girls laughed. "Look how easy it is!" she said while jumping and turning around in each direction. Then she jumped out and stood in front of me. "At least try it once."

I knew better, but she had issued me a challenge. I could do this, so I closed the car door.

"Scared? Yeah right. Let's go! Okay, how do I do it?" I asked. "Don't they have to stop the ropes first?"

They all laughed.

"No! You have to jump inside while they turn. Pay attention to the rhythm when each rope hits the ground and time it. Let me show you, and I'll count down for you," she said, ready to jump back in. "Three, two, one, now!" she said, and jumped in and stepped in rhythm between the two ropes. "Okay, Mr. Todd, I'm staying in, now you jump in on my count and follow my steps."

"All right I'm ready!"

I took my position and watched her feet and the ropes.

"Three, two, one, jump!" she shouted.

I jumped in on her mark…and the ropes tangled my legs instantly.

"Dang it!" I yelled and stepped out of the rope. "That's enough for me, I suck."

They laughed some more.

"You just need more practice, that's all. You did jump in at the right time, but you were too slow. You have to lift your feet higher, too," Dawn replied.

"Well I'm hungry and weak right now. Let me go fill up at the Waffle House and get my strength back. One day, I'll show you how the professionals do it," I joked.

"Don't blame it on being hungry! You're old and slow!" Dawn said as the other girls laughed.

"Hey! Old? Young lady, I'm not even thirty years old!" I protested as I opened the car door.

"Thirty *is* old, Mr. Todd." I couldn't take any more abuse from these young gals, so I shook my head and retreated inside the car.

"Mr. Todd, bring us something back from the Waffle House please?" Dawn asked.

I backed up and rolled down the window.

"Hurry up and tell me what you want," I replied. The group stopped jumping rope and happily ran up to the window, giving me their requests. I nodded and repeated their orders, but couldn't stop laughing.

"What's so funny?" one of the other girls asked.

"Well, right now I remember all your orders, but I'll probably forget every one of them by the time I get there. You know how old people are so forgetful," I said, watching the expressions of delight disappear from their faces. I laughed as I drove off. It served them right for calling me old.

• • •

I walked into the diner and sat at my usual booth. It wasn't crowded this time of the day. I checked my phone to see if Angie had texted me back. Nope. How busy could she be to not answer a text from this morning? It literally took seconds to do. This was one of my peeves about her, which aggravated me to no end. Dammit! I could feel my blood pressure and anxiety elevating again, every time I thought about how inconsiderate she could be. I needed to calm down, so I put my phone away and closed my eyes for a moment. I took several slow breaths and focused on more positive thoughts, which helped.

"Are you all right Todd?" Lisa asked.

I opened my eyes and leaned forward on the table.

"Oh yeah. It was a long day at work. I know you don't want to hear me complaining. I know my job is easy compared to yours. How is your day going so far?"

"I am so excited! I just finished my summer finals in two classes and got an A in both," she declared.

I shook her hand. "Congratulations Lisa! I'm happy for you."

"Thank you so much, and thank you for encouraging me whenever you come here. You always check on my progress. I look forward to seeing you. I'm going to have to do something nice for you next time you come in. I'll surprise you. One day you'll come in and I'll spring it on you," she said.

"You don't have to do anything for me. I know how hard you work, and I see how tired you are. I can only imagine how tired you must be for the rest of your day. My heart goes out you know. I mean, even though I'm a customer, we are kind of, sort of friends, right?" I asked.

Her smile broadened.

"Absolutely! You've shared things about your life with me too. You have a lot going on also, with Shady Meadows and being away from Angie, so I do consider you a friend even though we don't talk on the phone or hang out."

She was emphatic, and I totally agreed with her.

I stayed there for nearly an hour before driving back to my apartment, with a slice of apple pie in a carryout bag for later. It was time to kick back and have a drink, or two, or ten. Whatever amount was required to get me where I needed to be was the proper amount to me. I parked and headed toward the staircase when I smelled a bit of heaven. The aroma was coming from Ms. Pearl's apartment on the bottom left. I had to pass her door every day when coming or going from my apartment. The elderly woman's cooking was legendary according to Eugene and William, so I stopped momentarily and inhaled one more time.

I got to my apartment, changed, used the bathroom, and then poured a drink.

I had developed a new ritual just before I took my first drink of the day. I displayed a squad photo of me, Tom, Jay, and Tuck on my phone. Then, while playing our anthem, "Highway to Hell," I would salute and toast to our squad. It was hard to do when I first started a few months ago, but eventually, I was able to look at their faces in the photo. It was still painful, but I had to recognize them and keep their honor alive through remembrance. As I raised the glass to my lips, there was a knock at the door. I got up and looked out the peephole. It was Ms. Pearl. I opened the door to see her standing there, holding a large plastic container.

"Ms. Pearl, ma'am, how can I help you?" I asked.

"Hello, I baked you this cake to show my appreciation for all the good things you've done around here. You have been a blessing to all of us in this community. This is an old-fashioned buttercream and vanilla cake, handmade, not out of a box." She passed it to me.

"Wow, thank you! I could smell you cooking something when I passed your door a few minutes ago."

"Oh, what you smelled was supper for tonight. I baked that cake late this morning. Well, I need to be getting along now. Remember to bring my container back when you finish with it, or this be the last cake I bake for you." She winked and hobbled to the staircase. I watched her get to the railing and have difficulty negotiating the first step down.

I set the container on the table and darted out to meet her at the stairs.

"Ms. Pearl, wait, let me help you down these stairs."

I gripped her right hand while supporting her under the left arm.

"Oh thank you. I would've had one of my grandchildren bring this up to you, but they are all out playing. I got bad knees. I go up better than I can come down," she said. It was slow going, and it gave me time to feel how fragile this elderly woman was. When we arrived at the bottom, I walked her to the front door.

"Ms. Pearl, I thank you, but if you ever have anything for me, or need to talk to me, please call or send for me. I don't want you to risk falling on these stairs. Please ma'am." She turned around inside her doorway.

"I hated to bother you, Mr. Todd. You won't hear much from me," she replied.

"Ms. Pearl, you can never bother me. If you need anything—and I mean *anything*—just send word." This woman struck a chord in my heart. Sometimes you meet people in life that make an impression on you in an immeasurable way, but you just can't put your finger on why. She was one such person.

She looked at me, curiously, almost worried.

"Do you honestly mean what you just said?" she asked.

"Yes ma'am, I do! I give you my word."

"Are you busy this Sunday?" she asked.

"No, I'm free all day on Sunday. What do you need?"

"I need someone to take me to church this Sunday. Would you be able to?" she asked.

"Sure, just tell me what time."

"We need to leave here at ten o'clock. The church is only a fifteen minute drive from here, and devotion services start at ten-thirty. Thank you. That takes a load off my mind."

"You're welcome and have a good night."

I went back to my apartment, poured another drink, and looked out the window. Damn, I forgot to ask Ms. Pearl what time she wanted to be picked back up from church. How long do their services last? I once heard a black comedian joke how all African American worship services were extremely long; I didn't understand the joke. Anyway, she could tell me on Sunday. I looked at my phone and saw that there was a missed call from my Dad. I wasn't ready to talk to him. Not yet.

• • •

Just before midnight, my last bottle of Scotch sat empty on the kitchen table and I was numb. The warm sensation from the alcohol ran through my veins and eased the constant fluttery feeling of nervousness deep inside my gut. I hated running out of liquor. I should have bought some earlier. Hopefully, I'd be able to sleep through the night.

My phone rang, caller unknown.

"Hello?" I asked.

A female's voice answered. "Mr. Todd, this is Patricia Houston, I live in unit 510. I'm sorry to bother you this late, but those boys are at the playground again blasting their music. I have to go to work in the morning and can't sleep, and they woke my baby up! I've called the police and reported a noise disturbance, but that was forty-five minutes ago and no one has shown up. Would you please do something about this? Please!" she pleaded.

I could hear the desperation in her voice.

"Yes ma'am. I'll walk over there now and check things out."

"Thank you!"

I put on my sneakers and T-shirt, grabbed my pistol, and tucked it inside my waistband.

I headed across the parking lot toward building five and the playground. The music became louder as I walked through the building breezeway and turned the corner facing the playground. As I expected, the offenders were Derek Stephens and two of his brothers, along with two females I didn't recognize. They were sitting on one of the picnic tables, drinking, and smoking weed. One of the younger brothers saw me and turned the music down quickly, which caused Derek to look around until he saw me. He promptly extinguished the joint.

I walked up to the table. "Hello everybody. Two things: first, this playground is closed from 8 PM until 7 AM, so you all need to leave and take the party somewhere else. Second, the loud music during quiet hours violates the community noise policy."

Derek Stephens spoke up. "That's cool. We turned the music down and about to leave in a minute. We good," he replied.

I shook my head. "Negative, we are not good. This is the fourth time you personally have been in violation of the noise policy. I just gave your mother a final written warning today. Now, I have to file for eviction."

Derek jumped off the table and stepped up to me, crossing into my personal space. Six inches separated our faces and I could smell his sour breath as he tried to browbeat me. My heart rate jumped, and I began to get butterflies. I stood my ground so I could see the position of his two brothers.

"White boy, I swear on my kids, if you try to evict my mama you're done! Believe that!"

I saw his brother on the left begin to move out of my peripheral eyesight, so I took two steps back.

"You're the person causing your mother to be evicted, not me. These rules are for everyone, even me. You do what you have to do, just think really hard and consider the consequences of your actions. That's my advice. Take it or leave it." I walked away, listening for any movement behind me. There was a chance the brothers would try to jump me. I hoped not, for their sakes.

"White boy! Ooh! You gonna get yours, I promise. We gonna be here long after your pasty ass is gone. Punk ass boy!" Derek hollered.

I heard movement and footsteps behind me. I kept my pace slow and didn't turn to look, but I did reach under my shirt and grabbed the handle of the pistol. I wanted them to either come a bit closer or have them stop moving before I acted, though both scenarios could be the prelude to me being shot from behind. I felt my heart thumping and my neck tighten. The time was now, so I inhaled one last breath.

Suddenly, a police car pulled into the parking lot and their footsteps stopped. I moved toward the police car before looking behind me. Derek and company had retreated and were walking toward his apartment. The officer driving rolled down her window.

"Hey, Todd, we got a call nearly an hour ago for a noise disturbance at the playground, but we were tied up handling an assault," she said.

"No problem Shelley, I just took care of it, but I do appreciate you all coming out," I replied.

"Was that them walking away? Looks like Derek Stephens and his brothers," she said.

"Yeah. Hopefully they'll be out of here next month. Minnie Stephens was given a final written warning earlier today, so this recent episode is the final nail in the coffin," I replied.

"It would be nice to know where he moves to, being a known drug dealer with gang affiliations. They'll just leave here and set up shop somewhere else," she said, shaking her head. "We're going to hang out here for a while tonight. You be careful."

"Roger that, thanks for keeping up the presence around here, it's helped a lot," I said.

They both smiled as her partner leaned toward me.

"The complimentary coffee and Debbie cakes help too. Much appreciated," he said.

"Have a good night, and both of you be careful."

Back in my apartment I went to the bathroom. Sleeping would be impossible after what had just transpired. I was wired and needed to come down. There was no booze, but I needed something, anything, to get me numb again. Those fools in the park didn't know how close they came to getting shot. One or two seconds was all that separated them from this life and death. Strangely, I wished they had attacked me, so I had an excuse to rid the world of them. I paced back and forth, needing to release the energy inside me, then I dropped and started doing push-ups. My heart rate increased, and I began to feel my muscles pump up and swell. I stood up and did a set of jumping jacks, trying to release all the negative stress.

Fifteen minutes later I sat down at the kitchen table, sweating profusely. I scrolled through the pictures on my phone and pulled up the squad photo, enlarged it, and imagined the way things used to be. I looked at the time. It was 2:30 AM and I needed to make a beer run. It was going to be a long night.

• • •

I stumbled in late to the office the next morning with a major hangover, trying to perform my duties after only four hours of sleep. I poured a cup of coffee and sat down at the desk in a daze, daydreaming while looking out the window.

Andre was picking up trash around the grounds, his first duty of the day. It was to help keep the property cleaner. William and Eugene would be teaching him everything from drywall and carpet installation, along with the troubleshooting and repair of our HVAC systems. They shared their knowledge and weren't stingy with it. Andre soaked up the information like a sponge and seemed to be fitting in for the time being, which was fine with me, and one less problem on my plate.

My first priority was to begin eviction proceedings on the Stephens'. I completed the paperwork, drove to city hall, and filed the eviction with the magistrate's office. After returning to the office, I called William and gave him the eviction notice to hand-deliver it to Ms. Stephens.

Near lunchtime, FedEx dropped off a package containing two chess boards I had ordered for the media room. I set each board up in the back of the room, while a group of children continued watching a science documentary upfront.

I was hungry but broke, so there would be no more dining out until payday. Peanut butter sandwiches in my apartment were the lunch special of the day. While walking to my building, the laughter and screams of the children sliding down the makeshift slip-and-slide caught my attention and caused me to reminisce. This was one of William's ideas and worth every dollar. One garden hose pouring water down a rolled-out sheet of thick plastic on hill cost no more than fifty dollars and lasted for weeks. Two parents were chaperoning the activity with over two dozen kids participating. Everything was coming together nicely; not only looking different, but feeling different.

The office was hectic during the rest of the day. I hadn't realized the amount of traffic the media room and sports equipment sign out would generate. Then there was my own paperwork. This job was becoming a challenge. However, I felt it was worth the extra effort and since the community was supporting everything, I felt especially good about it.

Finally, it was time to get off work, but I needed to make a stop at the liquor store. Afterward, maybe I would take a drive to check on Tucker and his family. It was Angie's birthday next week and I needed advice from Reen and Tracy on what I should get her for a birthday present.

After locking up the office, I drove towards the store. The radio station was playing a heavy metal rock marathon, and they sure the hell were rocking out! I pulled into my usual spot in the liquor store lot and headed to the front door, but stopped when I heard some commotion coming from the side of the building. I peeked around the corner where the small awning and picnic table were located but didn't see anyone. I continued toward the back of the building and clearly heard the sound of fighting.

It was Cody, Toby, and Pete whaling away on a black guy. They had him surrounded and were punching and kicking him as he tried to cover his head. I stood paralyzed by this sudden display of violence, not knowing what the reason for it was, but found that it stimulated me. The shouts of the aggressors mixed with the groans and grunts of the subdued made my skin tingle and my rage boil. I wanted in, but this wasn't my fight. Besides, there had to be a good reason why all three of them were beating his ass. He must have done something awful to have these good ole boys working him over. I spoke up to let them know I was there because they seemed oblivious to my presence.

"Damn, boys, you all are putting a serious beatdown on him. What did he do?" I asked.

Surprised, all three stopped punching and kicking to look at me.

"Hey Todd! This gay boy wanted to run his mouth, so we shut it for him!" Cody snarled as Toby kicked again at the man who was now crouched on one knee and leaning against the building.

"That's a lie! I was mindin' my own business and you started with me! Then y'all jumped me! Get off me!"

The voice sounded like a young man, but I couldn't see him clearly as they hovered around him.

"Shut the hell up sissy!" Cody shouted. He looked at me. "Come on and get your licks in, Todd!"

The three began beating him again.

I finally caught a glimpse of the young man. He looked familiar, and then I realized was Chavis from Shady Meadows.

Without warning or explanation, I snapped and became enraged. I found myself involuntarily sprinting toward the fight, knowing it *was* my turn.

I shoulder blocked Toby, and I caught him flatfooted, knocking him to the ground. Then I turned toward Pete and front-kicked him in the solar plexus, sending him bouncing off the building. Cody was standing to my left, so I guarded my left side and pivoted, throwing a right hook which barely missed him. He backed away and tripped, nearly falling. He looked spooked; his eyes were open wide with surprise.

"What the hell are you doing! What's wrong with you man?" Cody yelled as Pete and Toby regained their feet and stared at me. I walked over to Chavis, who managed to stand up and was also gawking at me with the same shocked expression.

"You all right Chavis? Chavis is your name, right?" I asked.

He began brushing himself off, never taking his eyes off his three attackers.

"Yes sir. I'm good...I'm good," he replied. "They always calling me a faggot and a sissy, but they the ones who hit like girls!" he yelled defiantly.

Toby started walking toward him until I stepped in front of him and pointed my finger at him.

"Nope! You got to whip me first, boy!" I yelled. "Come on! You want to jump somebody? Jump me! Here I am, all by my lonesome, come and get some!"

The three men stood silent until Cody broke the silence.

"Oh? So you're a race traitor and sissy lover? You must be bending him over yourself," he said, and the rest chuckled.

"This ain't about none of that bullshit. This is about three grown men who are cowards and want to bully someone. Well, bully me then," I said, staring into their eyes. "I just witnessed you three chickens assaulting him and I think the police need to get involved. That's felony assault, and I'm not gonna let you all get away with it."

I took my phone out of my pocket and started to dial the sheriff's department before Chavis turned to me.

"No, don't call the police," he said.

"Why not? You can't let these jerks get away with this shit. They assaulted you."

He shook his head. "Don't call them Mr. Todd. I just want to get what I came for. I'll tell my cousins what happened when I get back. They'll take care of these fools." he said.

Cody and his crew began walking toward their van.

"Call the police! It's our word against yours!" Cody shouted as they climbed into their work van to leave.

"Go to hell! Gay monkey lover!" Toby shouted out the window as they spun their tires out of the parking lot.

I turned to Chavis.

"Are you gonna be all right, Chavis?" I asked.

"I told you I'm good. I just want to get my stuff and get home," he said and began walking toward the front of the building.

I still needed to buy my booze, so I followed him to the front and went inside.

A few minutes later, I came out with three bottles and got into the car. As I started the engine, I noticed that my shirt was soaked with sweat. When I turned the radio on, my hand trembled and wouldn't stop, so I made a fist, clenching it as tight as possible. I was wired now, and it would take time to calm down. I was worried the guys would come back for Chavis. After thinking about it I figured probably not tonight, though it was possible. The right thing to do would be to give the kid a ride back to Shady Meadows, just to be safe.

I saw him as he walked out of the convenience store with a bag. I rolled down the window.

"Let me give you a ride home, Chavis," I said.

He looked around and then back at me.

"Okay," he replied and got inside.

We left out of the parking lot and drove toward Shady Meadows. It was quiet in the car, as we both were processing what had just transpired.

Chavis broke the silence.

"You didn't have to help me, but you did. Thank you," he said while looking out the window.

"You're welcome. I didn't know who they were beating at first, but had I known, I would have stopped it earlier. That's my bad."

"I don't understand why you did help. Why did you?"

I didn't have a ready answer and hadn't really thought about it. Why did I help him? It wasn't any of my concern, but I made it my business. He waited for me to answer and I began to feel awkward. I glanced over to see him looking at me.

"I helped because it was the right thing to do," I said.

He nodded and stared out the window.

"I have a question for you. Those guys hang out behind that store all the time. So, why do you keep going to the convenience store right next door? Isn't that just asking for a confrontation?" I asked.

He turned to me.

"Mr. Todd, I've been dealing with these types of idiots since I came out in high school. I've been fighting for the right to be myself for a long time, and I'm not going to let anybody tell me where I can go or what I can do. I have the right to be left alone. I walk past them a few times a week and always mind my own business, but they always have something to say to me and call me names. They call me a punk, but I'm brave enough to accept who I am and not hide it. No, I'm not gonna hide from anybody."

After thinking about his answer, I understood what he was saying and he was right.

He was a brave young man, unlike my dad, who hid his true identity for over a decade and took the hypocrite's way out. Chavis stood up for his true identity with confidence.

"I can understand that," I replied.

"I carpool to work right now, but I've been saving my money to buy a used car. Once that happens, I'll be enrolling at Nashville State Community College and I won't ever have to walk past them again."

"It's good that you have a plan and goals. Just stay focused and you'll get there," I said.

We pulled into Shady Meadows, and I parked in front of my building. After all the excitement, I decided to cancel my plans of going to Tucker's house. I'd go tomorrow after I brought Ms. Pearl back home from church. For now, I needed to self-medicate in a big way. We got out of the car and went our separate ways.

"Mr. Todd, I'm gonna let my people know what you did for me tonight," he said while walking away.

"It's no big deal. Take it easy," I replied as I walked to my apartment.

Later, I lay on the living room floor after drinking nearly a fifth of Scotch whiskey. I was breaching the point of passing out when I noticed my phone ringing. I picked it up, hoping it was Angie, and deciphered the display. Closing one eye at a time, trying to focus on the name of the caller and finally realized it was my dad. I tossed the phone aside. It would have to go to voice mail. I wasn't in the mood to talk to him now and I wondered if I would ever be.

Chapter Nine

Oh, Happy Day!

The alarm woke me on Sunday morning at 9:00 AM to a bad hangover. I was seriously hurting and didn't want to get out of bed, but after contemplating excuses to give Ms. Pearl for canceling, I decided against it. I gave her my word and wouldn't break that for anybody. I got up and loaded my coffee maker, took a shower, and got dressed while it brewed.

I left my apartment at ten o'clock and walked down to Ms. Pearl's door and knocked. A few moments later, she answered.

"Good morning Ms. Pearl. I'm ready to leave whenever you are."

"Good morning to you, sir. Let me put on my hat and I'll be ready to leave," she replied.

I waited outside and smelled her cooking as it filled the breezeway, making me wish I had eaten something earlier. My stomach was rumbling. She came back and we walked to my car. It was best to support her and let her hold onto my arm while she used her cane. I helped her into the car, secured her seatbelt, and then we left.

We arrived at the church fifteen minutes later to a nearly full parking lot. Members were moving about, greeting each other with hugs in front of the entrance. We found a place to park, and I got out to open the door for Ms. Pearl and walk her to the front door.

The escort from my car to the front entrance took a while, as several people proceeded to hug and greet Ms. Pearl along the way, and so she could introduce me to each of the members. Finally, we arrived at the entrance. I could hear loud music and singing inside, which surprised me because it was so early in the morning. This wasn't like the Pearson's church or any other that I had visited as a kid. I didn't remember church ever sounding like this.

"All right Ms. Pearl, we made it. I got you here safe and sound. What time do you want me to pick you up?" I asked.

She looked at me with a blank expression. "What you mean, pick me up? You're coming inside with me," she said, her voice crackling.

I couldn't believe she was expecting me to actually go inside with her.

"Ms. Pearl, I didn't realize you expected me to go inside with you. Ma'am, we must have miscommunicated." It was evident she was getting angry, as her tiny mouth pouted, and she started trembling.

"I asked you to take me to church. What you think that means? If I asked you to take me to dinner, would you drop me off at the front door and leave? Don't play with me boy. Now come on," she said, gritting her teeth.

She was right, I should have known what she meant. My blood pressure began to rise as I didn't want to go to church today. Hell, I really didn't want to go with Tucker's family either. A reasonable excuse was needed to change Ms. Pearl's mind.

"You're right ma'am, it's my fault. I promise to go with you another time, but you see how I'm dressed today, it isn't appropriate for church. Look at how well everyone else is dressed. I look totally out of place."

Slam dunk! Or so I thought. I was wearing jeans and a polo shirt.

She looked me up and down. "Stop that foolish talk, you look fine. Come on now, you're gonna make us late fooling around."

"Ms. Pearl, everybody else has got on Sunday's finest. I can't go in there with jeans on."

I was getting anxious and angry and did not want to go inside.

"Shh!" she chastised. "Stop talking so loud. Are you gonna keep your word or not?"

I realized I had lost this battle and it was time to concede.

"Yes ma'am," I replied respectfully, initiating my military bearing. I took a deep breath and held the door open for her. Once inside, it was like stepping into another world. We stood outside the main sanctuary in the vestibule where ushers stood controlling access to the sanctuary doors. They were dressed in formal black and white and wore badges. Several other people were waiting with us. I looked through the small windows on the double doors and saw members standing up and singing along with a choir that faced the congregation.

Finally, one of the ushers opened the door and gave everyone a paper program with the order of service. Ms. Pearl took ahold of my arm and we strolled into the sanctuary. We were led to our seats by another usher. I was impressed by the orderly structure, having never seen anything like this before in the civilian sector. We were seated in a pew near the front, which Ms. Pearl had mentioned was her usual seat. I sat down and looked around, noticing the many eyeballs watching me, but glanced away when eye contact was made. Most of the onlookers were children, being nosey and gazing at me cow-eyed. I could understand why they would be curious about the white guy who came to church with Ms. Pearl. But I wasn't the only white person and noticed a white woman singing in the choir, along with another man sitting in the congregation. I didn't get the sense that these people were prejudiced toward whites.

The next few hours were charged with bible reading, announcements, a sermon, and lots of singing. I hadn't heard music like this before, but it sounded like a mix between rhythm and blues and something else. It was all foreign to me, yet also familiar in a strange way. I had entered with a headache and a hangover, but that was now long-gone. It had been drummed and pounded out of my skull by the energy. Nearly everyone at some point stood to sing, clap, and stomp to songs presented by the choir. I didn't feel a spotlight on me anymore, as the congregation looked forward and participated in something more substantial. The only reason I felt isolated was because I was the only person still sitting down. Surprisingly, I couldn't help tapping my foot and patting my leg to the rhythm of the music. There simply was no escape and who would want to? Even Ms. Pearl began to celebrate; she clapped and rocked back and forth on her cane, even shouting out loud. I remained alert to catch her in the event she fell or slipped, but she appeared to be perfectly fine and totally in control.

After the sermon, the service slowed down as the pastor invited people to come to the front and repent of their sins. I recognized this as the same sinner's prayer other churches conducted. One person walked down the center aisle, and the pastor laid his hands on him before directing him to sit on the front row, then invited anyone up to the front to pray for them. Members began to leave their seats and walk down the aisle until they formed a line consisting of at least fifteen people. One by one, the pastor held their hands with his eyes closed in what appeared to be fervent prayer. To say this place was filled with emotion would be an understatement. I fought against the feelings and thoughts triggered by this experience, which everyone in the sanctuary was sharing.

Ms. Pearl turned and pulled me to her. "Let's get in the prayer line. I need you to help me." I stood and escorted her to the back of the prayer line. While we waited, I noticed a stark difference in the atmosphere of the service. It was like a cool-down period. Most folks sat in their seats, singing with their eyes closed. Intermittently, people would stand up abruptly with their hands raised, crying out with phrases of gratitude. I couldn't understand why they were doing it. Although I was confused, I didn't see anything wrong or harmful in what was happening. It was as if the entire experience was immune from criticism. Despite the loud music and unexpected surprises, I was actually happy to be here and for the first time, without alcohol, I didn't feel anxious or stressed.

It was finally Ms. Pearl's turn for prayer. We stepped up to meet the pastor and he bent down so Ms. Pearl could whisper into his ear. He listened attentively and smiled as she stepped backward. The pastor reached out and motioned for me to come closer. I was confused and looked at Ms. Pearl, who beckoned for me to step forward. I did so and he grasped each of my hands and leaned forward.

"Mother Pearl asked me to pray for you. She says you are a blessing to the community over at Shady Meadows. Is that all right with you?" he asked.

What the hell? I thought to myself. *Why not? It couldn't hurt.*

"Yes sir, that's fine," I answered.

He grasped my hands tighter and closed his eyes as his nostrils flared.

"Lord God! Please bless this young man as he strives to improve the community that he has been entrusted with; Keep him from all hurt, harm, and danger that the enemy has sent against him! Please help him to continue doing good work within his community and help change the lives of all those who live under his hand of protection. Let him no longer be a stranger in a strange land, but rather bless him to become a righteous leader in his own land. To you, Father, we offer up these humble requests, according to your will. This we ask it in the name of Jesus, amen."

He opened his eyes, smiled, and embraced me. "Go forth in peace, young man."

"Thank you," I replied and nodded. Ms. Pearl grinned as she clenched my arm and we walked back to our seats.

Finally, we stood for the closing prayer, called the benediction in the handout program, which ended with the entire congregation singing the last word of the prayer, "Amen" in unison. I now understood the joke the black comedian told. The service was excellent, though really long. The next moment ushered in a period of Christian fellowship, where all the members greeted one another with a hug, followed by small talk. I was no exception to this rule and was greeted in the same manner by a multitude of folk.

When it was over, we left the sanctuary and walked to the car, where we encountered even more members who hadn't greeted us yet, and they came flocking. Once they were gone, I realized these were the friendliest people that I had ever met. I helped Ms. Pearl into the car and we drove back to Shady Meadows.

As we stopped in front of her apartment, she said, "Thank you for taking me to church. I won't ask you again, but now you know a place where you are welcome and can get yourself some strength and healing."

"You're welcome ma'am. It was cool. Enjoy the rest of your day," I replied.

"Wait. Come inside and have dinner with me. I'll fix you a plate."

"Ma'am, I planned to visit my friend after I dropped you off today, but I appreciate the offer. I mean, unless you don't mind making a plate to go. I can eat it when I get back home."

"Sure! You wait here and let me fix it," she answered.

Ten minutes later, she returned and handed me a warm dinner plate covered in aluminum foil. "Here, this is for you, chicken and fixings."

I took it and noticed the sheer weight of the plate, loaded with food, no doubt. My stomach hadn't stopped rumbling since we left the church.

"Thank you! I'll wash the plate and bring it back later if you don't mind," I said.

"It doesn't matter, I can wash it. Don't forget, you still got my cake container too."

I nodded and she closed her door. I skipped up the stairs to my apartment and went inside, then sprinted to the bathroom. My bladder was about to burst open. I washed up and looked at the clock, it was already 1:30 PM. I marveled that the service had lasted so long. I knew from living with Tucker that his family had long since returned from their church. I decided to leave right away, so I put the dinner plate inside the refrigerator and closed the door. I started for the front door but then stopped. I could still smell the aroma of country cooking in the air, and walked directly back over to the fridge, took the warm plate out, and sat down at the kitchen table.

I moaned as I devoured the meal in absolute contentment. The afternoon meal was a great ending to a pretty good morning. This day hadn't turned out as I initially expected; it was better. Within ten minutes, my plate was empty and I was burping from eating too fast.

"Damn, that was good," I mumbled to myself. After washing my hands, I locked up my place and finally left for Tucker's house.

• • •

I unlocked the front door and walked inside toward the kitchen.

"Hello everybody," I said.

Reen walked over and hugged me.

"Hey!" she replied.

Tracy and Mr. Pearson were sitting at the table with Tucker, then Tracy stood up and gave me a hug.

"Hey big brother number two," she said, looking up at me. I walked around the table and shook Mr. Pearson's hand.

"There's my prodigal son, done returned home. How are you?" he asked.

"I've been doing good sir. Working hard," I replied. Tucker rolled over to me.

"Working hard? You haven't known a hard day's work in your life," he joked.

We laughed and fist bumped.

"Oh and like you do? Give me a break!" I replied.

Mr. Pearson raised his hands.

"You two haven't been in the same room for one minute, and y'all are picking fights with each other already. On a Sunday, too. You both ought to be ashamed of yourselves. Shame!" he said jokingly, pointing the finger at each of us. I extended my hand to Tucker.

"Truce. Peace, brother from another mother," I said.

We shook as I sat down at the table.

"So, you been busy over there huh?" Tucker asked.

"Yeah. I've got a lot going on. Good and bad stuff," I answered.

"How so?" Mr. Pearson asked.

"Well, besides the improvements you already know about, we keep making good changes, positive changes, and the people seem to be much happier. They're getting involved and it shows. The place is totally different than when I first started working there. I'm super busy all the time, which is a good thing, but I got this one guy, drug dealer, gang leader…you get the idea, who's getting his entire family evicted. This guy has continued to push my buttons, trying to bait me into a physical altercation. My problem is that I hate his guts and am right on the verge of beating his heart out," I said.

Tuck shook his head.

"Don't you do it. I can tell this guy is already under your skin, but don't get played out of position, Marine. Like you said, they'll be evicted soon and not your problem to deal with," Tucker replied.

"Would you like something to drink Todd? Have you eaten?" Reen asked.

"Yes ma'am, I'd like some sweet tea please, and yes I've already eaten. Thank you," I replied.

Mr. Pearson leaned forward.

"Just stay disciplined son. You have too much to lose, so don't throw it away for a criminal. You have a future, remember that," Mr. Pearson said.

I nodded before gulping my drink.

"I copy that sir. Then this past Friday, I had to break up a fight at the corner store. One of the residents was getting jumped by three guys. They didn't like the fact that I broke the fight up and threatened to call the police."

Reen gasped.

"Oh my lord! Why were they beating him? What did he do?" she asked.

"Uh, he didn't do anything. It was mainly because of who he is," I replied.

Mr. Pearson looked puzzled, as did everyone else.

"Who was he? A rival gang member?" Tucker asked.

"No. The guy is gay and they didn't like him walking past their little hangout spot next to the store. I think some words were exchanged before they jumped on him. I gave him a ride home afterward. He seems to be a good kid."

"It ain't right to attack an innocent man like that, no matter what the reason. You ought to have called the law on them," said Mr. Pearson.

"Thank God you were there to stop them," Reen added. Tucker punched me in the arm.

"You're making all kinds of enemies bro. How about you try to fly under the radar, you know? Don't get caught up and mess up your future plans in law enforcement. The last thing you need is an assault charge. Think about that next time," Tucker said.

"It was the right thing to do at that time. I was letting them beat him until I realized he was one of my tenants. I kind of feel bad now, knowing I was just gonna stand and watch the show. I figured if three white guys are beating up a black guy, then it must be for a good reason—like they caught him stealing or something, maybe he deserved it, I didn't know."

Tracy tapped my arm to get my attention.

"I would've called the police right away and let them investigate. Most people won't even do that. I've heard of people getting raped and murdered, while onlookers just turn away and mind their own business. What if it happened to them or someone they loved? They'd want someone to help them. People can be very selfish!" she said.

Mr. Pearson reached over and rubbed her arm.

"You're correct baby girl. Don't get riled," he said, smiling.

I decided to break the next piece of news to them. "So today, I gave an elderly lady a ride to church. She asked me to go inside with her, so I did. In other words, I went to church today—an African American church."

Mr. Pearson leaned back and crossed his arms.

"Todd, I can't believe my ears. I am hurt, deeply hurt," he said, shaking his head.

I looked around the room and saw Reen and Tracy smirking, while Tucker could hardly hold back his laughter.

"Why? I didn't mean to disappoint you," I asked.

"Todd, you went to our church once after asking you for *months*, but when a dear elderly woman asked you one time, you went lickety-split! It hurts us to see that you favor that dear woman over us," he answered.

He picked up a napkin and began drying his eyes and whimpering. I was worried until everyone, including Mr. Pearson, burst out laughing. "Son, I'm just putting you on! It doesn't matter where you go to church. There ain't no division in heaven and there shouldn't be any down here either. Every true born-again believer knows that. Just so you know, Reen and I have been to African American churches throughout the years. We are sincerely delighted that you actually went to church!"

Reen sat down at the table. "Tell us about it."

"Yes, tell us everything! Is it just like they show on television?" Tracy asked.

I looked at Tucker. "You heard them Corporal. Give us a mission debrief, ASAP!" he said.

"Roger that, but first, I need Reen and Tracy to help me figure out what I should buy Angie for her birthday. Maybe send her some jewelry, or something else cool?"

Tracy grabbed my arm. "Oh! I know exactly what you should buy her! But tell us about your church visit first."

I spent the next few hours recounting the church visit, watching movies, and getting my butt kicked by Tucker playing video games. Finally, Tracy picked out an awesome necklace online and I ordered it to be sent as a gift. All in all, it was a good day, or maybe I should say it was a great day. It was one of the best days that I had in a long time. I felt almost normal.

• • •

The next week, I issued the first check to pay the new contractor. William, Eugene, and I were pleased with their work. Sherika had been in the office for a few hours, as she made her rounds around the district to gather financial files.

"Sherika, please don't forget to leave me those income verification forms before you go," I asked.

"I left them over there on the printer," she replied, pointing.

"Thank you ma'am," I replied.

"Oh, before I forget, I'm inviting you three to my wedding and reception tomorrow, but I don't have any more invitations printed. I apologize that I've been so busy, but I really would like you all to come. I wrote down the address of the church and the time it begins," she said.

"Tomorrow?" Eugene asked. "I'm taking the family out of town, dang it!"

William looked at Sherika and me.

"I can go. How about you, Todd?" he asked.

"Yeah I can go," I replied.

"Great!" Sherika said.

It might sound weird, but I had never been to a wedding before. Sherika was a great trainer, and I recognized that without her help I would have never lasted on this job. It was something to look forward to and might give me ideas about my and Angie's wedding day, whenever that might happen. Angie said we would get married after I graduated from the police academy.

My reporting date was getting closer and I remained focused on achieving that goal. Everything I had accomplished was moving me closer to the life and dream I envisioned. Dreaming; it used to sound stupid to me when I was younger, but the longer I lived, it brought me to understand that dreaming was really hope, and a little bit of hope never hurt anybody. It was fragile though, like the flame of a candle, easy to extinguish but helpful while it's burning.

When the workday ended, everyone left and went their separate ways, but wedding day excitement was in the air, you could almost smell it.

• • •

I arrived at the wedding on time and met William on the front steps of the church. He was dressed sharp, looking proper, and I barely recognized him out of his work uniform. I wore khaki pants, a button-down shirt with a tie, and a sports jacket; nothing too fancy. We stood to the side of the entrance for a few minutes before going in, surveying the other attendees. Everyone was dressed like the members at Ms. Pearl's church; neat and fashionable.

Will and I walked in and sat down. The music was some type of instrumental jazz, R&B love music or something like that. I didn't know what to expect before I arrived, but the whole event was quite modern and classy. The ceremony wasn't very long at all and consisted of two songs, the vows, and their kiss. Soon, everyone was on their feet, clapping and shouting at the newlyweds as they walked back down the aisle hand in hand. I was honestly happy for Sherika.

Everyone exited the church and gathered inside the reception hall, while the newlyweds took their wedding photos. The entrance of the bride and groom is the only clear memory I have of the reception. They had an open bar and William and I took full advantage of it.

Like a fool, I didn't eat before drinking, so by the time the music filled the hall I was drunk. By this time, maintaining my balance was my hope. I didn't want to embarrass myself or Sherika, that much I did know. At one point, I recall being pulled off my seat and taken to the dance floor. Me, not remembering how to dance but buzzed enough not to care, allowed some unknown smiling woman to throw me into the mix of bodies. My mind went back to technical school and partying with my buddy Reggie at the clubs. I looked around at everybody jamming and thought to myself, *I can dance, too!*

Eventually, the bar closed and most of the people had left. I looked around for William but couldn't find him. I needed to get back to my apartment but I was too intoxicated. The last thing I needed was to get pulled over. I shook my head at that thought. I was more concerned about getting a DUI when I should've been worried about driving drunk and killing somebody by accident. I rubbed the haze from my eyes and stood to check my balance.

Thirty minutes later I was at Shady Meadows parking my car. I stumbled out and tried to compensate for the equilibrium shift while standing. I fought through my double vision and eventually made it up the stairs, past the cat, and into my apartment. A minute later, I opened the door back up and set a can of tuna beside the doormat and refilled the water bowl.

"Goodnight Sam," I told him before floundering back inside to my bedroom.

I didn't bother to strip off my clothes before I collapsed on the bed and ultimately passed out.

• • •

I heard breaking glass and gun shots.

Shots fired! Was I dreaming? I opened my eyes and realized I was lying face down on my bed.

Rat-tat…rat-tat-tat…rat-tat-tat-tat.

I rolled off the bed onto the floor. It was the unmistakable sound of an AK-47 and this was no dream.

Where's my pistol? Think!

I reached down to my ankle holster and drew my gun. I heard my living room windows shattering, followed by the loud thuds of the rounds hitting drywall. I listened carefully and knew there were two active shooters, but there could be more. The barrage lasted about twenty seconds and was followed by the sound of a vehicle's spinning tires.

I crouched and rushed to the window in the spare bedroom. The blinds were shot to hell and the ceiling was peppered with bullet holes. I looked out the window. The parking lot was empty, but the air was filled with smoke from the gunfire. I checked my watch, it was 4 AM. I turned on all the lights and checked the rest of the apartment, then I called 911.

A damn drive-by? Incredible. I holstered my pistol and went down to the parking lot to examine the building. A visual inspection of the exterior showed only my apartment was hit, which meant I was the target. Who would do something like that? It was a dumb rhetorical question because I knew exactly who it was.

My heart dropped into my stomach as I glanced over at Tucker's car. It was also full of bullet holes, and the front and rear windshield were shot out. After examining the scene from the shooter's perspective, I determined where the car stopped, where they got out, and what directions they shot. Brass shells were spread out around the pavement, and I was careful to not step on any evidence to preserve this crime scene. I heard the police approaching, their sirens getting louder until three cruisers turned into Shady Meadows and parked in front of my building.

Lights came on in various units as residents started to stir and investigate for themselves. Within ten minutes, there was a medium-sized crowd of concerned residents standing outside. Everyone could clearly see the damage done to my apartment and to the car, and most of them gathered around me to check on my welfare and express their disgust. They let me know I wasn't alone and told me not to be discouraged. I appreciated their support, but I was more focused on giving some payback to those responsible. They had crossed the line this time and gone too far. This was now war and I was ready to kill or be killed. I knew who was responsible and he lived right across this parking lot.

Four hours later, William and Eugene reported for work and the last detective was about to leave the scene. A full crime scene investigation had been conducted. Shell casings and rounds were recovered, witness inquiries had been conducted. I hoped, but didn't expect, there to be any witnesses who were outside at four in the morning. The detectives asked me who I suspected or who might have a motive to do this and I told them Derrick Stephens, point-blank. This was ironic as he was standing across the parking lot with eyes on us when I told them. I pointed him out and made sure he saw me do it.

"There he is," I said. The detectives eventually questioned him and took his statement. He said he didn't see anything and, of course, he had an alibi, which they verified. He waited outside with his brothers, looking at me and laughing. Instead of getting heated and reacting to him, I nodded my head and returned to my apartment.

The Marine Corps had taught me a lot of beneficial things, valuable skills, and concepts. One of them was the importance of preparation. What no one knew was that I had an eye in the sky. The entire property was under surveillance by wireless video camera monitoring. I had the idea the night William and I hashed out our first contingency plan. The entire surveillance system cost less than $600, including the installation of eleven wireless cameras. The video feeds were transmitted to my laptop, which I kept inside my spare bedroom closet. I had the software to automatically backup the video every three days to a USB flash drive. The detectives waited while I made a copy for them to take and review.

"Here you go. I haven't looked at it yet, but I kept a copy for myself. Maybe you can get something from it. It's 1080p and should have decent clarity," I said to the detective.

"That's great. We'll call you soon, but meanwhile, we're also increasing our patrols here. We've talked and I'm well aware you can take care of yourself Marine, but try to lay low. Be aware of your surroundings. You copy?" the detective asked.

"Roger that. I appreciate it, but right now I need to eat some chow."

"Priceless," he replied, chuckling, and returned to his vehicle.

Honestly, I was dazed and confused. How could this be happening to me? I wasn't a drug dealer or in a gang. I was only doing my job and it came to this? My head began thumping with an incoming migraine about to land. Just then, William and Eugene walked up to me.

"Boss, I know you must be tired," Eugene said.

"Yes, and I got a killer headache too. I probably need to lay down and crash for a while. Do you guys need me for anything?" I asked.

"No, go get you some sleep. We got everything covered," William replied as I looked around.

"Where's Andre?" I asked.

"He's working. We got him painting this morning," he replied.

"Good. I'll see you all in a few hours. Let me get this power nap in."

I went into my apartment. I was more tired than hungry, so I went to the kitchen and opened a box of snack cakes and dumped them on the counter. I unwrapped each one and stuffed my mouth while sipping water from the faucet. It was déjà vu from a few hours earlier as I stumbled into my room and collapsed onto my bed.

Chapter Ten

Repel Boarders

I woke up at noon and rolled over on my back. There was work to do, and while staring at the ceiling, I started planning the rest of my day. First, I needed to write up a report and fax it to corporate. Then, I needed to call the insurance company to report the property damage and schedule a complete damage assessment. I also needed to call Barry Thomas and make him aware of the shooting. I looked at my phone and saw a text notification that a package was delivered that morning at 8:27 AM.

Package? What package? Then I realized Angie's birthday present had arrived at her place, and I needed to wish her a happy birthday. Throughout all the chaos, I missed her beyond belief and realized that she could have lost me last night. I wasn't ignorant of the possibility, but nevertheless, she didn't need to know about anything. Depending on her mood, it would either worry her to death or she would flip it around on me, making it my fault.

I dialed her number and waited. It was her lunchtime and I knew she always took extended lunch breaks.

"Hello Todd," she answered.

"Hey babe! Happy Birthday!"

"Thank you! I was going to take the day off, but I had some things to tidy up at the office. What have you been up to lately?" she asked.

"Not much, just working and staying busy. I sent you a birthday present; the text message shows it was delivered this morning. You can pick it up from the lobby office when you get home. I really hope you like it."

"I went into work late today so I already got it. Thank you," she replied.

"Well, how do you like it?" I asked. She paused and I heard her exhale.

"It's nice Todd, don't get me wrong, it's just that I don't wear that style necklace. It's a bit too gaudy for me, maybe even a little ghetto-ish?" she answered, trying to be polite in her own way.

"Okay, I follow. Tucker's sister helped me pick it out. I was positive that you would like it. Sorry about that."

"Maybe next time don't have another woman help you pick out a gift for your girlfriend. Do you think that might help? You've never seen me wear something like that before. What were you thinking?"

I was tired and worn out from everything. The job, the fights, and the drive-by shootings were enough to fatigue any fighting man, but I was finished fighting with Angie. I desperately needed her in my life, so I yielded. She was correct and I should've chosen a present personally and known what she would have liked.

"Darling, I'll buy you something else. Just send it to back and I'll file a return to get a credit."

"No, that's not necessary. It's 24k gold, so I can easily sell it. I'd rather have my birthday gift as cash anyway. Use your head next time. You're kind of smart when you want to be."

"I gotcha," I replied.

"Oh! Before I forget, the lease renewal is due and our rent has gone up by $100. You need to increase your share by fifty dollars. Do not forget," she said.

"Yes ma'am, that's not a problem. I got it covered."

"Don't call me ma'am, it makes me sound old. You've been down there way too long. You're starting to sound like one of those rednecks."

"Okay Angie. Hey, has anything from the NYSP come for me in the mail? I expected to hear something back from them by now."

"No, nothing has come yet and to be honest, I'm wondering if you really have been accepted to the academy. We've talked about this before and you know how critical this step is for our future. I've invested a lot of my own time, energy, and finances in this relationship. Do not make a fool of me! So, is there anything that you want to tell me?" she asked.

"Angie, you've seen all their correspondence just like me. Of course I've been accepted. Babe, I wouldn't lie to you. For Christ sake I love you! I've been ready to leave this place since the day I left you. Don't fret, the letter will come soon so please try to be patient."

"All right we'll see. Look, I have to get back to work. Take care of yourself, talk to you later!"

"I love you," I said.

"You too!" she replied.

I felt like we ended the call on a good note. Neither of us was mad, which was a win in my opinion. I ate, showered, and changed my clothes before leaving for the office. I planned to tell Tucker about the car this afternoon, but first I needed to see if it would start and drive. Dammit! How could I have allowed this to happen to my best friend's car? I hoped he would forgive me. I planned to pay for the damages out of pocket to keep Mr. Pearson's insurance premium from increasing. I decided I needed to focus on one task at a time, or I would be overwhelmed by everything. My luck had to change.

What else could go wrong?

• • •

It was the end of the workday before I finally had a chance to slow down. I had completed my list for the day and was waiting for Barry Thomas to return my call.

I was able to start Tucker's car and it seemed fine driving around the parking lot, so I left it running to see if it might overheat. The front door opened and William and Eugene came into the office.

"Are you guys about to leave for the day?" I asked.

"Yeah we're calling it quits. By the way, Ms. Pearl was asking about you. She slept through all the noise last night and didn't hear anything. I told her you were fine and working in the office. She wanted me to tell you that she is praying for you and will be checking on you soon," William said.

"She's a sweet old lady. So, where's Andre?" I asked.

"He's cleaning up the tools and such, putting them away in the storage building. He should be finished soon," Eugene replied.

"Have you heard anything back from the detectives yet?" William asked.

"No not yet. I guess it's still too early. Later this week hopefully."

"Hmm… we know who is behind it, but whether or not they can prove it is another subject altogether," he replied.

I sat back in my chair and thought about what he said.

"I need to tell you both something and I hope you don't get pissed at me. Okay? I've had this property under video surveillance for several months. I keep the server in my apartment with a rolling backup, and the police have the video footage from the last three days. They should be able to get some evidence from it. At least that's the way it works in the movies." I tried to lighten their moods with my weak attempt at comedy.

They both frowned and Eugene walked to the water fountain. William was clearly irate and it showed on his face and in the tone of his voice.

"That's messed up Todd. I can't believe you didn't trust us enough to let us know about this when you first had them installed! Why? What did we do man? I thought we were a team," William barked.

"I apologize to both of you. Honestly, I didn't know who to trust when I started working here. It's clear to me that's not the situation anymore. We *are* a team and I trust both of you, I swear. I've been avoiding telling both of you because I might get this exact reaction." I stood up. "But that was then and this is now. We can't change the past guys. Again, my apologies."

Eugene walked into the office with a devilish grin and stood next to William.

"I asked you about that fella on the ladder months ago. You said something about cable upgrade, but I thought something was fishy," Eugene said.

I came around the desk and extended my hand. William stared at me for a moment before shaking it.

"At least you showed us that you are man enough to apologize and admit when you're wrong. I can respect that. But from here on out, we don't want no secrets. If we are a team then we are a team," William said.

"We're good on this one boss. Just don't lie to us about a pay raise and not give us one!" Eugene added.

He laughed as William pointed at me.

"That's right, and don't invite us out to lunch and then stick us with the bill either! As a matter of fact, you know what I drink! I believe you owe us!" he said.

"I copy that fellas but you'll need to wait until payday, I'm broke. I'm going to check on Andre before locking up. Then I have to drive my buddy's bullet-riddled car to his house and try to explain what happened."

I cleared off my desk, washed up the coffee pot, then prepped it for the next morning before turning off the lights. The community room was empty now that all the kids were back in school, and there were no more scheduled room reservations for the day. I locked the front door and walked around to the storage building. Both doors were opened, and I walked inside to see Andre sweeping the floor.

"Hey Andre, are you about to leave?" I asked.

He was surprised to see me and was clearly uncomfortable. He stopped sweeping and stood up straight. His raised eyebrows and rigid stance told me he was intimidated by my presence.

"Yes sir. I'm almost finished sweeping."

"They told you to sweep the floor in here?" I asked.

"No sir, but the floor was dirty, and I had five minutes left before clocking out, so I'm taking care of it."

"Okay then, well done. Do you mind locking up when you finish?"

"No sir, I'll do it."

I nodded and turned to leave as he continued sweeping.

"Mr. Todd," Andre called out.

I walked back inside. "Yes sir?"

"I was talking with William and Eugene and they said you were in the Marines. Is that true?"

"Yes, that's true. Why do you ask?"

"Well, I was thinking about going into the service. I see those commercials about the Marines, you know, they're looking sharp in them uniforms. They have that sword and the rifle! I've been thinking about going to see the recruiter downtown. I can get paid, travel, fight…all that!" He confessed with enthusiasm, and after listening to him, I was the one stunned.

"Well, you rarely wear the full service-dress uniform or carry the sword, but those commercials are pretty cool, I must agree with you."

His expression changed, and now he looked alive and excited like he was ready to be the star during a sports event.

"If you got time, I'd like you to tell me about it. What do I gotta do to get in? What's it like being a Marine?"

I was still in shock that he was considering the Marines, but I didn't have time to talk to him. Then I had an idea, but I needed to check with Tucker first.

"I can't talk right now Andre. I'm on the way to my friend's house, who also happens to be a Marine veteran. I want to check with him first, but how would you feel about going over his house this week to meet him? Then we can talk about the United States Marine Corps all day."

"That's what's up! But I don't have a car. My girlfriend does and she could give me a ride, but I don't want her there. It's gonna be about man's talk, right?" he asked.

"I'll tell you what, ride with me there and I'll bring you back. That's no problem for me."

"Cool, and thanks Mr. Todd," he said as I left.

I got into the car and looked around the interior at the cracked windows and bullet holes. I drove off and practiced what I would say to these people who were like family to me. It wasn't difficult to love them like my own, they had extended a helping hand to me even while their own son sat wounded in a wheelchair. This was one of the worst situations possible, in my opinion. I was responsible for what happened to us that day, and now for his property being damaged. It was a damn shame to ruin their day with this terrible news.

• • •

I opened the front door and walked to the kitchen. There was nobody there, so I walked to the den while announcing myself. Then I heard voices from outside at the back of the house. I looked out the window and saw the entire family sitting under the gazebo in the backyard.

I went out the back door and walked over to them as Tucker called out, "There's my buddy! What's up, bro? We were just talking about you."

I walked up the steps to the gazebo.

"Hey everybody," I said and gave Tucker a handshake while Reen and Tracy hugged me. I waved to Mr. Pearson.

"Sir, I need to tell you and Tucker some bad news. This morning, around 4 AM, someone shot up Tucker's car and the front of my apartment."

I said it and waited for the hammer to come down on me.

"Dude, are you serious? Tell me you are joking," Tucker asked.

"Nah man. I'm sorry about your car bro…I didn't expect anything like that to happen. When I told—"

"Todd! Are you all right? Damn the car man! How are you?"

"I wasn't hit, only my apartment and your car. The police collected evidence and are working on it, but I promise to pay for all the repairs, and I'll give the car back. I should have gotten my own vehicle a long time ago. I don't want to come across as a user, taking advantage of your kindness…"

Mr. Pearson interrupted me.

"Son, we don't care about the damn car, we care about you. You don't need to apologize about anything."

He walked over and embraced me. "I don't want another one of my sons hurt or killed! Don't you know we love you?" I could hear him sobbing and began tearing up myself.

He pulled back and looked at me. "Are you sure you're okay?" he asked, sitting back down.

"Yes sir," I replied.

I looked at Reen. She was standing with her arms crossed, weeping gently. Abruptly, she raced over to me and hugged me again.

"They could have killed you. Please be careful Todd. Don't leave us!" she cried until Tracy gently pulled her back.

Tucker rolled up to me. "Who did it? Did you get a look at them?" he asked.

"I think I know who did it but I can't prove anything. The police have some video camera footage from that night, and I'm still waiting to hear back from them."

"Maybe you need to consider quitting. There ain't no amount of money worth your life," Tucker said.

"Amen to that!" Mr. Pearson added.

I sat down at the table and began to massage my temples. "I've got a lot of time and energy invested at Shady Meadows, and now I can add blood and tears, too. So, someone there doesn't like me. Why? What did I do wrong? Help people? Try and rid the community of criminals and thugs who have made life there unsafe for the entire community? What about the children? I haven't done anything wrong, and I just don't feel like I should retreat. I'm not trying to be a Rambo, but now it's my turn."

I looked at Reen, who was still crying. "Don't cry Reen, I promise to be careful. But those thugs who tried to kill me have some world-class payback coming."

"Now son, you ought to not be thinking of revenge and such. Leave it to the authorities to find these rascals and bring them to justice," Mr. Pearson said.

"Yes sir, I'll let the police do their job, but I'll stay on alert. Now, I don't want you to have to report this damage to your insurance company and need to figure out the repair costs."

"I won't allow you to pay a dime. Come on, let's take a look at this beauty," he replied.

We all went to look at the car in the driveway, while Mr. Pearson and Tucker gave the vehicle a thorough inspection. Tucker rolled up to me, laughing.

"Boy, it's a good thing you weren't inside, you would have been ripped to shreds. It looks like you dodged another bullet. I'm gonna have to nickname you 'Lucky.'"

I shook my head and turned away. He had no idea his words were like nails of guilt being driven into me. Mr. Pearson walked over.

"I tell you what Todd. You said it drives fine, no funny noises, no smells, right?" he asked.

"Yes sir. It runs great. I thought something critical would have been damaged with all those bullet holes."

"Come back over here tomorrow after you get off, and we'll get all the outside holes covered with Bondo and putty. We'll get the front and back windshields replaced by the insurance company. Don't worry, the rates won't be affected, it's a safety requirement on the policy. All you'll need after that is a paint job. And it just so happened that Tucker and I were talking, and he wants to give you his car, free of charge," Mr. Pearson said.

Tucker rolled up. "Congratulations buddy, and thanks for saving me a hundred bucks a month on car insurance! Ha!"

I felt ambushed by this, and I felt strange accepting it. It was a great car, and after covering the holes up and adding a new paint job, it would look like new.

"No way, let me pay you for it. Just give me a price and I won't haggle with you," I said.

Mr. Pearson patted my back. "Nope, it's already been settled. Let's go inside so Tucker can sign the title over to you. Just let me know when you get the car insurance transferred over so I can cancel mine."

Everyone moved back toward the house.

"Hey Tuck, let me holler at you for a sec," I said.

He rolled to a stop as I joined him. "There's this kid who I hired at Shady Meadows, and after watching a bunch of commercials about the Marines, he wants to enlist. He's asking me for advice, words of wisdom, and such, but I had to run over here and didn't have time to chit-chat with him. I thought maybe he could come with me tomorrow and we give him a full report on what he's getting himself into. The kid's got a baby already and needs to put bacon on the table, but he ain't gonna be able to do that just working as a maintenance helper. I thought it would be cool for us to take him under our wings and let him know what the Marine Corps is all about."

"Hell yeah, bring him over. I'd like to meet him. He needs to see what the other half of the commercial looks like. The half that they don't advertise." Tucker chuckled. "You know, veteran tombstones and wounded warriors haven't gone anywhere, but sometimes it feels like we are on the dark side of the moon. Everybody likes to see the moon shining, but what folks don't see, they don't think about, even though it's still there. Kind of like me; out of sight, out of mind."

"Cool. I'll tell him tomorrow. He'll be riding with me over here and then I'll drop him back home."

"Ten-four Corporal," Tucker replied as we fist bumped and went inside.

Mr. Pearson found the title and Tucker transferred the vehicle into my name. It was an expensive gift that I didn't know how to repay. They let me live with them, Tucker let me drive his car, and now he was giving the car to me. I appealed to him one last time.

"Man, please let me give you something for the car. Dude, come on," I pleaded.

Tucker smiled. "I've been reading the bible, okay? It says in there somewhere something like this: freely you receive, freely you give. Man, if this car is a blessing to you, then one day you pass the blessing off to someone else. That's what you can do. You copy me?"

"I copy bro."

An hour later I drove back to my apartment. As I drove through the complex, I could see and feel all the changes we had made for the better. Groups of children were playing in different areas. Residents were enjoying the view from their shaded balconies. There was no loud, disruptive music. Most importantly, there wasn't a drug dealer, gang member, or prostitute in sight. Shady Meadows looked like a brand new apartment complex, and I hoped it would stay this way after I was gone. After taking in the view and observing the new environment, I realized this was the type of place I should have grown up.

Back in my apartment, I changed into shorts and a tank top while warming up two frozen dinners. Who can eat just one? I turned on the television, sat down with a tray on my recliner and didn't waste any time devouring my food. The sooner that I finished eating, the better, so I could start drinking. I knew to eat first or risk getting sick and puking my guts out.

Ten minutes later, I poured my first triple shot of the night. I turned off the television and played my squad's favorite songs while pulling up my team's picture, performing my ritual out of love, respect, and honor for the lost. Tears streamed down my face as I sat motionless remembering Tom and Jay. I poured another drink, sat back down, and closed my eyes for a moment to remember.

• • •

I woke up a while later to the cell phone ringing. It was Barry Thomas. It was about time he returned my call, but damn, too bad it was after working hours just as I was getting my mind right with Irish whiskey. Against my better judgment, I answered his call.

"Hello Mr. Thomas."

"Hello Mr. Goodson! We need to talk young man. I've heard some disturbing news concerning you at Shady Meadows and I need your undivided attention. Are you able to talk right now?" he asked. His voice was elevated.

"Yes sir, I'm free right now." I sat up in my recliner, ready to let him know everything about the shooting and who I believe was behind it.

"I received a call from the contractors who I personally approved to perform the renovations and unit upgrades at Shady Meadows. They told me you did not renew their contract this fiscal year. Now at first, I thought this was a mistake because you're new and must have gotten confused. But then I checked your petty cash disbursement reports and see that you've been paying a different contractor out of there. Petty cash is not the authorized method of payment to contractors for long-term work. You and I have an explicit understanding of the duties you are to perform and not perform. I have been using those contractors for over seven years at Shady Meadows, so I want you to explain to me what you know about this?"

Huh? He caught me off guard with his question. "Sir, what about the shooting I reported? Aren't you concerned about that?" I asked.

"I know about the shooting and read the report you sent. No one was hurt and the property damage is being covered through our property insurance. Is there something else I'm missing? You're supposed to be a big, bad war veteran, right? A little gunfire shouldn't spook you, so don't try to change the subject. I asked you to explain yourself. Quit stalling," he replied.

Stalling? All right then, it was go time. I didn't have anything prepared for this inevitable moment, so I decided to be brutally honest. I had known this moment of truth would come one day, but also believed the work I had done at Shady Meadows was necessary. I decided to adhere to the old adage: It is better to ask forgiveness rather than to seek permission. Now I would stand tall in front of the man, but I wasn't worried. This wasn't my first rodeo.

"Yes sir, it's true. I didn't renew their contracts. They were too expensive, it's that simple. I found a contractor who is doing the same work but at forty percent less cost. They have already turned several units and their work is very professional. All of us are happy with it."

"Us? I'm talking to you, not us! You had no authority to make that decision. You were insubordinate, that's clear. So, this is what I'm going to do tomorrow morning, I am going to fax you a written reprimand for insubordination which you are going to immediately read, sign, and fax back to me. Then you are going to call my preferred contractors back and inform them that their contract is renewed. Going forward, I advise you to stay within the boundaries that have been set. Next time, you will be terminated. Do you understand me?"

I didn't answer him right away; I couldn't. He was talking down to me like I was a child and it didn't sit well with me. I began feeling flush and hot, even insulted. Who did he think he was? I got up from the recliner and swallowed the whiskey still in my glass.

"No sir, I don't understand at all. Do you mind if I speak freely?" I asked, as a formality only, because regardless of his answer, I would be heard.

"Speak. What do you have to say?"

"To be honest sir, I think you're the one that needs to do some explaining, not me. I'm just doing my job, and part of that is cleaning up the mess that you left for me."

"What? You're being very disrespectful and treading on thin ice young man. You better start explaining yourself."

"I will if you'll let me finish. Look, let's just cut the shit, Mr. Thomas, the game is up. Those contractors have been billing Shady Meadows for years, just like you said, but they haven't completed any work. They've been getting paid tens of thousands of dollars while defrauding the company. I've verified it and know it for a fact."

"I don't know what you are talking about! How do you know all this? Where is your evidence?" he asked.

"You don't know about this? Come on, Mr. Thomas, be honest. You have access to the same invoices and past budgets as I do. What you don't have are the affidavits from company employees who state that they informed all the previous managers, as well as yourself, of the ongoing fraud! Now, you want to write me up for stopping their gravy train and correcting the problem? I don't think so. I'm not signing shit. I'm doing my job the right way; the legal way."

I heard him chuckle under his breath.

"You need to fax me your resignation tomorrow. I appreciate your hard work, but it's time to part ways. You are not a good fit for this position. I won't bother sending you the reprimand."

I could tell he was in retreat, but I wasn't willing to let him go. No, this was a skirmish and I decided to pursue him. I had the offense now and would keep it, and the momentum, so I pursued him like he was an enemy combatant.

"I'm not resigning. Why would I do that?" I asked.

"Fine! Tomorrow I'll fill out the paperwork and terminate you. Get ready to move your belongings out of the office and out of the apartment. You'll hear from me by noon. This conversation is over!" he said, ending the call.

I walked into the kitchen and guzzled the whiskey straight from the bottle. This was a good job while it lasted, but like the saying goes, all good things must come to an end. I laughed at first, then felt a sense of relief, knowing I would be going back to Angie. Of course, she would want an explanation of what happened, but I was sure she would take my side. Or maybe not, but what else could I do?

Then I remembered that I had one last card to play. If I was going down, so was the opposition. I grabbed my keys off the table and went down to the office.

I sat down at my computer and logged into my email. Barry had made a mistake by letting me know how and when he would attack, so I launched a pre-emptive strike on his position. I wrote an email addressed to the company's CFO, Daniel McFarland, and Human Resources, outlining the history of the financial fraud perpetrated by the contractors and Barry Thomas and attached all relevant documents, along with the scanned affidavits from William and Eugene to support my claim. After proofreading the final letter, I sat with my finger on the mouse button, imagining I was about to launch a Tomahawk missile strike from a Navy ship. I smiled and I clicked send.

I went back to my apartment and continued drinking into the night. I had done it now. I had screwed up again. But it didn't matter if I went down, as long as I went down with a fight.

• • •

I woke up exhausted. I had two separate nightmares which interrupted five pathetic hours of sleep. Regardless, I reported to the office and began my workday as usual. Barry said he would call by noon, but until then it was business as usual.

I didn't let any of the staff know about my conversation from last night and that I was a short-timer, mainly because I wanted to avoid all the questions they would ask. I had previously talked William and Eugene into signing affidavits stating they notified the previous managers, along with Thomas, about the contractor fraud. Those guys had no incentive to lie and the money trail didn't lead back to them. It did lead to the contractors and whoever was enabling them, despite the staff's warnings.

Both William and Eugene needed their jobs, and if they found out I was in the hot seat and about to be fired, they would no doubt worry about their own careers. All our jobs were in jeopardy, but I was the one mainly responsible. I worried that talking them into backing me up might have been a bad idea, and I started to feel I probably shouldn't have involved them. But they were adults and had to accept responsibility for their own actions.

Noon came and went without a call from Barry Thomas and soon it was time to clock out. I wondered what could have happened. At least the car insurance company had sent the technicians out earlier to replace the front and rear windows on my car, and the property insurance adjusters had completed their damage assessment.

I heard someone open the front door. It was Andre.

"Hey Mr. Todd. Uh, you told me to get with you after work about going to holler at your buddy. You still want to do that?" he asked.

"Yeah, I talked to him yesterday. We're good to go. Like I said, you can ride with me and I'll bring you back. Ready?" I asked.

"Yes sir, I'm ready but, um.... Well, I told my girlfriend Kim about it, and now she wants to come. She wants to drive her car, and we'll follow you. I didn't know if that was okay with you?"

"Sure man, that's fine. What about your baby? Do you need to get a babysitter first?" I asked.

"No sir, we need to bring the baby with us. If that's all right?"

"No problem Andre. I'm ready when you are."

I locked up the office and a few minutes later, Andre and Kim pulled up next to my car. I waved to them and backed out while they followed me.

Thirty minutes later, we all were walking in the front door of the Pearson house. This time, I rang the bell as a courtesy because we had company. Reen met us in the hallway.

"Hello, I'm Reen and welcome to our home!" she said, shaking hands with Andre and Kim.

"Hello ma'am, I'm Kim Reynolds."

"Hello ma'am, I'm Andre Greene."

Reen smiled and then focused on their baby.

"It's nice to meet you both, but who is this precious little angel?" she asked while lightly rubbing their baby's foot.

"This is little Megan Olivia," Kim replied.

Reen clearly adored the baby. "I'm sorry for asking and I understand if you don't want to, but may I please hold her?" Reen asked.

Kim smiled and handed the baby to her. The transition didn't seem to affect the baby's happy mood, and soon Reen was rocking the baby in her arms. "Everyone is in the family room. Tucker is waiting to meet the young man who wants to become a Marine." Reen smiled at Andre and then led us to the family room. "Forgive my manners. Would either of you care for something to drink?"

"No, thank you ma'am," Andre and Kim answered in unison.

Mr. Pearson and Tracy stood up and walked over to us with Tucker following, and Reen introduced everyone.

"Kim, Andre, and Megan, meet my husband, Henry, my daughter, Tracy, and my son, Tucker," she said while steadily rocking the baby.

Everyone shook hands. Tracy began baby talking with Megan and looked at Kim.

"Kim, may I please hold her?" Tracy asked.

"Absolutely," she replied.

Reen handed the baby to Tracy.

"Oh my god she is so beautiful!" Tracy said as if mesmerized by the infant.

"Thank you!" Kim answered.

Mr. Pearson leaned over to the baby.

"You two have been blessed with a beautiful baby girl. Look at her eyes!" Mr. Pearson said.

I couldn't understand the infatuation with the baby. Yes, the baby was cute, and I had expected the women to make a big to-do about her, but not Mr. Pearson. Maybe, it was because he was an old-timer. I noticed older folks seemed to act differently as the years passed.

Suddenly, he seemed to snap out of the baby's spell.

"Todd, how about we get started patching those holes in the car while Reen and Tracy talk to Kim in the kitchen. Sound good to everyone?" he asked. Everyone nodded in agreement.

I pulled the car into the backyard workshop, and Mr. Pearson and Tucker got to work, sanding around the bullet holes and filling them with putty. They made sure Andre got involved with the bodywork after showing him the process. After finishing this first step, we needed to let it dry and harden, then I could bring it back over next week so it could be sanded smooth. I moved the car back into the driveway and met Tucker and Andre in the family room, while Mr. Pearson went into the kitchen with the others.

Tucker turned on the television and game console.

"Hey Andre, you ever play the *Call of Honor: War Battalion*?"

Andre's eyebrows lifted.

"Yes sir, I played it a couple times. I'm not that good at it though," he answered.

Tucker tossed him a game controller.

"Cool, let's play a couple games. I'll make sure we are in the same unit. Just stick with me, it'll be fun bro," Tucker said.

Andre sat down on the couch as the game was about to start.

"What about me?" I asked.

Tucker looked over at Andre.

"What about him? What should he be doing?" Tucker asked.

Andre looked puzzled.

"I don't know," Andre replied.

Tucker looked at me.

"You'll be our spotter. We can't catch everything on the screen, so pretend you're a drone and be our eyes in the sky, copy?" he asked.

"Ten-four," I replied.

They played desert warfare for nearly an hour as Tucker led and directed Andre through the game. I watched Andre immerse himself, ducking and dodging on the couch with the occasional verbal shout out as his character would get cornered and killed.

Listening to Tucker give commands among the game explosions began to irritate me, and I could feel my heart rate increase. I had played this same game with Tucker a thousand times before and never reacted this way, but that's when I could control part of the game. It was different sitting beside them, basically helpless because I wasn't in the match.

I finally had enough and stood up.

"I can't take no more of this shit! I'm going in the kitchen!" I yelled.

Tucker and Andre stopped playing and looked at me. Tucker turned to Andre.

"Good games bro! Let's shut it down now, we've played for long enough," Tucker said.

Andre nodded as Tucker turned off the console and put up the controllers, then rolled over to the couch. I sat back down next to Andre and tried to relax.

"So Andre, the game is pretty intense, huh?" Tucker asked.

I could tell by the boyish grin on Andre's face that he was relaxed and enjoying himself.

"Yeah, for sure. That's the best I ever played, but you were helping me out a lot. Dang, that was fun," he remarked.

"It is fun, but keep in mind that it's just a game, man. Real combat is nothing like that. There are no resets, no restarts. I want you to listen to me young brother, really listen, and I'll break it down for you. If you go into the Marines, be prepared to go overseas, either to Iraq or Afghanistan, or maybe both. We are there to stay, so don't listen to the news reports. Let's say you qualify and actually make it and become a Marine. When you leave the States and land in-country over there, you'll be in harm's way. Whether it's close-quarters combat, driving down the road, or stopping to give a candy bar to a kid while a sniper peels your cap, it's all the same. It's a serious business. I'm not trying to scare you; I'm only telling you the truth. Take me, for example. How did you think I got this way? This is from real combat. No reset. No restart. So, I'm just curious, why are you considering the military?"

Andre's posture and demeanor went cold.

"Real talk? I got a little girl to support. Don't get me wrong, I appreciate Mr. Todd hiring me, but I can do more than being a maintenance helper. My homeboy's big brother is in the Marines, like Mr. Todd and you were. So yeah, I was thinking about it," Andre said.

"I can respect that. Just understand the oath of enlistment. You pledge to defend and protect the Constitution of the United States of America against all enemies, foreign and domestic. Those words mean something. Are you prepared for the possibility of losing your life for those words, and never living to see your woman or your daughter again? Because that's a real possibility, but you can also serve thirty years and retire without a scratch, man. I just want you to know that enlisting in any branch of the military is an important decision. You've got to weigh the cost and be all-in because you'll have a team that depends on you. Once you're in, there ain't no half-ass about it or changing your mind. It's all-in. You get me?" Tucker asked.

Andre nodded as they fist bumped.

"I probably should think more about it. Thanks for the advice. Good looking out," Andre replied.

"Andre, you're welcome to come by here anytime bro. I'll be here," Tucker said.

"That's a bet! Cool." Andre smiled.

I stood up and stretched. "All right Tuck, we're gonna head out now partner."

"Todd, you ain't the boss of Andre. He came with his woman and can leave when he damn well pleases! Ain't that right, Andre. Tell him!" Tucker joked while Andre laughed.

"Man, Mr. Todd is still my boss. I got to respect him," Andre replied.

I patted Andre on his back.

"Good answer, Andre!" I said and looked at Tucker. "You're a punk for trying to turn one of my team against me. Let's get out of here Andre."

I turned around and fist bumped Tucker.

"All right Tuck, take it easy bro," I said.

"Drive safe, buddy. I'll see you later." Tucker looked at Andre. "You know where I live. Don't be a stranger."

"I gotcha," Andre replied.

Fifteen minutes later, Reen and Tracy finally released baby Megan as their hostage, and after saying their goodbyes, we walked to our cars. I noticed Kim was beaming.

"Thank you for inviting us to visit. The Pearsons are super nice people," Kim said.

"You're welcome. Yeah, they're like family to me, and I could tell they were happy to meet both of you, but they went crazy over Megan." I said.

"I know right! But that's fine," she replied.

They laughed, got into their car, and pulled out of the driveway.

"See you tomorrow Andre!" I shouted.

Their horn beeped twice. I started my car and pulled out behind them.

I had set my phone to silent, so I checked for missed calls. Nothing. I hated not knowing Barry's next move and didn't want to stress about it, but I couldn't bury my thoughts, the what-ifs. I needed a drink and the sooner the better. I passed Kim and Andre at the first opportunity and sped up to get back to my place sooner. I was late for my daily ritual.

CHAPTER ELEVEN

SUN SHOWERS

The next morning I was late getting to the office, but William had opened for me and started our coffee brewing. Eugene and Andre were putting duct tape over the holes in my apartment windows as a temporary fix, while I waited for the contractors to replace them and repair the damage to the interior.

I sat at my desk, still waiting on the phone call from Barry. I knew it would come today, but I was determined to keep doing my job regardless. My main concern was explaining all of it to Angie. She was already frustrated because the letter from the academy hadn't come yet. Our last conversation might have pacified her temporarily, but I knew that wouldn't last.

I heard police sirens blaring at full volume on the property. I stood up and hurried outside to see what was going on. Four police cruisers sped down the driveway before separating into pairs and surrounding building number five. They ran inside the breezeway and stopped at unit 515, the Stephens'. When the door opened, they all rushed inside. I looked around and saw William, Eugene, and Andre walking toward the parking lot. Several residents came outside to watch, while others peeked out their windows.

A few minutes later, the police walked Derek Stephens outside in handcuffs and sat him inside the back of a cruiser. I called out to William and the guys and waved them over.

"Team!" I said and poured my coffee out in the grass. We huddled in a circle.

"Looks like they got him boss," Eugene said.

"Yeah, but for what? The detective told me his alibi checked out and he wasn't a suspect. Drugs maybe?" I asked.

William looked at me. "If they stay a while and come out with sealed bags of dope, then we'll know right away. They'll barricade the apartment too. They should let you know before they leave. Unless it's something else we don't know about, then they probably won't tell you anything."

The officers got back into their cars and left, leaving Ms. Stephens standing outside her door. One of her other sons poked his head out the door and said something to her, and she turned to go inside. She stopped and saw us looking at her.

"You gonna get yours!" she shouted before walking inside and slamming the door behind her. The team was quiet, looking to me for my reaction.

"She has a date with the magistrate in three weeks, and then this entire community will be rid of them. She needs to worry about where to move to next and save her threats for someone who gives a damn. She did this to herself," I said and walked back to the office. Nobody commented and we all went back to work.

At noon, I ate lunch at my apartment while sitting back in my recliner. There were thirty minutes left on my break, so I decided to decompress while looking at the sky through my cracked living room window. I felt like crap being in limbo and waiting, not knowing when or what was going to happen with me. Would that gang of cowards be bold enough to come back again and play Cowboys and Indians? Or would they be smarter and be more precise when they tried to kill me next time? Something was changing inside me, causing me to feel different, off-balance.

I stayed flush and anxious most of the day. The condition had snuck up on me, and I gradually adjusted to the effects. Underneath the disordered thoughts in my active mind, there were two questions fueling my anxiety: *Who am I?* and *Why am I still alive?* They were stupid questions, I thought, but I felt like an idiot for not being able to answer them.

I remembered better times when I was a kid. The best memory from those days was my mom's smile.

I picked up my cell phone, scrolled through the contacts, and dialed. A few moments later, it connected.

"Hello?" It was Herman.

"Hello Herman, this is Todd. How are you today?" I asked.

"Todd? I'm fine, thanks for asking. How have you been? Are you calling from the academy? Your mother mentioned you were accepted."

"I'm doing good. No sir, I haven't received my reporting date yet, but it'll be soon," I replied.

"That's great! I sure hope you'll invite us to your graduation. At least invite your mother. I don't want to impose on you, and I can understand me not getting invited, but it would mean so much to her. She's always been very proud of you."

"Herman, when I graduate, you and my mother will both be invited. I give you my word on that," I said.

"Thank you, Todd, I appreciate that very much. It was great speaking with you, take care of yourself and good luck. Hold on for one moment while I call your mother."

"Thank you sir."

A minute later my mother answered.

"Hello Todd, how are you dear?" she asked.

The sound of her voice uncovered cherished memories and feelings from the past. I felt like I was eleven years old again, calling my mom at work when I got home from school. She would ask how my day was and if I had homework to do. I realized the love she showed me throughout my life was unmovable and dependable, like the sun and moon. The kind of love one expects to last a lifetime.

At that moment, I was filled with gratitude for my mother despite my current troubles.

"Hi Mom, I'm fine. I was thinking about you and decided to give you a call while on my lunch break. How's everything with you," I asked.

"Aww, you're so sweet. Everything is fine with me. God is good," she replied.

"I told Herman I would send an invitation to the two of you for my graduation, but I haven't received my reporting date yet. It should be soon. I'm still working at Shady Meadows, for the time being."

"How is Angie doing?"

"She's fine. Waiting for me to come back."

"I know she misses you dearly. Be patient. Soon you'll be reunited. Then you'll have the rest of your lives to have children and make me a proud grandmama," she said and began giggling.

"One day Mom, but first let me graduate from the academy. I still need to clear that hurdle."

"You're going to do great at the academy, and I have no doubt that you will be at the top of your class," she replied.

"Thanks Mom. Well, I just called to check in on you and Herman. I need to get back to the office now."

"Herman was so excited when he handed me the phone," she whispered. "I don't know what you said to him, but he'll tell me when we get off the phone." Her voice returned to normal. "I love you Todd. Take care."

"I love you, too Mom. I'll talk to you later. Be careful out there," I replied.

After the call, my attitude and emotions were back in balance and my focus returned. I looked through the window again and stared at the sky, which was brighter than before. I looked through my contacts again and found my dad's phone number. Was I ready to talk to him? I dialed.

"Hello?" he answered.

"Hello Dad."

"Todd! How the hell have you been? I've been calling you for weeks. What have you been up to?"

"Sorry Dad, I've been swamped. There is so much going on here, but I'm good. How about you?" I asked.

"I can't complain son. Same old shit, different day. So, the slaves on the plantation are running you crazy, huh?" He laughed.

"I've had a ton of work to do, that's what I'm saying," I replied.

"Well, don't let them savages run you ragged. You're the manager, the overseer. Remember that you have the power, so don't let them jungle bunnies make your life difficult. They will if given a chance. We both know firsthand they don't mind breaking up someone else's happy family."

My serene mood disintegrated and anger took its place.

"No, that's not true. We both know that's a lie," I snapped.

"What? What do you mean?"

"I mean exactly what I said. You lied! You told me a fairy tale nightmare about why you and mom split up. But guess what? She told me the truth about what happened and why it happened, and her story doesn't match up with yours. In fact, I call bullshit on you, Dad!"

"Dammit! You watch your mouth, boy! Mind who you're talking to and have some respect!" he yelled.

"You shut your mouth! Shut your damn mouth! I don't want to hear another word from you! Mom didn't cheat on you. It was you who cheated on her! I believe her, every word. She said you wouldn't stop cheating, even after she begged you to. Now be a man and admit it!"

There was silence for a few moments.

"Yes, I made mistakes. I'm sorry. You're right, I didn't tell you all of the truth—"

"You didn't tell me any of the truth!" I said, interrupting him.

"I apologize. I didn't want you to think bad of your old man—"

"What are you apologizing for? Because you lied to me? Or because you're a hypocrite?" I asked.

"Hypocrite? Why are you calling me names? I can't believe you're talking to me like this Todd. I'm disappointed in you."

"Yes, you're a hypocrite. Ever since I was a kid, you've been raising me to be a monster, a racist, and a gay basher, but then I come to find out that you were cheating on mom with men! That's being a hypocrite! You're disappointed in me? Good, because I'm disappointed in you! Not just because you lied to me about mom, but because you lied to me about who you really are!" I could hear him sobbing, but I wouldn't relent. "Where is your courage? I always looked up to you like a hero. A person who stands up for what they believe in, but you broke that picture. The other day, I helped out a young dude because he was getting beat up for being gay. And guess what? I respect him a hell of a lot more than I respect you. He accepts who he is and makes no bones about it! He's willing to fight for the right to be who he is, regardless of what other people think. But he shouldn't have to! And unlike you, he's honest to himself and to the world about who he is."

I could hear my father crying now.

"I can't...I got to hang up," he whimpered.

His desperation caused me to pause my attack and I became conflicted. I hated what my father had done to my mother and me, but I still loved him and his pain became my pain. He was my father.

"I love you Dad, whether you are gay or straight. But you need to make this right. You need to own this. Mom didn't deserve to be slandered by you and she should get an apology. Until you do that, we don't have anything else to talk about. I have to go back to work now. Goodbye," I said and ended the call.

I noticed my hand was trembling.

I couldn't hold my emotions back any longer and broke down crying. I knew my dad was hurting because of me, but Mom was the real victim. Still, I cried for several minutes before drying my tears and returning to the office.

• • •

As soon as I sat down my cell phone rang. It was the corporate office number.

"Hello, this is Todd Goodson."

"Hello Todd, this is Deborah Randel calling from Human Resources. How are you today?" she asked.

"I'm fine, thank you."

"The reason for this call is to let you know that we have received the complaint and documentation that you emailed us concerning your district manager, Barry Thomas. We take these accusations very seriously, and since you also sent the email to our chief financial officer, we decided to investigate this matter immediately. We understand Mr. Thomas has asked for your resignation, which you declined. Yesterday he submitted paperwork to our department for your termination. We would like you to report to the corporate headquarters today at 2:30 PM, so we can discuss what actions we intend to take going forward."

"Yes ma'am, I will be there," I replied.

"Good. We will be waiting. Thank you."

We ended the call.

"Son of a bitch!" I yelled.

I felt exposed, like a student being called to the principal's office while the entire class sits by and watches. It was no surprise Barry had somehow wiggled his way out of trouble, but I knew it was only a matter of time for him. I checked the time and decided to leave immediately. There was no need to be late for my own firing; it was better to get it over with.

I called William on the office walkie-talkie and let him know that I had to run to corporate and he needed to lock up. I turned off the office lights and looked around as I went to my car. All in all, the job was good while it lasted. I was satisfied with what the team and I achieved here, and the difference was like night and day. I started the car and turned up the radio. "The Ticket" by Joe Cocker began to play as I drove off. At least the waiting game was over, which was a relief, and I could begin rehearsing my explanation to Angie.

• • •

I walked into the corporate headquarters and signed in with the receptionist.

"Please have a seat. Mrs. Randel will be out shortly," she said.

"Thanks." I sat down and thumbed through the outdated magazines on the coffee table beside me. The door behind the receptionist's desk opened and a woman walked out.

"Hello Todd, we are ready for you," she said.

I walked over to her and we shook hands.

"Deborah Randal." She smiled.

"Nice to meet you Mrs. Randel. Too bad it's under these circum-stances," I said.

She looked puzzled, but said, "Here, this way." She led me through the door and down a corridor until we came to a large conference room. We entered and she closed the door behind us. I looked around and saw a man sitting at the table, but no Barry Thomas. The smiling gentleman walked over and shook my hand.

"Hello Todd, I'm Dan McFarland, and it is a pleasure to meet you. Please, have a seat."

I sat down, and Mrs. Randel sat down next to me.

"Would you like anything to drink? I know it's hot out there and you've just got off the road," he asked.

"No, but thank you sir. I'm fine," I replied.

He was making me feel uneasy with all this fluff. What were they up to? I wished they'd just fire me and get it over with.

"Then let's get started. This won't take long." He sat down at the head of the table. "First of all, we want to let you know that we have investigated all the complaints and accusations against Barry Thomas. This included allowing him to address those accusations and to defend himself by submitting any evidence to the contrary. These are severe charges which border on criminal negligence. Deborah?" He turned to Mrs. Randel.

"Barry Thomas no longer works here. After reviewing everything and investigating the staff at other properties in his district, we found more evidence of the same contractors billing for work that was never performed. Also, we have contacted the district attorney's office and have a meeting scheduled with them about this matter. They have the authority to depose and interview witnesses and audit all parties involved, including their financials and phone records. We wanted to let you know the result of our internal investigation personally," she said, and looked at Mr. McFarland.

"And I wanted to especially thank you Todd, for having the integrity and courage to bring this matter to our attention. It's not an easy thing for a subordinate to go against their superior. In many cases, or rather in most cases, that amounts to career suicide. But I commend you," he said.

I was in a daze. I couldn't comprehend what they were telling me. It was beyond surreal.

"So, I'm not being fired?" I asked, hesitantly.

They both laughed and shook their heads.

"No Todd, you are not being fired," he said. "Actually, if I could promote you right now, I would. The vacant district manager position will be offered to Sherika Jones when she returns from her honeymoon." He turned to Mrs. Randel. "When is that?" he asked.

"She is scheduled to return in five days, on the sixth," she said.

"Good," he replied. "Todd, please report to her when she gets back. Sherika knows the position better than most DMs. She has worked very hard and deserves the offer."

"Yes sir, I agree."

"So, what are your future plans and goals? What would you like to achieve with this company? I can tell you right now that you are definitely on my shortlist for really great upcoming opportunities," he said.

"To be honest Mr. McFarland, I have other obligations, which Barry Thomas was made aware of before hiring me. I don't plan on remaining in the state for more than another four months, maybe five at the most. I've been accepted to the NYSP training academy and I'm just waiting on my reporting date. I intend to become a state trooper and hopefully getting married right after that. But I really appreciate how this whole matter turned out. I feel a lot better now that the pressure and stress are off me, and not having to worry about getting fired for doing my job."

He walked over to me and shook my hand.

"I wish you the best in your career. Law enforcement needs more people like you. Integrity is everything, isn't it? What are you without it? Good luck!"

"Thank you sir," I replied.

Mrs. Randel shook my hand.

"Thank you for driving up here on short notice. And I'm sorry I gave you the impression you were getting fired. You're doing a great job." She smiled.

"Thank you. And have a great day. Goodbye!"

I walked back down the corridor and through the lobby until I burst through the front doors and stopped. My entire body was tingling from the adrenaline rush.

"Yes!" I clenched my fists and yelled. "Hell yes!"

I had won. Barry had the advantage, the elevation, and the fire-power to put me down, but he missed. I stayed focus and prepared, and when the time was right, I double-tapped him. Game over Barry Thomas, game over.

I drove back to Shady Meadows, riding a rush and a high I had not felt in years! My heart was thumping in my chest, but this time, it felt good and I felt redeemed.

• • •

My news definitely deserved to be celebrated. I stopped at the corner liquor store on the way back and bought two bottles. I wasn't boozing it up this time to self-medicate because of my anxiety or feeling depressed. I didn't feel the need to drink at this moment, but I was going to anyway. I left out of the parking lot and noticed Chavis walking on the side of the road. I pulled over and rolled down the window.

"Hey Chavis, you want a ride?"

He looked startled. "Okay, thanks."

He got in, and I sped off.

"Hey, have them guys bothered you again?" I asked.

"Nah, I've been going to the store every day and haven't seen them at all."

"Me neither," I replied.

"Forget about them fools. I meant to tell you; I think that's just wrong how they shot up your crib. Your car, too," he said, peeking around the interior and noticing the two holes in the dash panel. "I hope they get caught."

"Yeah man, thanks. It could've been worse. Now I got a car that looks like something from the movie *Mad Max*. It's getting repaired, slowly. Maybe you noticed the putty covering the holes. I'm gonna be getting that sanded next week and then eventually painted."

"What? There ain't nothing wrong with this car. It still drives and looks good. I would drive it!"

I laughed.

"You're right, there's nothing wrong with it. I thought the bullet holes made it look bad ass, myself. Are you still saving for your car?" I asked.

"Yes sir. I figure that in six months, I will be rolling."

"Six months goes by fast," I replied.

I drove slowly through the entrance and down the road. The children were home from school, and although they didn't typically play in the driveway, a stray ball or child could quickly dart out. I had zero tolerance for anyone speeding through the complex, as were most of the residents. I parked and we got out.

"Thanks for the ride, Mr. Todd."

"No problem, Chavis. Take it, easy dude."

Once inside my apartment, I changed clothes and sat in my recliner. Everything felt like it was falling into place, no more waiting and wondering. I felt I had finally gained back complete control over my life. It was six o'clock and usually, I would have knocked back several shots by this time, but I didn't feel my usual impulse. I tried but couldn't remember the last day I had gone without a drink.

I had been drinking every day since stepping foot back on American soil. Some would say drinking that much would make me an alcoholic, but I didn't feel like one.

I walked over to the refrigerator and opened a bottle of water while staring at the liquor.

No, I wasn't an alcoholic, and to prove it, I decided not to drink anymore today. My mood was excellent, so I sat back down to relax and turned on the television.

An hour later my phone rang. It was Mr. Pearson calling.

"Hello Mr. Pearson."

"Todd, I need you to come to the house now if you can."

"Yes sir. I'm on my way, give me thirty minutes. Is everything all right?" I asked.

"Please, just come over and don't rush. Drive safe son," he said.

His voice was trembling.

"Is something wrong with Tucker?" I asked.

"Please come to the house."

He hung up.

CHAPTER TWELVE

BELLY OF THE BEAST

As I drove down the street toward Tucker's house, I saw an ambulance in the driveway without its lights on. I began to panic and sped up, skidding to a stop at the curb. I jumped out and ran across the yard up to the front door, looking at the empty ambulance sitting with its back doors open. I opened the front door and stopped.

The entire family was standing around a covered gurney, crying, while two paramedics stood by.

"No...No." I dropped to my knees and howled. "Tuck!" I was suddenly lost in grief with no sense of time. I felt someone pull me upright and I recognized Mr. Pearson's voice.

"It's all right, son. He's in a better place now," he said.

He hugged me and we cried together. Then I felt Reen's and Tracy's arms around me, and all of us mourned as one family. It may have lasted minutes or hours because time seemed to stop.

"Do you want to see him before they take him?" Mr. Pearson asked.

I wiped my eyes and inhaled, still crying.

"Okay."

The paramedic carefully unzipped the body bag halfway and laid the flap back. Tucker looked peaceful, like he was asleep.

My best friend was gone.

"I love you Tuck!" I cried out and fell on top of him, sobbing uncontrollably. I felt hands rub my neck and pull me away from the gurney. The paramedic zipped the bag up, and I watched in tears as they wheeled his body through the front door. Mr. Pearson stepped outside for a minute and then came back and locked the door. I composed myself enough to speak.

"What happened?" I mumbled.

Mr. Pearson took his glasses off to wipe his eyes.

"Reen found him in the family room when she went to vacuum. She thought he was asleep, but when she called out to him, he didn't answer." Reen began sobbing loudly. "Everyone, if there ever was a time needed for prayer, this is one." He grabbed one of my hands and one of Tracy's hands, and Reen completed the circle.

"Almighty God of love, we thank you for all that you have given to us. We thank you for sending us Tucker! The love and joy he brought to this family and this world are enough to last a thousand lifetimes. We cry and weep in grief right now because he is gone from us in the body. But we know that the love we shared with him will never die and will last forever! Please let your love rain down on this family and help us through this difficult time. Amen."

Mr. Pearson walked into the kitchen and I hugged Tracy and Reen.

"Will you stay with here with us? At least until after the funeral?" Reen asked me.

"Yes ma'am. I'll drive to my apartment tomorrow and pack some clothes, then come back."

"Thank you," she replied, and we hugged again.

Everyone went to their own rooms while I went into mine and closed the door. I laid down on the bed, devastated. I couldn't accept that Tucker was dead. It didn't make sense, but I knew I had to accept it.

I desperately needed a drink, but there was no way I would leave the house tonight and drive to my apartment to get it. I knew Tucker had a stash in his room that he kept out of sight from his parents, out of respect. They knew he drank, but they didn't want to see it in the house. I got up and went into his room and opened the bottom door of his nightstand. I found a full bottle of Jack Daniels and grabbed it. I stood up and a wave of grief hit me without warning. I started to cry and did my best to be quiet so I didn't disturb the Pearsons. It was as if Tucker's presence was all around me, as long-forgotten memories relentlessly flickered through my mind. I reluctantly went to my room and closed the door behind me.

I drank half the bottle before falling asleep around midnight. That night, I didn't fear to have nightmares; I prayed for one. Any horror-filled dream would be better than accepting the reality that Tucker was gone.

. . .

The next three days were a blur to me. The last clear memory I had was calling headquarters to request three days off for bereavement. Everything else consisted of repetitive bouts of crying from all of us, followed by moments of normalcy. I remember a continuous flow of visitors who paid their respects, bringing both food and support. Tucker's girlfriend was overwhelmed. I was surprised to see Andre and Kim at the house because they had only met Tucker once, but I was glad they did.

The funeral was the hardest part for us all. The casket sitting above the grave. The American flag presented to Reen. The jolt that radiated through my body from the Marine Corps rifle salute. The finality of it all.

After the funeral and gathering, I had the impulse to leave the others so I could be alone. I changed my clothes, packed my bag, and brought it to the front door. Tracy was in her room with the door closed. Mr. Pearson and Reen were in the family room.

"Sir...ma'am, I'm going to head back to my apartment. Do you need me to do anything before I leave?" I asked.

"No sir, thank you. But are you gonna be all right?" Mr. Pearson asked.

"I'll hold it together. If you all need me just call. I'll come back over tomorrow."

They both stood up.

"Thank you Todd, for being here with us. We love you," Reen said and hugged me tightly. "You need time alone for yourself. Be safe while driving back."

Mr. Pearson hugged me and patted me on the back.

"Tracy is asleep in her room; we won't bother to wake her up," he said.

"Okay, goodbye," I replied.

I left the house and drove to my apartment. The sky was overcast and it began to sprinkle, but heavy rain was forecasted. Earlier, we were worried that the funeral might get rained on, but nature smiled on us and not a drop fell.

I pulled through the front gate just as lightning lit up the sky. The residents were prepared for the storm and I didn't see anyone outside. I went to my apartment, straight to the kitchen, and drank a double shot of Scotch. I changed into jeans and a T-shirt, then grabbed the bottle off the counter and sat in the recliner.

I started my ritual with my music playlist and pulled up our group picture. I drank and stared at the team photo, transporting myself back in time and bringing my squad back to life in my mind. We were just some guys trying to survive and make it back home alive, but accepting that if we couldn't make it back then we were honored to die together.

I turned up the bottle and drank long and hard, letting the sour whiskey burn through to my gut. Memories of each squad member rotated in my brain. A smile, a laugh, a fart during roll call, they all brought me to tears and laughter.

I lifted the bottle again to quicken my arrival to unconsciousness, but it was slow-going getting there. The combination of pain, rage, and guilt kept me awake. It's impossible to sleep when you're being tortured or torturing yourself. I laughed and cried for hours, and then the laughter stopped, leaving only grief.

I went to drink again from the bottle, but it was empty, so I stumbled to the counter and opened the second bottle. This time, I poured some on the floor first, then lifted it in the air.

"For my brothers who ain't here!" I shouted and then drank.

I slumped down on a kitchen chair. Something needed to change. I was alone, the last one alive. There was still Angie. I reached for my cell phone and dialed her phone number. It wasn't midnight yet, but it was late for her. I didn't give a damn if she got mad. She hadn't returned any of my calls from the last few days. I refused to send her news of my best friend's death by text. Hell no. But I needed to hear her voice, even if she was fussing at me. I could always blame it on being drunk.

The phone rang a few times until her voicemail answered. I ended the call and tossed the phone across the table. I was restless and needed something new to occupy my attention. I unpacked my bag and found my pistol. I brought it back to the table, dropped the clip, and checked the action a few times. I replaced the clip and put one in the chamber. I always carried it that way, locked and loaded. Always faithful. Always loyal. Semper Fi.

I raised the bottle again and decided I had enough. The rain began pouring down in buckets as the roof rumbled.

I put the gun to my head and wondered, *Why was everyone dead except me? I'm here, and they're...wherever.* But it didn't feel like this was the way their lives were meant to end. I was comforted to know that I was still in control and could simply pull the trigger and instantly be where they were. That would be easy.

The sound of thunder brought me back to reality as I thought about the rain. I felt numb and imagined the cold rain hitting me in the face and reviving me. I stood, put the pistol in my waistband, and stumbled out the front door. Somehow, I blundered down the steps to the bottom landing without falling. The parking lot lights were made dim by the pouring rain and it drew me closer. I stepped out from under the building and was instantly soaked by the downpour.

I held my arms out and faced the sky while water pelted my face. I was thankful for my life, but I didn't want to live this way anymore. It was time to say goodbye to this world and rejoin my squad. I had done my best, so I lowered my arms and turned to go upstairs. I heard someone yelling from across the parking lot.

"What you doing, bitch? Singing in the rain? Stupid ass!"

I turned back around and peered through the downpour. It looked, and sounded, like Derek Stephens, standing across the parking lot in the opposite breezeway.

"You look like you saw a ghost. You look scared as shit. I should come over there and beat your ass right now! You thought they could keep me locked down? Wrong!" he yelled.

I didn't say anything, but it was clear to me what needed to be done.

"Like I told you before, white boy, I'm gonna be here long after your ass is gone. Eviction my ass! I promise you, next time they won't miss!"

He started howling.

I turned around, reached inside my waistband and pulled out my pistol, but faced him with the gun behind my back and slowly began walking toward him.

"Oh shit! You want some? I'm gonna break your goddamn jaw white boy! Bring your ass over and get some of this!" he shouted.

My destiny was manifest now. I would finally join Tucker, Jay, and Tom, but only after I killed this last enemy combatant. He wasn't a civilian, he was a terrorist, wreaking havoc on the community. I knew this man must die. I stepped onto the parking lot and stopped about seven meters from him. At this range he couldn't escape. He stood in the breezeway nodding his head, before stepping forward into the rain, ignorant of his fate. I relaxed and exhaled just before pointing and aiming.

"Mr. Todd! Mr. Todd!" I heard a woman's voice call out from behind me. "Please, I need help!"

I turned my head and looked through the rain to see Ms. Pearl at her door. She was waving at me to come.

"Please hurry!" she yelled.

I lost all sense of focus and intention. I glanced at Derrick but started walking toward Ms. Pearl, putting my pistol back into my waistband under my shirt.

"Oh! You scared now, punk? You better walk away! Anytime you want some, you know where I'll be!" he yelled out, never knowing he'd only had a few moments longer to live.

I decided I would help Ms. Pearl then come back and complete the mission. She stepped back inside and held the door open for me. I stumbled inside and she quickly closed and locked the door behind me.

"What's wrong?" I babbled.

"Give it to me," she said, holding out her palm.

"Give you what?"

"Don't you raise your voice in here boy, the children are sleeping. I said, give it to me. You know what I'm talking about." She stepped closer, her palm nearly touching me.

"I don't know what you're talking about. If nothing ain't wrong, I got something to do!" I yelled.

"Shh! I told you to keep your voice down. You're not going nowhere. I ain't gonna tell you again, give me that pistol. I'm gonna put it up for you." She jerked up the front of my shirt and almost managed to pull the gun out. I jumped back.

"Stop! No!" I yelled and staggered toward the door, but she scurried past me and blocked it. She grabbed for the gun again and caught hold of it, but I snatched it from her and held it by my side.

"Enough of this shit! Move out of my goddamn way!" I yelled.

Without warning, she slapped me across my mouth, leaving me stunned and shocked. I felt rage overtake me as I leaned over her and screamed.

She slapped me across my mouth again, even harder.

"Fool! What's wrong with you! In the name of Jesus, I rebuke your murderous spirit! Come out of him!" she screeched.

I didn't understand what she was talking about, but her second slap woke me out of the fog I had been in. I felt embarrassed and ashamed, wondering why I was yelling at this old woman.

"Now give it to me," she demanded.

I slowly raised my arm and she took the gun from me.

"Thank you! Now sit down on the couch and take your shoes off. I'm gonna bring you a blanket and pillow. I'll put this up for you. You can have it back in the morning." She left and came back with the linens. "I thought I told you to take off your shoes. You ain't putting them on my couch, now take them off."

No matter how much I struggled to resist her demands, I was helpless. Her words seemed to put me in a trance. I took off my shoes and sat there, looking at the floor as a child would. She set the pillow and blanket on the couch and put her hand on my shoulder.

"Do you want to tell me what's wrong?" she asked quietly, rubbing my shoulder.

I shook my head, knowing there was no way to explain what even I couldn't understand. I looked up at her through tear-filled eyes.

"Everything Ms. Pearl."

She started humming one of her church songs and kept rubbing my back. I dropped my head and started sobbing. I didn't hold back. I released everything.

"Yes Lord, bless him. Bless him!" she shouted.

We stayed like that until I began feeling sick.

"I need to lay down. I don't feel so good," I moaned.

"You're drunk. You need to sleep the liquor out of you. That's an easy way for the devil to get into your mind. You would do best to cut that out. Now go on and stretch out."

I laid along the couch on my back and closed my eyes as she put the blanket over me. I heard her turn off the lights and walk away.

"Ms. Pearl…" I slurred, feeling more nauseous with each word.

"Hmm?"

"Sorry I yelled and cussed."

"You know better next time. Good night," she replied.

Despite the chaos and grief going on around me, I felt at peace in her home as I fell asleep on her plastic-covered couch.

• • •

I woke up to the faint sound of gospel music and the smell of bacon. I lay on the couch with my eyes closed, reluctant to open them and face the inevitable embarrassment from my actions the night before. I didn't remember much, but I knew that besides disrespecting Ms. Pearl, I had almost committed a murder-suicide. It was hard to accept, but my pathetic condition was staring me in the face. How could I recover from this and make sure it never happened again? I could never let this happen again! But, honestly, how could I stop it?

Maybe not tonight or tomorrow, but someday this would happen again. I had to find a way to keep my life together. If the NYSP had sent my reporting date out by now, I could've been out of here months ago and none of this would've happened!

I heard a little girls voice. "Mr. Todd! Grandma said to wake up and come eat breakfast!"

I opened my eyes and saw two girls and a small boy. They stared at me with a puzzled look. I sat up.

"Hey, kids. Thanks," I mumbled in a hoarse voice. I stood up and walked to the kitchen where Ms. Pearl was putting food on the plates. "Good morning," I said.

"Good morning. Go and wash your hands and sit down at the table."

"Yes ma'am." I went to the bathroom, washed my hands, and rinsed my face. It was 7 AM, but it might as well have been midnight because I had no sense of time.

We all sat down and ate breakfast together quietly. When we were finished, the children cleared the table and went into the living room, leaving Ms. Pearl and myself alone.

"Ms. Pearl, thank you for breakfast and uh…looking out for me last night. I apologize for being disrespectful," I said.

"I forgive you. It wasn't you; it was the demon inside you that had you talking crazy like that and blaspheming. That's why the Lord sent you here, so I could get that devil out of you. I'm going to keep praying for you, but you need to pray for yourself too. You need to be going to church."

I didn't pay attention to all her religious talk about demons and all that, but I appreciated that she helped me and saved two lives last night.

"Yes ma'am, but I have to leave now," I said.

"All right, you have a good day and let me know if you want to go to church with me this Sunday."

"Uh, Ms. Pearl, I need my pistol back."

"What do you need that for? That ain't gonna do nothing but cause you trouble," she said, shaking her head.

"Ms. Pearl, it belongs to me and I need it back. I won't do anything stupid like last night. I'm going to straighten up, I promise."

"I ain't gonna steal from you, it belongs to you. Just don't you be a fool," she said and walked away. She came back with the pistol, wrapped in a plastic shopping bag and gave it to me, then walked me out.

"'Bye!" She said and closed the door.

I looked across the parking lot where Derrick Stephens had stood, and the memories of the near-tragedy became more apparent to me. I walked upstairs to my apartment. The lights were still on and the window blinds open, so I turned them off and closed the window blinds to darken the room.

I went to my room and set the gun on my dresser before I laid down. I was exhausted and hungover. There was work that needed to be done today, which would keep me busy and my mind occupied. However, I had a dark, nagging feeling of dread in the pit of my stomach, and it wouldn't go away. It had started the moment Tucker died and got worse every day. I decided I couldn't work today, there was no way. My head felt like it was going to explode and I had pain shooting through my chest. I started to worry.

I changed my clothes and left in a hurry. It was too much for me. I felt like I was slowly drowning alone. I needed to get to Tucker's house and be with his family; they were the family I wished I had. I started the car and began to leave when I noticed William walking with the other guys, flagging me down. I rolled down my window and William extended his hand through the window.

"I'm sorry to hear about your friend. My condolences to you and his family," he said. Eugene and Andre did the same. I could barely fight back my tears as their sincere concern struck a chord in me.

"Thank you guys, thank you. I'm sick today and won't be working. William, you're in charge. See y'all later," I said.

"Don't worry, we'll hold down the fort. Take your time, handle your business," William said. I nodded and drove off.

• • •

The kitchen was empty and quiet when I arrived. I walked into the family room and saw Henry and Reen sitting together, watching television. Reen turned around to look.

"Hello dear, come on in and join us," she said.

"Todd. Come on in son. Have a seat."

I walked over and bent down to hug them both, then sat beside Reen.

"How are you doing?" He asked.

I didn't know how to answer him. I couldn't tell him the truth. It would shock them both. They were going through enough.

"I'm trying to hang in there," I said. "Where's little sis at?"

"She's over her friend's house trying to get over this loss," Reen answered.

"Yep, everybody grieves in their own way and in their own time. We all need our own space, to be alone and deal with it," he said. "You know the saying 'time heals all wounds'? Well that's true, but there's a second part to that saying that I found: 'but the wounds leave scars, so one can forget that time.' Now that's the truth."

His words triggered a flood of grief inside me and I broke down in tears. I hated being like this! I hated showing weakness! But it didn't matter what I thought or wanted; the grief was smothering me. Reen put her arms around me and pulled me to her. I even felt guilt that she was consoling me when I should be comforting her! I had to calm down. It was best to be alone right now.

I sat up and wiped the tears from my eyes.

"I miss him," I said.

"We all do son. There's nothing wrong with that. It means you love him," Henry said.

"Amen," Reen replied.

We sat there a few minutes more before I became restless and needed to move.

"I'm going to lay down for a while if you don't mind. I didn't sleep well last night."

"Mind? Todd, you are family to us. Not 'like' family, family. That's your room. We'll be here; you get some rest. We might take a nap shortly ourselves," he replied.

I went to my room and laid down. Lying in bed next to Tuck's room was bittersweet. There was comfort from being near, but the closer I got, the more I missed him.

My eyes were tired and I dozed off for a little while, but when I woke, I had an undeniable urge to have a drink. Just one to get me by. I stepped out of my room and down the hallway to see if Reen and Henry were still in the family room. It was empty and their bedroom door was closed, so they probably were taking a nap.

I went to Tucker's room and closed the door, hoping he had more liquor stashed somewhere. I searched through his other nightstand, his hutch, and inside his closet, but there was nothing. Suddenly I realized what I was doing and what I had become. I fell onto his bed, wailing.

"Tuck! Man! Help me, bro! Tell me what to do man!" I groaned and clutched his pillow.

Eventually I opened my eyes and was blinded by a ray of sunlight. I lay still. Tucker's picture on the nightstand came into view as I blinked and wiped the tears from my eyes. I could almost hear his voice, whisper trying to tell me something. I felt like I was in a comforting dream or trance; I didn't stop to question this moment.

A wrinkled piece of paper beside the picture came into focus and I picked it up.

It was the business card of his therapist, Josh, the one I had crumpled up and thrown away in my trash can. Tucker knew about it but hadn't said anything to me. I stared at Tucker's picture and I understood.

"Roger that Tuck. I copy," I said to him and rolled onto my back, took out my cell phone and dialed the number.

I decided at that moment that *this* was going to be my last mission. Whether I lived or died, there would be no retreat and no surrender.

CHAPTER THIRTEEN

HOME SWEET HOME

(Three months later)

It was Monday morning, and I woke up at 5:55 AM, just before my alarm was set to go off. I used the next five minutes to set my intentions for the day by meditating and beginning with a positive attitude. Today was a brand new day. I didn't worry about what occurred yesterday or what might happen tomorrow; my focus was on the present and staying in the moment.

I got out of bed, went to the bathroom, then began my daily exercise routine of stretching and pedaling thirty minutes on my exercise bike. I moved to push-ups, dumbbell work, and pull-ups before jumping in the shower. It felt great to be alive as I hung my head down to allow the warm water to massage my neck.

I had traveled a long way to appreciate this moment, but the tough times were worth it. It had taken every ounce of strength for me to face myself and dare to push through the façade that was Todd Goodson and honestly accept who I was as a person, and not who or what I portrayed myself to be. Most of my life had been spent on being who my father wanted me to be, a reflection of himself. Even though he sowed the seeds of racism and homophobia within me, I couldn't blame him. Who and what I had become was my sole responsibility and I admitted it.

The call to Josh Eshelman at the VA Hospital was the best decision of my tumultuous life because it was the day my new life began. He talked to me for an hour on the phone that day and then came over to the house and picked me up. Henry and Reen were surprised to see him, but thankful I had decided to reach out to someone for help.

They had sensed my desperation in trying to deal with Tucker's death and stood together at the front door in tears as Josh and I drove off.

After divulging to Josh the details of my near-fatal intentions, he recommended, and I consented, to be placed on a 24-hour psychiatric hold for observation. As my road to mental and physical recovery began, it was no surprise to be diagnosed with extreme Post Traumatic Stress Disorder and depression.

After submitting FMLA paperwork from the doctor to corporate headquarters, my request was approved for two weeks of medical leave, which was the amount of time needed to complete stage one of intense substance abuse therapy.

After achieving that first goal, I returned to work.

It was emotionally challenging as Thanksgiving and Christmas rolled around without Tucker. We had spent many holidays together overseas and his absence bothered me. To deal with that, the doctor prescribed a low dosage of anti-anxiety medication to help stabilize my mood and impulsive behavior, with the future goal of eventually weaning me off them completely.

Initially, Josh and I began my recovery plan with three therapy sessions a week for the first month, then it dropped to two, and now we were down to once per week. All of this was in conjunction with a veteran's support group, which I continued to attend twice a week. Every minute of time and energy that I put toward the program paid dividends, and I felt almost born-again.

I didn't feel the need to tell Angie the extent of my rehabilitation. To her knowledge, I was already supposed to be in counseling, so there was no need to hit the hornet's nest.

I got out of the shower, brushed my teeth, and got dressed. After cooking and eating a spinach omelet, I left for the office. The March air was warming up quickly, and spring was definitely around the corner as I opened the office and started the coffee. I still had an hour before the workday began, but I liked to walk to the school bus stop and wait with the kids. It became another routine I had adopted. It was little things like that which made a big difference for the kids and me. Besides making sure that there would be no bullying or fighting, it was a choice that made me feel happy, so it was a double win.

There were usually three or four parents who would wait with me. The morning conversations we engaged in gave me an understanding of how things were going in the community from their perspective, which in turn helped me to be more proactive and nip any resident concerns in the bud.

The bus arrived and we waved the children off to school. I returned to the office and prepared my Monday morning report.

My occupancy rate was excellent and my budget was in the black once again. Ms. Stephen's and her family had been evicted last month, and the apartment renovated and leased to another family. As for her son, Derek Stephens, he had his own problems to deal with. He was arrested again, but this time he was refused bail.

Fortunately, my video footage from the night of the drive-by shooting led to the arrest of three other gang members, who in turn snitched on Derek and were going to testify against him. Facing fifteen years in prison for conspiracy to commit murder, he opted to plead guilty to a lesser charge in hopes of a reduced sentence. He wasn't coming back anytime soon. Three months ago, I would have been happy to hear that news, but not now. I felt relieved that I didn't have to deal with him again, but there was no joy in knowing that another mother had lost her son. In Derek's case, the prison was his intervention and hopefully he would hear the wake-up call. It was disturbing to know she wasn't the only mother living at Shady Meadows whose children were waist-deep in the gang and drug life. The single redeeming aspect to me was that she had other sons, and that maybe they would learn from their big brother's situation and choose to walk down a different path. In the end, it was their responsibility and, just like me or any other person, they had to accept the consequences for their actions.

The office phone rang.

"Hello, thank you for calling Shady Meadows, this is Todd Goodson. How may I help you?"

"Good morning Mr. Goodson," Sherika said.

"Good morning Mrs. Taylor. How are you?"

"I'm fine, thank you. How are you?" she asked.

"I'm fine ma'am, thank you!"

"Ma'am? Todd! You're making me feel old! You know better than to call me that," she replied, laughing.

"Okay! I'm fine boss lady! Now, what do you want?"

"All right, now don't run out. Don't let me have to write you a reprimand for disrespect," she laughed.

"No ma'am! Uh, I mean, please no, Sherika!"

We both laughed, which was always the best way to start the workday.

"I wanted to call you because I just received an email from the licensing division and was notified that you have passed the property manager's licensing test successfully. Congratulations!"

Her news caught me by surprise. I had forgotten about taking the test with everything else going on. I didn't need the license but had studied for it anyway. It was an excellent short-term goal that I knew was attainable, besides occupying my time. Idle time was something I needed to avoid so I could become more productive, and less time sitting around stagnating. Life was short and the next minute wasn't guaranteed, so maximizing every day became my priority.

"Cool! I hadn't checked all my emails yet but I'll look for it. Thanks for letting me know," I replied.

"This calls for a celebration. Pick a day and I'll drive down there and take you to lunch. You can pick the place. My treat!"

"That sounds good, thanks. Let me check my schedule and I'll get back with you this week."

"Good. How is everything else going down that way? The reports have been looking great," she said.

"All is good. We are making steady progress on the renovation schedule. The staff is happy and Andre is working out really well. Besides that, same ole Meadows, you know," I replied.

"Same old Meadows? No, I don't think so. Shady Meadows has made a 180-degree turnaround under your management, so don't sell yourself short. I still remember the first few weeks after you started there. I have to admit I had my doubts and you can't blame me for that. You were a mess! But you got yourself together and handled your business, and now it shows. You should be proud."

"I wouldn't have made it without everyone's help. You, the team, and everyone in the community who helped with the vision deserves to be proud," I replied.

"Yes, we are proud, but you should be too."

"I'm happy and grateful that everything is working out for the best," I said.

"Awesome! Okay, I'll let you go and get back to work," she replied.

"Talk to you later. Goodbye."

We ended the call and a few minutes later I submitted my report. The front door opened and the guys walked in.

"Morning," William said, followed by Eugene and Andre.

"Good morning fellas. How is everybody?" I asked.

"Tired. Wifey woke up at three o'clock this morning wanting to renew our wedding vows. I don't know if it's her hormones or what, but she's killing me. Boss, she wants it all the time. I'm shriveling up, no matter how much water I drink," Eugene said.

I smirked at him.

"You say that like it's a bad thing. If you weren't getting enough, you'd be complaining; you get too much, and you still complain. Man, you better tighten up and get you some of the little blue pills to keep up with her," I replied. William patted him on the back.

"Wow Eugene, I'm sorry you got so many problems. Take Todd's advice; Keep it up and while you're at it, shut the hell up. Nobody wants to hear you complaining about getting too much loving!"

Will shook his head in disgust and Andre and I couldn't stop laughing.

"Eugene, if you want, I can give you some tips," Andre said.

"Boy! You ain't even twenty years old yet! When I was your age, I was rocking the boat too, just like you! Don't get it twisted!" Eugene replied as we all burst out in laughter.

"All right guys, you're killing me this morning. Coffee is ready and daylight is burning. Let's earn our paychecks," I said.

They all filled their cups and left, but Andre came back.

"Mr. Todd, do you have a minute? I need to talk to you about something," Andre asked.

"Sure, sit down. What's up?"

He was smiling but looked uncomfortable as he sat down.

"Sir, I really appreciate you hiring me for this job. Mr. William and Mr. Eugene have taught me a lot about maintenance. It's like they opened my mind to another world of how things work. So, I thank y'all for the opportunity." He lowered his head. "Do you remember when I needed to take the day off from work last month and go to the doctor with Kim and the baby?" he asked.

I thought and barely remembered it.

"Yeah, and?"

He raised his head.

"Well, that was a lie, and I apologize. Actually, I had an appointment to take the ASVAB exam for the military. I wasn't sure if I was gonna pass it, so I kept it quiet and didn't tell anyone. Well, I found out that I passed! Mr. William and Mr. Eugene know, but I made them promise not to tell you. So I'm letting you know that I'm joining. I leave for basic training in July."

Andre was stoic. His transition to manhood was obvious, as well as his boldness, both marked by this monumental decision. I stood up and put my hands on my hips.

"What branch of the military?" I asked.

He also stood.

"The United States Marine Corps," he replied.

At first, his answer broke my heart as I wondered why? He could have chosen any other branch of service, but he wanted the Devil Dogs. Why? I tried to find the right words to encourage him, which led to an uncomfortable silence. His eyes widened as he stepped up to the desk.

"After I met Tucker, even just that one time, I looked at everything differently. When I went to the funeral, I knew what I wanted to do. I've seen it happen in the movies, but never thought that I would meet a real-life hero. All the stuff he did, fighting for our country, and even after he came home all messed up, he still acted like a Marine. Look, it's a done deal for me. Kim is with me on this and this is what I want to do. I thought you would be happy for me," he said.

He had made his choice and his words resonated with me. I walked around my desk and shook his hand, then pulled him close and patted his back.

"Congratulations future Marine. Remember to be always faithful. I support you."

He drew back from me grinning.

"Semper Fi. Yeah, for sure. All right then, let me get to work," he said and left.

I sat back down and took it all in. I was happy Andre was going to fulfill his dreams, but from the moment he told me, I became deeply concerned about his well-being. After growing to care for him like he was my kid brother, I had to accept that these were the feelings that came with it. My cell phone rang. It was Angie!

"Hello babe! What's up?" I asked.

"Sweetie! The letter just came from the academy! I opened it and you are to report in three weeks, on March 25th! Oh my god!" she screamed.

I dropped into my chair.

"Oh my god! Yes!" I shouted at the top of my lungs. "I can't believe it! It's about time!"

"Check your personal email too! Oh baby, finally!" she moaned. "I can book a ticket for you tonight and get you back here in one or two days."

"No don't do that, I need to give my two weeks' notice first. Besides, I planned to buy a truck down here after I got the reporting date. Everything is cheaper down here, price, taxes, everything. After I buy the truck, I'm giving Tucker's old car back to his folks. They can keep it or sell it. Don't worry about booking a flight, I plan to drive back."

"What?" she asked. I could tell by the tone of her voice that she was irritated. "Screw the two-week notice! You don't owe them anything! Okay, the truck idea is smart because we can save thousands if you buy one from down there, but just do it today. I want you here as soon as possible. Sweetheart, I miss you so much," she pleaded.

"Listen, I'll give my notice now and look for a truck. It will take me a week to really shop around, giving me one more week before I would leave anyway. What's one more week? Besides, a two-week notice will give Sherika enough time to find a replacement," I replied.

"Sherika? What kind of ghetto ass name is that? That's your boss now? Whatever happened to the other guy?" she asked.

"It's a long story, but yes, she's the district manager. Anyway, I'm happy about the news, babe. Where are you?"

"I took today off work. Don't try to change the subject. I told you what I want, so you need to think about it. Think really hard about it," she said.

"Okay, I'll talk to you later," I replied.

I ended the call, then jumped up and pumped my fist like a cheap Tiger Woods imitation. I couldn't believe the day had finally come. I called Sherika and let her know, and then radioed the guys to come back to the office and told them. Everyone was happy to hear the news.

Later, I became sick with truck fever and began searching local truck dealerships online. What would it be? Dodge, Chevy, Ford, or Toyota? No longer would I have to wait next to a full-sized truck at traffic lights and be suffocated by its exhaust fumes. There was no shortage of deals for new or certified pre-owned vehicles on the web, and for two hours, I sat in front of the computer like a little kid in a candy store, mouth drooling and mesmerized. Ultimately, I chose the perfect pre-owned truck and went with Dodge. It was noon so I shut down my computer and went to lunch.

• • •

I walked into the Waffle House and sat in my regular booth, waiting on Lisa to get free. A minute later, she walked over to my table, smiling.

"Hey Todd, your regular order?" she asked.

"Yes, thanks. By the way, I have some breaking news for you. I got my reporting date from the NYSP. I start in three weeks." I said, smiling.

"Wow, that's a shock. I had forgotten about you leaving. I'm happy for you," she said, before walking behind the counter.

Ten minutes later, she returned with my order.

"Here you go," she said and walked away.

"Lisa," I called, but she hurried into the kitchen. She was acting weird today, maybe on her menstrual? Probably. But I was still excited about the news and looking forward to a new truck. I scarfed down my meal like a recruit in boot camp, before sitting back to let the swelling in my belly subside. Lisa still wouldn't talk to me. Most times, she would sit down across from me and chat for a minute, and the diner wasn't very busy today.

Finally, I caught her attention and hailed her down for the bill, and she came over to cash me out.

"Thank you and have a nice day," she said and headed toward the register.

This pissed me off. We had known each other for almost eight months and I had never seen her act this way toward me. I remained in the booth and stared at her until I got her attention and called her back over.

"What's wrong with you, Lisa? What's with the cold shoulder?" I asked.

"You tell me. You walk in here after almost a year of us knowing each other and tell me you're leaving in a few weeks. What, that's not supposed to affect me? Please!" She answered with attitude, holding her hips.

"I don't understand. You knew I was waiting and would be leaving one day, so why are you treating me like this?" I asked.

"You're right. I shouldn't be treating a customer this way. I apologize, *sir*! Is there anything else?"

I sat quietly while looking into her eyes, until the right words came to me.

"Lisa, you are a beautiful woman. You're intelligent, funny, independent, but most of all, you have a loving heart. You're always giving to others and you don't complain about much. Any man you choose to be with would be lucky. He'll have hit the lottery. Even if it was me. But I have someone who's waiting on me to come back to them. None of that matters when it comes to how much you have meant to me as a friend. You were the only person who had the time to listen to me, even if only for a few minutes. Lisa, you mean the world to me."

Her expression and posture changed as her hands went behind her back, and she sighed.

"I'm acting like a spoiled child. I'm sorry. I'll miss you coming in here every other day, telling corny jokes and all that. But most of all, I'll miss the way you look at me and ask me how I'm doing. because you really want to know."

As tears filled her eyes, I grabbed her arm.

"Hey Lisa. I'm gonna miss you too."

I stood up and hugged her and opened my eyes to see the cook spying on us, before looking away at his grill.

"I have to get back to the office, but I'll be back again before I leave town. Let's not get all mopey and sad, okay?" I smiled.

She looked at me and laughed.

"All right Todd. Drive safe. 'Bye."

I drove back to work and considered calling Henry and Reen to tell them the news but decided it could wait until I got to the house after work. I saw Chavis checking for mail as I parked in front of the office.

"Hey Chavis, what's up?"

"Nothing much Mr. Todd. Just getting the mail for my mom," he replied.

"I was wondering if you'd bought a car yet?" I asked.

"No sir. I probably got like three, maybe four months left to save."

"Okay cool. Pretty soon you will be rolling," I replied.

"I hope so."

We shook hands and I went back to work. Time was flying by and minutes seemed like seconds. A few months ago, I would have been craving a drink after work, but not now. The thought alone nauseated me.

When it was time to clock out, I locked up the office and drove to see Henry and Reen; Tracy too, if she was there.

Thirty minutes later, I pulled into the driveway. Henry was cutting the front lawn on his riding lawn mower, while Reen sat in a chair under a shade tree. I walked over to her as she called out.

"Tracy! Come out front! Todd is here!" She looked at me. "How are you, dear?"

"I'm doing good," I replied as Tracy came out of the house. We met on the front steps and hugged. "Hey little sis, what have you been up to?" I asked.

"I've been doing good. I finished moving to campus and have started all my classes. I came home today to visit mom and dad and I'm so glad to see you!" She hugged me again.

I heard the lawn tractor shut down and Henry climbed off and walked over to us.

"Hey there bubba! What are you doing around these parts?"

We shook hands.

"I came by to let you all know that I finally got my reporting date for the academy. I leave in three weeks."

"Oh! That's great news Todd! I'm so happy for you!" Reen said as she grabbed my arm. Henry pushed back his glasses.

"Well congratulations son!" he said.

"Thank you sir," I replied and looked at Tracy.

"Oh that's good," she said, and walked back into the house.

I looked at Henry and Reen. "Did I miss something?"

"She doesn't want you to go. In her eyes, she's losing another big brother," Reen replied.

"That sounds about right," Henry added.

"I'll be right back," I said before going to find her. She was in her bedroom with the door closed, so I knocked.

"Tracy?"

A few moments later, she responded. "It's not locked."

I walked in and sat down on the bed next to her and kept quiet, waiting for her to speak when she was ready.

"I'm sorry for acting like this Todd. I had hoped that you wouldn't leave, but I knew better. You have to live your own life. It's not fair to want to keep you here for myself. That's selfish on my part."

I put my arm around her. "I'm sorry sis. But I promise to stay in touch and come back and visit one day. Until then, we're gonna be doing a lot of facetime and texting. You'll see, it'll be like I'm right around the corner."

"You better call me!"

"I will. I promise."

I gave her a firm hug and she walked me back outside to Henry and Reen.

"I see y'all done got it all straightened out," he said.

"Roger that," I replied.

"Good! None of us need to shed any more tears than we already have. I'm surprised we haven't caused a second flood by now!" he joked, as we all said our goodbyes.

I stayed a few more minutes before driving back to Shady Meadows. When I got back, I changed my clothes and began exercising. The day had gone well, but I started feeling my anxiety level rise for some reason. I worked my body to exhaustion to ward off the impulses of the past. Those days of self-medicating and getting wasted were over and I wasn't going back.

• • •

The following week was a blur. Sherika had her new assistant design farewell party flyers for my last day of work, with Eugene and Andre putting them on all the residents' doors. I told her it wasn't necessary, but she insisted on having a party in the community room for me. She was my boss; how could I refuse? I invited Henry, Reen, and Tracy, as well as Lisa. Everyone but Tracy said they were able to come. She was going to be at Spring Break.

On Friday afternoon, I got off the phone with the sales manager at the car dealership after making the final arrangements for my truck. I took my car title out of my desk and locked up the office. I went across the property, past the playground, over to unit 414, and knocked on the door. A woman answered.

"Hello Ms. Harper. Is Chavis home?" I asked.

"Hi Todd. Yes he is. Come inside. Is something wrong?" she asked.

"No ma'am. I want to ask him for a favor."

"Okay." She smiled. "Chavis! Come here!" she shouted. He came down the hallway with a puzzled expression.

"Hey Mr. Todd. What's going on?"

"Chavis, I need a favor from you. I need someone to take me to the car dealership so I can buy a truck. You can drive my car and drop me off. The only thing is, I won't need the car anymore and was wondering if you might take it off my hands. It sure would help me out a lot."

He frowned and cocked his head. "What do you mean by 'take' it off your hands? You want me to buy it from you? How much do you want for it?"

"I'm not selling it to you, it's free. Just take it off my hands," I replied and showed him the title. "Here's the title. I've already signed it. You just need to date it and have your mother sign as a witness." I looked at her.

She nodded and looked at him. "The man is giving you a car for free. It's a blessing. What do you say?"

Chavis rubbed his head as his eyes began watering.

"Why you doing this for me?" His voice trembled.

"Why not you Chavis? You're as good as any other person I know and you stand up for yourself. I'll tell you like the former owner told me: freely I receive and freely I give. So, are you gonna help me out or what?"

He walked up to me and shook my hand.

"Thank you," he said. "Let me get my shoes on."

He ran down the hall.

"Thank you!" Ms. Harper said before she walked over and hugged me.

Chavis came back, and we signed over the title at the kitchen table. He held it up and smiled.

"You just helped me get my own apartment. Now I have extra funds for school and can get furniture for an apartment. Thank you Jesus," he said.

"Great. We need to be going. Are you ready?"

"Yes sir," he replied, and we left.

• • •

Two hours later, I pulled into my parking space in a new Dodge Ram truck. I jumped down and walked to my apartment, passing some children playing.

"Mr. Todd, is that your truck?" a little girl asked.

"Yes ma'am, it is!"

"It's nice," she replied.

"Thank you little lady," I said and walked upstairs.

I called my mom and Herman and told them about the academy and my new vehicle. They were excited for me, of course. After we finished talking, I checked my voicemail, hoping my dad had left a message. It had been over three months since we last spoke. I decided to call him, regardless of the ultimatum I gave him. The call went to his voicemail and I hadn't intended to leave a message, but I did anyway. Screw the ultimatum, this was my dad.

"Hello Dad, this is Todd. I was calling to check on you. Call me back when you get a chance." I hesitated for a moment. "I love you Dad. 'Bye," I added, and ended the call.

• • •

The next week kept me busy. I said farewell to my support group and called Josh to let him know I would be leaving. He gave me information for several support groups within the state of New York.

I stopped by the Waffle House and Lisa gave me an awesome going away present. It was a gold-plated bracelet that displayed the acronyms, POW and MIA with the words 'Never Forgotten' in between. She gave it to me along with a hug, and let me know that she wouldn't be able to come to the party. I wanted to know the reason, but I didn't ask. We both knew why. Had things been different, we could have been a couple. She was perfect for me.

The day of my departure, I went to Tucker's grave and paid my respects, since it might be a while before I could come back. I knelt at his grave in silence and promised myself I wouldn't cry, but should have known not to make promises that I couldn't keep. I cried like a baby anyway. I wasn't crying out of guilt or anguish anymore. I cried because I missed my buddy.

"I know you're not down there in the ground. I just wanted to tell you that I'm doing good Tuck. You don't have to worry about me anymore."

They were the only words I could utter.

I slowly picked myself up and walked to my car. There were only a few hours left in the day before I would be on the road back home.

Everything I was going to take was packed up and loaded on my truck. I left the rest of the furniture for William and Eugene to distribute since they knew people who could use it.

I got back to the office and noticed the residents were already bringing food into the community room. I knew there was a committee Sherika had organized, and they weren't wasting any time setting up. I decided to take a break and check back later when the party was close to starting.

While taking a nap, my phone rang. It was Angie.

"Hello babe, what's up?" I asked.

"Hey sweetie! Real quick, I found two amazing houses upstate that are a complete steal! I don't want to lose them, so I'm signing a contract to hold both of them. I'm emailing you the listings, so let me know which one you like best. I'm going to tell you right now that I like the first one, but let me know what you like anyway," she said.

"Okay babe. I'll take a look at them. But shouldn't we wait until I actually graduate and begin working first before we start looking at houses?"

There was silence, which told me a storm was brewing.

"You know, it's just like you to rain on my parade. I'm just sending you the goddamn listings Todd, for Christ's sake, don't be so negative."

"You're right. I apologize sweetheart. I'll look at them in a minute. I'll see you tomorrow afternoon anyway. I'll be leaving here and hitting the road in a few hours. It's all good," I replied. "I love you."

"You too! Drive safe! 'Bye!" She ended the call and I went back to sleep.

• • •

I woke up to someone knocking at my front door. I checked the time. It was already six o'clock! I jumped up and rushed to the front door to find William and Andre standing there.

"Boy, what are you doing? Everybody is waiting for you at your party! You got other guests that came too. Come on now, tighten up short-timer!" William barked.

"Man, I took a nap. Damn, I was in a deep sleep. My bad. Let me get my phone and turn off the lights," I replied and gathered my things.

I turned off the last light switch and locked the door, then took all the access keys off my ring and handed them to William.

"Here you go man. Thanks for everything William. I never would have made it without you bro," I said.

"You just make sure to keep in touch. Give the old man a call sometime," he replied.

We shook hands, then I looked at Andre.

"And you? I'm gonna keep close tabs on you until you raise your right hand, you hear me?" I said.

"Yes sir," he replied, chuckling.

"Let's go the party," I said.

We walked down the stairs and toward the community room. The parking lot was full, which was odd to me. I had never seen it that packed. As we approached, I saw a large group of residents talking outside and heard music playing inside. It was beginning to look like a party. I stepped inside and was greeted by people I knew, but also some strangers. I bent down and hugged Ms. Pearl, who I had mistakenly passed by without seeing until she tugged on my back pocket and got my attention. Reen and Henry were there, and I eventually made my way over to them.

"I appreciate you both coming. I laid down earlier to take a nap and just woke up ten minutes ago," I laughed.

"We haven't been out to a shin-dig in years. Glad to come and see you off!" Henry yelled over the music. "You will be keeping in touch with us, right?"

"Yes sir! Don't worry!" I replied.

"The music is so loud," Reen said.

I looked around and saw Eugene and motioned him to bring the sound down, while Sherika came up and hugged me.

"We want you to say a few words, and then the children want to present you with something they made," she said.

I excused myself and followed her to the front of the room. The music was turned off as Sherika quieted the room.

"Okay everybody, the guest of honor is here now and would like to say a few words. We all know him: Todd Goodson."

Everyone began to applaud. It was a bit too much. I wasn't a celebrity; I was the same as them. The room became silent.

"I would like to thank everyone who came out here tonight, and even those who wanted to come but couldn't. Some people have to work and some folks aren't feeling well, so please make sure you take some cake home tonight for them and try not to eat it yourself!" I said as laughter filled the room.

"Seriously, I can say that when I first came to work here, I was a different person. Most of you remember that guy. Most of you couldn't stand that guy. I don't blame you; I didn't like him either!" I laughed and they laughed with me.

"But then one day, I opened my eyes and looked at myself and decided to make a change. I wanted to be more like the people around me; the people in this room. I've had struggles and challenges in my life, but so does everybody else. It made sense to me that since we were all struggling then we should struggle together, instead of struggling against each other. Right?"

People clapped and some shouted out.

"Amen!" and "Brother Todd, preach!"

"I'm not going to hold y'all long because, well, I'm starving." Chuckles and laughter followed. "But I want everyone to know that you are more than residents to me. We are family and this is our community. I wish everyone the very best. Until we meet again!"

I held up my hands as the room erupted in applause and cheers. Next, a little boy and girl walked out from the crowd carrying a massive piece of decorated card stock by each end and handed it to me. On it was written, "Thank you Mr. Todd" and "We Love You!" It was completely covered with children's names. I was touched to the core and nearly got choked up, but I was able to hold my emotions at bay as I hugged them. Then Sherika handed me a large present.

"This is from all the residents. They took up a collection and we bought you something," she said.

I handed her the large children's card and opened the box. It was a very nice leather jacket which I took out and put on.

"It fits great. Thank you sincerely," I said.

The music was turned back up and the lights were dimmed as the real party began. I sat down and ate at the guest of honor table with Reen, Henry, and the staff. It was a bittersweet time and reminded me of leaving behind comrades when deploying to a new duty station in the military. I was happy and sad.

By eight o'clock, I said my final goodbyes to everyone and closed the door to my truck. I let out a deep breath and sat there for a few minutes while looking in my rear-view mirror, watching the party continue. I smiled, started my truck, and drove off.

When I got to the front entrance, I stopped my truck. I had the feeling I was leaving something behind. I wracked my brain but couldn't think of anything. After looking both ways, I pulled out.

"Sam!"

I slammed on the brakes, backed up and turned around. With so much happening these last few weeks, I completely forgot to think about what would happen to Sam. It was too late to make arrangements with someone to keep him, and I wasn't going to leave him behind and alone. He wasn't skinny anymore, but it wouldn't take long for him to shrivel up again. I hadn't planned to keep him, so I never took him to a vet for a check-up or shots. Besides, Angie would never allow an animal in the apartment.

I parked the truck and left it running while I jogged up the stairs, hoping he would be sitting in his usual spot on my mat. When I crested the last step, I was relieved to see him lying in front of my old door, just as he had been doing when we first met. I walked up to him slowly and bent down to rub him.

"It's time for me to leave Sam and I don't want to leave you little buddy. So, how's about you come to New York with me? I'll take you to a vet and get you checked out like I should have done months ago. I'll buy you some proper cat vittles too. Come on." I picked him up and carried him back to the truck and set him on the passenger's seat.

"You know, Angie is gonna flip out when she sees you. But I'm not leaving you behind bro," I said.

We drove out the front entrance of Shady Meadows and headed toward the interstate and our new life.

CHAPTER FOURTEEN

THE AWAKENING

After driving for most of the night and into the early morning hours, I found myself passing through Baltimore. I needed a rest stop for myself and for Sam. I searched for a local Wal-Mart on my cell phone. I could use their restroom and also pick up some pet supplies; namely a pet carrier, cat food, kitty litter, and a container to hold it. A collar and leash would be a good idea as well since I didn't want Sam wandering off in curiosity when out of my grasp. After locating the store, I used my GPS which led me to a surprisingly busy parking lot. I stepped out of the truck. "I'll be right back Sam, gotta take a leak. Your turn is next," I said and closed the door as he trotted inquisitively across the seat toward the driver's window and stared at me.

Thirty minutes later I walked back to the truck with Sam's new gear. The collar was a good fit and he didn't appear to mind it much. I opened the kitty litter and poured some into the tray beside the truck, connected the leash to his collar, and opened the door. He didn't seem to notice the leash at all as he carefully climbed over the seat and hopped onto the parking lot pavement. To my surprise, he walked directly to the tray, casually sniffing the kitty litter before stepping inside and urinating. A few scratches of litter later, he was finished and stood before me meowing. I knew he was hungry, he had to be, so I picked him up and set him back in the passenger's seat and closed the door again. I let down my tailgate, slid the tray inside before closing it back, and got back in the truck. Sam's meowing was becoming incessant, so I rushed to open up a can of cat food for him.

"Alright buddy, some premium vittles for ya, enjoy."

He wasted no time and began to devour the contents as I started the truck and got back onto the road. Next stop, home. Even though it was early in the morning, I called Angie to give her a heads up on my progress and possibly brunt the news of our new pet, but my call went to her voicemail. In a way, it was a welcome relief that she didn't answer. I was in a great mood and didn't want this peaceful time of tranquility to be shattered. Not yet anyway. The next call to my dad sent me to his answering machine. Not a big deal. We would get our issues settled soon. I knew he was hurting. I was as well.

Four hours later, I arrived at Angie's apartment building and exited the elevator. As I walked down the once familiar hallway, everything appeared foreign to me, including the way I felt inside. Anxiety tickled the back of my neck as I held the carrier with Sam inside with one hand and my duffle bag around my other shoulder. The hallway became narrower and my breathing shallower with every step as I wondered why I was feeling this way. I should be happy, ecstatic even, but I wasn't even close.

Don't mess this up, Todd. Show her how you've changed. Let her be proud of what you have accomplished. It's all good Marine, it's all gravy from here on out. I was determined to believe it. I stopped in front of her door and set the carrier and my bag down, inhaled deeply, and rang the buzzer. A few moments later I heard the door unlock before she opened it.

"Todd!" She shouted and threw her arms around me and squeezed me tight. I returned the same energy and held her tightly, lifting her up and off the ground. Our lips met in a deep, wet kiss and once again I became lost in her passion. After setting her down I gently held her face with both hands, gazing into her eyes.

"I'm back babe. I'm back and born again. You are looking at the new and improved edition," I said smiling.

"Well, I am ready to see what you got for me, you badass Marine. Come on and bring your stuff inside."

Meow. Meow. She looked down at the carrier.

"Todd. What the fuck is that? Don't tell me you bought a damn cat!"

"Uh, Angie I tried to call you earlier and let you know I was bringing him with me. This is Sam. I've been taking care of him for a while now and I didn't want to leave him down there. He's my cat. I'm sorry about not—"

"What the hell is wrong with you Todd? Are you retarded? I don't know what you were thinking, but that damn cat is not coming in this apartment, so you might as well go find a shelter, cat pound, dog pound, or whatever and drop it off there!"

I stood there for a moment, speechless, dumbfounded.

"Angie, please. Let's discuss this without all the yelling and hollering. I apologize for not—"

"No! No! No! There is nothing to discuss! Get rid of it, now!"

I stepped backward and began to control my breathing and my thoughts, forcing myself to stay calm. I had come a long way and didn't need to fuel this fire by reacting out of anger. There was too much to lose. *Stay calm Todd.*

Angie turned and walked into the apartment, leaving me standing in the open doorway. I picked up the carrier and my duffle bag and walked inside.

Angie stopped suddenly and turned around. "Are you deaf Todd? I just told you that damn cat is not coming in this apartment and I meant it!"

"He's in the carrier Angie. Please, just let me bring him in for a few minutes while we talk."

"There's nothing to talk about! My decision is final!"

"Please Angie, you don't need to yell, I can hear you."

"Evidently not! I thought you were supposed to have changed. You left here a mess, and you come back here trying to pull some off the wall shit like this?" She shook her head in disgust. "Go, get rid of that frickin cat first, and then we can talk." She walked up to me with her arms crossed. "What happened to you down there? Too much time living with those ghetto jungle-bunnies has totally screwed your head up. I was expecting a serious change for the better, instead, I get this. You would have been better off to have stayed here and worked under that spook Reggie."

"Angie. That racist language isn't necessary at all. I've changed for the better and if you allow me to speak, I can show—"

"Racist? I'm no racist you ignorant prick!"

"I've changed Angie, but you need to change your negative behavior as well if we are going to be together."

"Oh! So that's a threat? Huh? I am absolutely perfect the way I am and not changing my views for you or anyone else! Do you understand that, asshole?"

"Angie, I'm not asking you to change for me or anyone else. Make a change for you. It won't happen overnight, but I promise to be right there and support you every step of the way. Babe trust me and hear me out, please." I was calm and direct, but most of all as honest as I could be.

"Get out of my face!" She screamed.

I stood motionless while trying to find the words to express the feelings that sincerely needed to be conveyed. I picked up the carrier and my bag and remained silent, not having a clue of what to do next. She closed the door halfway.

"Leave now and do not come back here with that damn cat. It's that simple Todd. Bye!" She said and slammed the door. I waited there for a couple of minutes, hoping that she would calm down and possibly reconsider her ultimatum before shutting me out. My mind raced during the elevator ride down for a possible solution. I had come too far and gone through a living hell to be in this position, risking life and limb to get back here. I couldn't lose it all now, not this way.

• • •

Thirty minutes later, I stood at my dad's front door, and again sat Sam and my duffle bag down and knocked. A perverse sense of *deja vu* darted through my mind as I waited for dad to open up. *What would his reaction be? Would I be in two arguments in one day with the people I loved and cared for?* The entire day felt surreal as the unpredictability of events continued to mount, building an internal pressure within my very soul. I was battling anxiety on a new level and found myself with the only weapon I now had command of; honesty. Being honest to myself and others in my life was my foundation and I was determined to hold on to it. It was all that was left inside of me. This was supposed to be home, but ironically, I felt more like a stranger in a strange land.

I knocked twice. No answer, but I could hear the sound of his television inside. He was home and probably already looked out the peephole at me. I didn't want to use my key and barge in on him. *Maybe he had company over?* I thought about it and decided I wasn't going to leave until we made things right. I missed my dad and hoped he missed me too. I unlocked the door and walked inside with Sam and my belongings.

"Hey, Dad! It's me, Todd." No answer. I walked into the living room and saw him sitting in his chair, watching television. Without responding and without looking at me, he stood up, switched off the TV, walked into his bedroom, and shut the door. The silence was deafening, and my excitement quickly turned melancholy. But I pressed on in optimism and began setting up Sam's litter tray, opened up a can of cat food, and let him out the carrier. I sat down on the couch and looked around the apartment. Everything looked the same.

There was a peculiar sound, which I couldn't identify. It was coming from my dad's bedroom. I walked to his door and heard him quietly crying. I knocked.

"Dad, open up."

The crying became muffled before it stopped, but still he didn't answer.

"Come on Dad, open up, please."

A few moments later, he whipped open the door and stood before me, his face wet with tears. "What do you want from me, Todd? Do you want to yell at me some more? Go ahead then and give it to me! I'm gay! Alright? There it is! Yes! I didn't do right by your mother either! I admit it! Okay! That's what you want to hear, so there it is! I'm sorry! It's all on the table now! Now, what do you want to tell me? Go ahead boy and let me hear it!" He cried out, sniffling.

As the tears streamed down my face and our eyes locked together, I unleashed the words in my heart which mattered most. "Dad, I love you! I love you!" I grabbed him by his shoulders, pulling him close and embracing him with all my might. There we stood, hugging each other and sobbing uncontrollably. I refused to release his trembling body until both of us were free of the pain which had separated us. Time stood still in that moment, as we both were purged the lies, hypocrisy, and the judgment from our past.

"I'm so sorry Son," he croaked. "I'm sorry for hurting your mother. For the lies. I'm sorry for teaching you to hate. Please, please…forgive me!" His weeping became profuse. "I'll apologize to your mother, I promise. I'll try to make things right."

"I forgive you and know you will make it right Dad. I believe you. After you do that, you're gonna have to forgive yourself too."

We stepped back from each other and tried to compose ourselves, wiping our tears, both exhausted from the intimate release of shared emotions. "Dad, where are the tissues at? We are both leaking snot like damn fire hydrants," I joked, and we chuckled.

"Tell me about it," he sniffled. I hadn't realized that much water was inside of me. Sorry about the boogers on your shirt," he replied, while attempting to wipe off my collar. We couldn't help but smile and laugh.

A few minutes later, we sat on the couch together to decompress.

"Do you want a beer son?"

"No, thanks anyway. I stopped drinking months ago. But I'll take a soda if you have one. Any kind will do."

"Sure thing," he replied before returning with two cans of soda for us both. He held out his can and toasted. "Here's to new beginnings."

"Roger that. To new beginnings."

We tapped our cans and sipped our drinks without speaking a word. The moments of silence which followed were comfortable, even tranquil.

"I see you bought a cat. What's the name?"

"That's Sam. He was a stray cat I found a while ago. I've been taking care of him ever since and decided not to leave him down South."

"Good for him and you. He's a good-looking cat."

"Thanks. Yeah, he is a handsome dude."

"So, I'm sure Angie is glad to have you back home. How is she doing? You have been over there, right? I figured you must have visited her first."

"Angie is Angie. She is already at my throat, mainly because of Sam. She told me not to come back over until I get rid of him."

He began motioning to Sam in an attempt to lure him over to the couch. "Come here kitty. Here kitty. Come, Sammy." Sam stopped and stared, before leisurely walking over to the couch, allowing my dad to pet him. "Oh, you're a good cat," he smiled before turning to me. "Are you sure he is a male? Sam and not Samantha? I can't see his balls."

"Yep, he's a boy."

"You know he can stay with me here if she has a problem with him. I don't mind it at all," he smiled.

His invitation was the perfect remedy for my situation, but I had mixed feelings and doubts.

"Thanks for the offer Dad, but Sam is my cat and my responsibility. I do any and everything that Angie wants me to do. I've bowed down every time, even when I shouldn't have."

"Todd, you'll be starting the academy soon and things will get better, trust me on that. Your life is going to change."

I sat with a silent frown that couldn't be hidden, and my dad knew me well. He didn't push for a response, knowing it would come naturally.

"I'm not sure that I am ready for any of that yet. I'm doing great, emotionally, physically, but every day is still a battle, a struggle. Everyone is expecting me to become someone or be something. I'm just not sure of the future at this point in my life. I don't want to disappoint you, mom, or Angie. I just don't—"

He reached out and squeezed my knee.

"Enough. Todd, don't make my same mistake. I followed in your grandpa's footsteps in every way. I look back now and wonder how life might have turned out for me; hell for you and your mom too if I would have followed my dreams. Truth be told, I was cowardly and afraid to stand up to those same expectations and go my own way. So, go your own way son!" He grabbed my hand. "Whatever you do, academy or not, married or single, straight or gay; I will always love you boy, and will always support your decisions. Have the guts your old man lacked when it counted. There's not a dam thing holding you back." He smiled. "Life is short, so make the most of it."

"Thanks, Dad. I appreciate you."

• • •

I spent the rest of the day talking with my dad about the future and tried calling Angie a couple of times. She wouldn't answer my calls or return any texts, so I ended up sleeping at my dad's place. He stayed up most of the night, playing music in his room and I could feel that he was happy. He cleaned his conscience and was on his new path in life, free from judgment.

The next morning, we said goodbye. I loaded my truck and headed down the street toward the highway, ready to confront Angie face to face with Sam by my side. I rehearsed my apology to her, along with my explanation and reasoning why I wanted to keep him.

Unexpectedly, I found myself pulling off to the side of the road.

It was then that the most important answers to my life's questions finally dawned on me.

Who was I? What is my purpose? Why am I still alive? Those unanswered questions continued to haunt me, even after months of therapy. But I could see clearly now and past any immediate future with Angie. I loved her for what I wanted her to be, and not for who she truly was, and she loved me back that same way. Those fictitious people never actually existed. They were only portrayals in our minds of the qualities which we both sincerely wanted to have in a mate. But she wasn't ready to look inside herself and do the hard work needed to change, and it wasn't my place in life to force her. Our paths were headed in different directions; for the time being.

Honesty taught me that all of the hate, ignorance, and fear in my life which separated me from the world was my own fault. For that, I was sincerely repentant. I built those crooked fences with my own hands. They didn't need to be made straight; they needed to be torn down, and that's what I accomplished. Since there was no one blaming me for the past, I stopped blaming myself. It was time to live my own life, and there were no more fences to keep me out or hold me in.

Sam meowed. When it was safe, I made a U-turn. I knew a place existed for me that I could call home, so I headed back to those very people whom I loved, and who loved me; the real me.

I didn't have to become a police officer with a badge and a gun to protect and serve others; I had been doing that all along.

This is who I am, and the love from God, the Marines, and my country is the reason why I am still alive. I was on my way home. *Finally, home sweet home.*

THE END

I thank you for reading Crooked Fences and hope you enjoyed this novel! If you would like to leave an honest review, please take a minute of your time to review the book.

Other novels by C.J. Heigelmann: An Uncommon Folk Rhapsody (Historical Fiction).

If you would like to sign up for my email list (we never spam) to receive news on other novels by C.J. Heigelmann, free book giveaways, book signings and new releases, you can sign up here: https://www.cjheigelmann.com/contact/

For all other inquiries, please contact me personally at: cj@cjheigelmann.com

ABOUT THE AUTHOR

Author C.J. Heigelmann is a writer and multi-genre novelist of Contemporary, Literary and Historical fiction. Heigelmann's style of writing is marked by cultural and social diversity and inclusion. His focus on perspective and realism separates him from other mainstream contemporary authors.

Comparable authors: Charles Martin, Robert Whitlow, Denise Hildreth Jones, Therese Anne Fowler.

"I express my characters in their pure flawed form because all of us are flawed. I don't shrink from using stereotypes whether positive or negative. Instead, I promote them and in the next breath completely shatter them. This exposes the error of subjugating individuals to intellectually lazy social labels, compelling the reader to confront the empirical nature of a character while lending insight into true understanding. I write to expand the perception of one's self, the human family, and the world around us."

C.J. Heigelmann

Made in the USA
Las Vegas, NV
15 August 2023

76149145R00144